# A Letter from Nana Rose

BOOKS BY KRISTIN HARPER

*Aunt Ivy's Cottage*

*Summer at Hope Haven*

# A Letter from Nana Rose

KRISTIN HARPER

bookouture

Published by Bookouture in 2021

An imprint of Storyfire Ltd.
Carmelite House
50 Victoria Embankment
London EC4Y 0DZ

www.bookouture.com



ISBN: 978-1-80019-562-2
eBook ISBN: 978-1-80019-561-5

*For my father*
*and in memory of my "Little Grandma,"*
*who saw the ocean first*

# PROLOGUE

She woke from her nap with a gasp. She'd been dreaming about her twin again, a dream so real it could have been a memory…

It was a hot, dazzling day in July, 1948. The sisters had just graduated high school and they were summering at their family's bayside estate on Dune Island, off the Massachusetts coast. They'd spent the morning strolling along the flats and combing tidal pools for treasures: an amethyst-colored piece of beach glass. Two bay scallop shells as big as their palms. A stone shaped like a butterfly.

When the tide rolled in and the water was deep enough, Hattie and Rose swam and dived and floated until their fingers pruned and their teeth chattered. Then they climbed the wooden stairs up the steep dune and followed a narrow path through sea lavender and beach grass to the rustic, two-bedroom cottage. After serving themselves large squares of strawberry shortcake, they carried their plates out to the patio.

Seated in brightly painted Adirondack chairs, the twins could smell honeysuckle and wild-rose scent intermingling in the breeze. They listened to the gentle swells folding against the shoreline, the gulls squawking in the distance. The sisters ate slowly, savoring their dessert. In between bites, they talked about their futures, which seemed to stretch before them endlessly, shimmering like the bay…

*Life certainly didn't turn out the way we imagined it would,* she thought, now ninety-one years old. Although it made her breathless, she hefted herself out of the recliner and shuffled to the desk for a piece of paper and a pen.

It was time to share her secret.

# CHAPTER ONE

## *Saturday – June 18*

"First things first," Jill Sampson announced to herself after she got out of the car in front of Nana Rose's house on Sea Breeze Lane.

That was what her grandmother used to say when Jill and her two older sisters, Rachel and Brooke, arrived at her Hope Haven residence on Dune Island when they were girls. They'd scramble out of the back seat, nearly suffocate her with embraces, and then one of them would urge the others, "Let's go down to the beach!"

"Not until we unload the trunk," their father invariably objected.

"First things first," their grandmother always countered. "They've got their priorities straight, Jimmy—they've said hello to me and now they've got to go say hello to the bay. You were the same way when you were a boy. You'd race off and I wouldn't see you again until suppertime. The unpacking can wait."

By the time they'd get back, their father would have already emptied the trunk and taken their suitcases to their rooms for them. *He was as happy as Nana was that we were so excited to see the beach again*, Jill realized, overcome with loneliness.

It had been nine years since she'd lost her mother. Her father had died from a heart attack six years ago now. And Nana had passed away in March.

Because Jill's sisters hadn't arrived on the island yet, there was no one there for her to embrace. No one there to embrace *her*.

She couldn't face going into Nana's empty home by herself, so she trekked up the driveway and followed the crushed-shell path around the house.

In contrast to the flat, neat rectangle of tree-shaded lawn in the front yard, the sandy back yard was a wild composition of beach grass and beach plum, bayberry and bearberry, sea lavender and seaside goldenrod. In the right-hand corner, an ever-spreading thicket of wild roses filled the air with its sweet fragrance.

Jill surveyed it all, but she didn't stop walking until she'd reached the upper platform of the wooden staircase leading down a steep dune to a private beach where the water nearly lapped the dunes at high tide and receded at least a quarter mile at low. Right now, it was coming in. The sweep of royal blue water was crinkled by a gentle breeze and fringed in white along its edges. Some ten yards to the south, a dense patch of seagrass swayed with the nearly imperceptible motion of the tide, but the surface was otherwise unbroken from here to the horizon, and beyond.

"I'm back," she whispered to the seascape, a tradition she'd practiced ever since she was a young girl. "I've really missed you."

It felt like forever since she and her sisters had returned to Nana's place, even though it had only been three years. Prior to this lapse, they'd always spent at least two weeks together there every summer. Often they stayed longer, depending on their individual schedules.

But three years ago Nana had fallen and broken her hip. Afterward, she'd had to move out of her off-island duplex, so she could move into an assisted living facility. It was so costly, she'd had to lease out her summer place on Sea Breeze Lane to year-round tenants. Even then, she'd barely been able to cover her expenses, but she was more concerned that her granddaughters had to cancel their annual vacation to the island.

"I feel terrible about this," she'd cried. "You girls love getting together at my place in the summer and so do your families. And I loved having all of you there with me."

Jill's heart cracked a little at the memory of her elderly relative, only thinking of her family, grandchildren and great-grandchildren even when she'd gone through so much pain and upheaval.

Jill, at thirty-nine, was single. Or, as some people annoyingly put it, she was *still* single—as if she needed a reminder that she was behind schedule.

Forty-one-year-old Brooke and forty-three-year-old Rachel were both married, with teenage children. And their husbands and kids enjoyed going to Hope Haven as much as Rachel and Brooke did. But the three women insisted the most important priority was that their grandmother's health-care needs were being met.

"Renting out your home year-round is a necessity, Nana. There's nothing to feel bad about on our account," Rachel had told her during one of their four-way video chats.

"Rachel's right. We love vacationing together at Sea Breeze Lane and we'll miss going there, but we want you to do whatever it takes to recover," Jill had agreed. "And we'll still all come to visit you in Worcester."

"It's only for a year or two. Once your health has improved and you're caught up financially, we'll have a big celebration on Dune Island with you, Nana." Brooke's sense of optimism had always bordered on denial, but Rachel and Jill had suspected their grandmother wouldn't be returning to her summer home again.

Sadly, they'd been right. Nana never did regain enough mobility and strength to live independently again. In March, she'd died of congestive heart failure, leaving her granddaughters grief-stricken and without any surviving blood relatives except each other and the children.

Shortly after her burial service, Nana's attorney had informed the three sisters that they'd inherited their grandmother's summer estate, just as she'd told them they would. "Rose knew that her time had come," he'd said candidly. "She was aware that her current tenants are preparing to move out in mid-June. It was her final wish that after they leave, the three of you spend two weeks together on Dune Island while you come to a unanimous decision about what to do with the house next."

At this, the sisters had raised their eyebrows at each other in puzzlement.

"Just be sure to let me know the dates you'll be there and what you end up deciding," the lawyer had continued.

"Why would Nana feel it was necessary to put a formal request like that in her will?" Jill had asked her sisters later, as they were eating lunch in a nearby bistro.

"She knew how difficult it's going to be for us to go to Sea Breeze Lane without her. This was probably her way of making sure we return as soon as possible, no matter how sad we are," Brooke had guessed.

"Yeah, that sounds like Nana's reasoning. But what I meant was why did she require us to make a unanimous decision about what to do next with the house? Obviously there's no need to cover her assisted living facility expenses any more. It's not as if we have to rent the house out again, so what is it we're supposed to decide?"

"Well, I think..." Rachel had hedged. "I think Nana wanted to give us the option to sell the house. Otherwise, she would have stipulated that we keep it in the family."

"*Sell* it?!" Jill had exclaimed so loudly the man at the table beside them had whipped his head around to look at her. She'd lowered her voice and repeated incredulously, "You want to *sell* Nana's house?"

"It's not that I *want* to," Rachel had sounded a little put upon, a little defensive, even though she'd kept her volume down to match Jill's. "But it is something I think we need to consider. Derek and I can barely afford to pay our mortgage and property taxes in Maryland. And they're even higher in Massachusetts, especially on Dune Island." Rachel and her husband were making boatloads of money from their furniture restoration and importation business; recently they'd even expanded to include an additional shop. But they'd struggled when they were first starting out, so she had a tendency to act as if they were still living paycheck to paycheck.

"We'd be splitting the expenses three ways," Jill had pointed out. "Can you realistically afford that? Aren't you saving up so you can put a down payment on a house or a condo or something?"

Jill was a tech writer for a major appliance company and although she earned a decent salary, she lived in Boston, where housing costs were through the ceiling. At Rachel's urging, she'd looked into buying a place of her own in the suburbs. But the only houses Jill could afford were so far outside the city that she would have had to commute over an hour each way for work, as well as to go out on the weekends.

Not that she'd really felt like socializing very much that spring. In addition to losing her beloved Nana, Jill had been reeling because Brandon, her boyfriend of eight months, had just dumped her in favor of his twenty-three-year-old personal trainer. That was one more reason she couldn't wait to retreat to Sea Breeze Lane: experience had taught her that there were few problems in life that couldn't be alleviated at least a little by spending time at the ocean with her family.

"I could be happy renting forever as long as I have Nana's place to go to," she'd said.

"For two weeks out of the year?"

"And on weekends, like I used to do when Nana still summered there." Although Jill had moved several times since graduating college, for the past five years, she'd lived in Boston. So during the two summers before Nana's accident, Jill had travelled to the island almost every weekend, as well as the two weeks she'd spent there vacationing with her sisters. All that time had made her grow even closer to her grandmother, and to the island.

"That might work out okay for you, but what about for Brooke and me and our families? It's an eight-hour drive from my house—and the flight from Oregon is almost six. It's not as if we can just drop everything and pop over to the island for a couple of days of vacation whenever we want."

Somehow, the way Rachel had put it made it seem as if Jill didn't have a care in the world compared to her sisters. True, it was to her advantage that she lived closer to Dune Island than they did, but they had more flexibility in their summer schedules than Jill. As business owners, Rachel and Derek relied heavily on their staff to carry out the daily operations, so they were free to take their vacations as they pleased. Brooke was an occupational therapist at an elementary school, so she had a long summer break. Her husband Todd was a graphic designer who worked remotely anyway.

Suddenly, Jill had an idea. "If you guys stayed for a month or two every summer, would that make it worth it to keep the house?" she'd asked eagerly.

Brooke sounded equivocal. "It might… although I don't know if Todd and the kids would be on board with that plan. We've kind of gotten used to vacationing in the mountains for the past few summers." Before Rachel could voice her thoughts on the matter, Brooke questioned, "But why are we discussing this already? Nana wanted us to spend two weeks in Hope Haven while we make up our minds one way or the other."

At the mention of their grandmother's request, both Jill and Rachel had fallen silent and resumed eating their lunches. Before departing for their homes, they'd all promised not to talk about the subject with each other until they arrived on Dune Island in June.

But Jill had worried about it constantly since then. Although she and her sisters had had their squabbles and minor sibling rivalries over the years, they'd never disagreed about anything as important as this. The possibility that either Rachel or Brooke would even *consider* selling Nana's place had put Jill on edge for the past three months.

And if all that wasn't stressful enough, the week before she'd left for Hope Haven, Jill had heard through the grapevine that her department at work was being downsized. Although her manager hadn't confirmed whether the rumors were true yet, she'd been on tenterhooks waiting to find out whether her position might be eliminated.

Yet as she stood on the lip of the dune breathing in the faintly briny air, Jill felt considerably calmer. Nana's place had always had that effect on her; it was one of many reasons she couldn't bear to give it up. Not for any amount of money.

*As soon as Rachel and Brooke are here again, they'll feel as strongly about keeping the house as I do*, she told herself. *We've been away for so long that they've probably forgotten how beautiful it is.*

Nana's parents had purchased a little cottage on this property in the 1940s specifically because of its remote location. In the sixties, the cottage had been claimed by the bay during a winter storm, so she'd had the current house constructed farther back from the edge of the dune. By the mid-1980s, the island's summer population had increased exponentially and much of its land had been developed, but Sea Breeze Lane was still very secluded.

Nana's house was the last of four residences on the one-sided dirt road; the closest neighbor was two acres to the right. To the left was a half-mile expanse of uninhabitable dunes, which were eventually interrupted by a tidal river and marshland. Except for an occasional boater who'd come ashore to fish, it was rare to cross paths with anyone at that end of the beach. Jill had always felt a little smug that Nana's modest patch of property offered more privacy than some of the most exclusive waterfront communities on the island.

She turned and squinted in the opposite direction, toward town. Dune Island was made up of five villages, collectively forming Hope

Haven. While they were all breathtaking, each one had a unique identifying feature. Benjamin's Manor was an historic fishing village with a small, quaint harbor. Port Newcomb, the island's largest town, was home to the major ferry dock. Highland Hills's plunging oceanside cliffs were spectacular, and the cranberry bogs in Rockfield were as scenic as they were fruitful.

And then there was Lucinda's Hamlet—also called "Lucy's Ham" by the locals—which was where Nana's house was located. Lucy's Ham was known for its bayside boardwalk about a mile and a quarter north of where Jill stood now. She used to love browsing its shops and playing games at the arcade or getting a cone at Bleecker's Ice Cream Parlor with her family when she was a kid. But as an adult, she rarely went into that part of town any more. In fact, she rarely went *any*where beyond her grandmother's place if she could help it.

As Nana used to say, pointing to the scenery, *Why would I leave when I have all of this right at my doorstep?*

Jill kicked off her sandals and hurried down the stairs, fingering the thick rope handrail strung from post to post on her way down. She hopped off the bottom step into the warm, fine sand. Although the sky was supposed to cloud over later in the day, the sun was currently blazing, so she scurried to the water and waded in until it reached the hem of her cotton capris.

As a girl, she would have worn a bathing suit beneath her shorts and shirt so she could have flung them off and raced her sisters into the water. Brooke usually was the first to submerge herself and Jill would dive in second. Even though Rachel was the oldest and succeeded at nearly everything she did, she was always last in this particular contest because it took her a long time to adjust to the chilly water.

A lump swelled in Jill's throat as she remembered how Nana used to drape fresh towels over the deck railing so they'd be warm from the sun by the time her granddaughters—and later, her great-grandchildren—came upstairs to dry off. Jill glanced over her shoulder, wishing her sisters would arrive soon so she wouldn't feel so lonely.

Brooke was flying from Portland into Annapolis, because Rachel didn't want to drive all the way from Maryland to Massachusetts by herself. Their husbands and children were involved in work, various end-of-year school activities, trips and camps. So it would just be the three sisters for the start of the vacation.

Jill was really going to miss hanging out with her nieces and nephews—there was never a dull moment with them around—but she had to admit she was relieved that no one else was coming for a while. She remembered how emotional they'd been the first time they'd visited Sea Breeze Lane without their father. Being at Nana's house had triggered so many memories of him that it had felt as if they'd just lost him all over again. So Jill was glad she and her sisters would have time alone to try to adjust to their grandmother's absence.

And although she was genuinely fond of her sisters' spouses, she was also glad that they wouldn't be there while the trio discussed what they wanted to do with the house. *Nana would have specified if she'd wanted Todd and Derek to have a vote in the matter*, she reasoned.

Her grandmother may not have always been politically correct—after all, she still referred to Jill and her sisters as *girls*. But she was a strong, independent woman who didn't think men should be in charge of making all the financial decisions, the way they usually were when Nana was growing up.

Jill also figured her grandmother hadn't wanted Brooke and Rachel to have an unfair advantage in the event the three of them didn't agree on what to do about the house. Nana had always been sensitive to Jill's heartache over the fact that she hadn't met a man she considered her soulmate yet. A man she'd loved enough to marry, and vice versa.

*I knew from the start that Brandon and I didn't have a future together, so why did I waste so much time with him?* she brooded.

"You beat me into the water for once!" someone called, interrupting her self-recrimination.

Jill spun around to see Brooke bounding down the stairs, her hair flying out behind her. She didn't have time to wade to shore before her sister splashed out to greet her. "I'm so glad to see you," Brooke said over Jill's shoulder, enveloping her tightly.

"So am I." As Jill returned her hug, she could feel Brooke's scapula sticking out. She pulled back to look at her and was surprised at how sharp her features appeared, too. Brooke's shoulder-length locks, once threaded with gray strands, were thoroughly brunette—almost as dark as her teenage daughters' hair. Yet instead of making her appear younger, the coloring job had aged her beyond her forty-one years. Or was that only the effect of taking a red-eye flight?

After they released each other, Brooke looked Jill up and down and declared, "You look beautiful, as always."

Jill knew she didn't look beautiful. She looked puffy and pale and her dishwater-blond hair was in need of highlights and a trim.

Physically and emotionally, she was thoroughly washed out. But she understood that Brooke's remark was a reflection of how happy she was to be with Jill in person again. She twisted sideways to point to the bay. "Now *that's* beautiful…"

"Mmm," Brooke murmured, her eyes brimming. Of the three sisters, she was the most sentimental, so Jill assumed they were happy tears, but it was just as likely that she was on the brink of crying because she missed Nana. If she started, Jill would, too, and she didn't want that to happen already. Or to happen *again.*

"Where's Rachel?" she asked.

"She was calling Derek to tell him we'd arrived safely and then she was going to have to take off her sneakers and socks, and I didn't want to wait for—oh, look, here she comes now."

Jill glanced up to see her lithe, willowy sister descending the staircase, her sunglasses perched atop of her cropped auburn hair and her pants legs rolled up to her kneecaps. "Hi, Rach," she called, waving. "C'mon in. The water's fine."

"It's freezing," Rachel exclaimed as soon as she dipped her toes in, but she continued inching forward.

"Here, I'll warm you up." Jill quickly splashed through the shallows until they were close enough to wrap their arms around each other.

"Together again at last," Rachel said.

Then Brooke came up from behind them and elbowed her way into their embrace, the waves lapping at their ankles. They used to call this kind of hug a "sister-braid" when they were girls. It had always made Jill feel three times as strong as she was on her own and today was no exception; after they let go of each other, she finally felt ready to enter Nana's house.

"Before we unload the cars, let's go inside to get a drink and open the windows," Jill suggested. After they'd climbed the stairs, she retrieved the key from its usual hiding place beneath a large quahog shell on the deck. Then she went around to unlock the front door so she could come through and open the sliders for Rachel and Brooke.

Nana's house originally was one story tall, with two bedrooms and a bathroom in what everyone considered the back of the house, the side closest to the road. In the front, the open-concept kitchen, dining area and "great room" faced the bay. Bordered by floor-to-ceiling windows on both ends, the large space also contained four sets of sliding doors, which opened to a deck stretching across the length of the house.

When Jill and her sisters were young, Nana had added a second story to the house. It had two bathrooms and four bedrooms, each with its own balcony. Whether upstairs or down, the expansive views from the front and sides of the house were so spectacular that Nana hadn't seen any reason to fill the house with paintings or other ornamental accessories.

Her sparse décor was both functional and elegantly understated, and its palette imitated the surrounding scenery: hardwood floors and jute rugs the color of damp sand. Overstuffed sofas reminiscent of summer clouds. Accent pillows as bright as seagrass and light fixtures and doorknobs the same pewter blue as the ocean after a rainstorm.

Jill paused in the great room and glanced at the two pearl-white, scallop-shaped swivel armchairs situated where the sliding door and side window met in the far right corner. That was her favorite spot in the house. Sitting there, slowly twisting from side to side as she viewed the bay always gave her the sense of being on a ship. Jill could lounge in one of those chairs and gaze at the water and sky and dunes from now until Labor Day, and she'd never get her fill of them.

"I can tell you've been staring at the beach grass again," Nana used to tease her. "Because your eyes are even greener than usual."

Remembering, Jill's vision blurred with tears again, so she hurried to open the sliders for her sisters.

"Ah, home sweet home," Rachel said wistfully as she stepped across the threshold.

"It would be a lot sweeter if Nana was here with us," Brooke lamented.

"Mm-hmm," Jill murmured, afraid if she said anything else about Nana one of them would burst out crying. The three women quietly began opening the windows, tiptoeing through the downstairs rooms, almost as if they didn't have the right to be there without their grandmother.

"Looks like the cleaning crew did a great job," Brooke commented blandly when they'd all circled back to the kitchen.

"Considering how much they charge, they *should* do a great job," Rachel replied.

Jill had been the one to arrange for the cleaners to come in after the year-round tenants moved out, and felt she had to defend her decision. "We were lucky to schedule them. This is their busiest time of the year."

Rachel shrugged. "We could have cleaned it ourselves."

"After a cross-country flight and then ten hours on the road? No thanks," Brooke said. "It was worth every penny to have the house deep-cleaned before we got here."

Jill was about to echo her sentiment, when Rachel slid an envelope out from under the napkin holder on the breakfast bar. "Look, it's addressed to all three of us. Probably a note from the tenants. You want me to open it?"

"Sure." Brooke perched on a tall stool and Jill sat beside her, resting her elbows on the mottled turquoise-colored quartz countertop.

Facing them, Rachel began to read, "*My darling girls.*" She sucked in a loud breath. "Oh—it's from Nana!"

Their grandmother had referred to the trio as, "my darling girls" for as long as Jill could remember, so she knew Rachel was right, but she still asked, "Are you sure?"

Her sister showed her the piece of paper. "It's her handwriting, see? And her signature."

"When did she write it?" Brooke's eyes were already filling.

"I don't know. It isn't dated. Obviously she must have made some arrangement to have it waiting for us because she says, *Welcome back to Dune Island! I'm very glad you're here again, so please don't ruin my joy by crying because you've received a posthumous note from me. Especially you, Brooke.*"

Nana knew each of her granddaughter's personalities so well that it wasn't surprising she'd anticipate Brooke's weepiness. But the truth was that Jill also felt close to tears at seeing her grandmother's penmanship and hearing her words. And from the way Rachel's voice sounded, she did, too. She read:

*I imagine you're wondering why I included a clause in my will requiring you girls to vacation on Sea Breeze Lane for two weeks while you decide what to do with the estate.*

*In part, it's because it's been three years since you've reunited here and I was concerned you might postpone your trip this summer because you're grieving. (All the more reason to have some sister-time by the sea again!)*

"Didn't I tell you?" Brooke interrupted. She pulled a napkin from the holder and dabbed her eyes while her sister read on.

*I also wanted you to be here while you consider what to do with the house because certain decisions shouldn't be made from afar. They shouldn't be rushed. And neither should certain stories, including mine.*

*That's why I've arranged for my attorney to have a letter delivered from me almost every day while you're staying in Hope Haven; there will be ten more, after this one. (Check the mailbox each morning, as that's where the courier will leave them.) These missives are for your eyes only. Whatever you choose to disclose after you've read them in their entirety is up to you, but please wait until then to divulge anything I've written. I think it's important for you three to absorb this story, first.*

*I'm sure that your parents mentioned bits and pieces about my background, including my parents' automobile accident and my sister's untimely death. But they undoubtedly also told you that my generation didn't usually talk as freely about our families' business as so many people do these days. Or maybe your parents warned you that the past was too painful for me to discuss and they discouraged you from asking me about it, which I appreciated.*

It was true that Jill and her sisters knew very little about their grandmother's background. They were aware that her parents had died in an automobile accident when Nana was just eighteen or nineteen. They also knew she'd had a twin sister, Hattie, who'd passed away in her early twenties. And that Nana's husband had divorced her to marry another woman. But the details were sketchy and the sisters' parents had, indeed, forbidden them to question Nana about her family. While they may have been curious, from a young age the girls had understood the subject was off-limits and that they'd get in trouble if they brought it up, so they didn't. Out of respect for Nana's feelings, they'd never inquired about it as adults, either.

So it was a shock to hear Rachel continue, *But now I need to tell you a story about my past. It's something I've never told anyone else before—a secret, in other words.*

*I would have taken it with me to the grave if your father hadn't died before I did. But now it seems as important to share it with you girls as it was to keep it from him. For better or for worse, the past is part of your family history and you deserve to know about it.*

*Or maybe that's just an excuse. As close as I am to death, I'm selfish enough to want to leave with a clean conscience, yet cowardly enough to wait until after I'm gone to reveal my secret.*

*I'll tell you more in my next letter. For now, please make yourselves at home and go enjoy the beach.*

"She signed it, *Your loving Nana*," Rachel ended.

"Wow." Jill blew the air out of her cheeks, stunned. *The way Nana wrote about wanting to die with a clean conscience makes it seem like she felt guilty about whatever story she's going to share with us*, she thought.

"Yeah. Wow is right." Rachel shook her head, running a finger back and forth across the page as if to find something she'd missed the first time she'd read it. "I can't imagine Nana ever intentionally doing anything so shameful it required a lifetime of secrecy. Something she couldn't even tell her own son."

"She didn't say the secret was something *she'd* done. She said it was a secret about her past," Jill reasoned aloud for her own sake, as well as for Rachel's. "Maybe it was something about her parents. Or her sister."

Brooke, who had been uncharacteristically quiet, suddenly crossed her arms on the countertop and dropped her head against them. "That letter makes me really sad."

"You mean because Nana must have been dying when she wrote it?" Rachel asked.

"Or are you sad that she was carrying some kind of secret burden for so long?" Jill guessed.

"Both." Brooke's voice was muffled. "And because the letter sounds exactly like her. It makes me miss her even more. It's hard enough coming to Nana's house without her here, but I'm not sure I can handle reading a letter from her every day. It just seems to emphasize the reality that she isn't with us."

"Hearing Rachel read Nana's words makes me lonely for her, too," Jill acknowledged softly. "But it was obviously very important to her to tell us whatever it is she's going to disclose. I know she wrote that certain stories take time to tell and time to absorb, but I have to wonder if sending us a letter each day is also her way of helping us feel as if she's here on vacation with us."

Her head still buried in her arms, Brooke gave a horizontal shrug, unconvinced.

Rachel suggested, "Maybe once you get some rest, you'll feel like you can manage everything a little better?"

"Yeah, maybe." Brooke sat up and wiped the skin beneath her eyes with her fingertips. "I'm pretty jetlagged. But if I nap now, I'll never sleep tonight and I've had terrible insomnia lately."

"How about if we bring our suitcases in, change into our swimsuits and take a nice, relaxing dip in the bay before the sky clouds up?" Rachel suggested. "It might be our only chance until Monday. It's supposed to rain tonight and tomorrow.

"Oh, all right," Brooke reluctantly agreed, rising from the stool. "It is awfully hot out."

"Good." Rachel's enthusiasm sounded forced. "You heard what Nana wrote—she wanted us to go enjoy the beach. So let's try to put all the sad stuff out of our minds for now."

*Easier said than done*, Jill thought. But she rose and followed her sisters outside to unload the cars so they could finally begin their long-awaited vacation together on Dune Island.

# CHAPTER TWO

*Sunday – June 19*

Although she'd left all three windows and the sliding door to the balcony open when she went to bed the previous evening, Jill woke in the morning feeling clammy and hot. A marshy smell hung in the still, humid air; a sure sign a thunderstorm was coming. Groggy, she sat up and listened for Nana stirring in her room on the other side of the wall. *Nana's not here*, she suddenly realized, falling back against her pillow again and burying her face in the crook of her arm.

Jill, her grandmother and her father had always been early risers. From the time she was young, she'd accompany them on their morning walks along the beach. Avid birders, her dad and Nana had taught Jill how to identify sanderlings, terns, ospreys, egrets, herons and numerous other birds by sight, as well as by call. The fact that she hardly heard any birds chirping now was another indication of an impending storm.

*I'd better check the mailbox before it starts to rain*, she thought. She'd tossed and turned long past midnight, reflecting on her grandmother's letter and wondering what her secret was. Although she regretted that the secret had been so troubling to Nana, Jill had a hunch that there might be something about the disclosure that would help influence her sisters to keep the house. Why else would their grandmother have chosen to reveal her secret at the same time the three women were supposed to make a decision about the estate?

But that wasn't the only reason Jill was eager to get the mail; as she'd told Brooke, receiving a letter from Nana almost made it seem as if she was still there, conversing with them. So she threw off her sheets and hopped out of bed. She barely paused to glance at the thick band of purple clouds bruising the horizon before she padded downstairs. To her surprise, Brooke was seated at the breakfast bar, typing on her laptop.

"I didn't think you'd be up already." Noticing damp marks on her sister's shirt, Jill asked, "Did you go for a run?"

"No. I'm just sweaty because it's like a sauna in here. I hope the storm clears the air."

Jill dashed outside to check the mailbox and when she returned emptyhanded a minute later, Rachel was in the kitchen, too. She said she wanted to get eggs and vegetables at the farm stand down the road so she could make veggie egg scramble for breakfast.

"I might as well go to the grocery store while I'm out. Do you two want to help me make a list? We can take turns preparing meals," said Rachel.

"Hmm. I just assumed we'd want to order takeout or go to restaurants while we're on vacation," Brooke replied without looking up from her laptop.

"That will be too expensive," Rachel argued.

"It would be too expensive if we did it at every meal for our entire families. But one of the best perks of not having the men and kids with us is that we don't have to cook."

"I rarely have any men or kids with me, so I don't mind taking an extra turn," Jill offered. "I like to cook when I'm cooking for someone other than just myself."

"What about—" Brooke started to say but then she interrupted herself. "Oh, that's right. I forgot that you ended it with what's-his-face."

"Actually, Brandon was the one who ended it with me," Jill clarified as she popped a pod into the coffee-maker, trying to ignore the fact Brooke hadn't remembered his name. Because Brandon had dumped her shortly after their grandmother had died, Jill hadn't confided the details about her breakup to her sisters the way she would have done if they hadn't been mourning for Nana. "It seems he preferred his personal trainer, who's half his age."

"Loser," Brooke uttered in disgust. "You're better off being single."

*I'm definitely better off without* Brandon, *but that doesn't necessarily mean I'm better off being single*, Jill thought. Why did it have to be an either-or situation anyway? *Either* she was with someone who wasn't quite right for her, *or* she was alone. Why couldn't she be happily married to a terrific guy, like each of her sisters and most of her friends were?

Pulling a pad of paper from a drawer, Rachel commented, "Brooke and I talked so much about the kids last night that we didn't get to hear what's new with you, Jill. How are things at work?"

"Oh, you know," she replied vaguely as she followed Rachel into the living room area to take a seat on the large sectional sofa.

Ordinarily, she would have told her sisters about the rumors circulating in her office and the possibility that she could lose her job. But a fear had crept in that if they knew she might be unemployed soon, they'd use that as a reason to justify selling the house, even though Jill would have done whatever it took to pay her share of the expenses. "My deadline schedule has been crazy, but that's nothing new."

"It can't be that awful—you've been there, what, four years? That's a record for you, isn't it?" Rachel questioned.

Her sister was right that Jill hadn't ever stayed with one employer for more than three and a half years, but Rachel's comment made her feel like a slacker. Another statement from her sisters to try to ignore. Sure, Jill had changed companies and jobs more than Rachel, but it wasn't because she couldn't handle the workload—it was because she was restless.

As a student at a small, liberal arts college, Jill had been an English major, primarily because she loved to read and write. Also, because she was young and naive and no one had advised her to do anything different. But if she had known then how limited her career options were going to be, she would have specialized in something more practical.

After graduation, she'd taken a variety of roles until she stumbled into becoming a technical writer for a retailer of ready-to-assemble furniture. Once she'd mastered the necessary skills, she'd grown bored writing the same kinds of manuals, so she'd moved on to a new corporation, where she wrote end-user documentation for office equipment. And then she'd resigned from that role and so on. Technical writing was fulfilling to a point, but she considered it a job, not her life's calling. *Do I even* have *a calling?* she often wondered.

"Changing jobs frequently isn't necessarily a bad thing. It's important to keep growing and acquiring new skills," she said brightly. "And it keeps me from getting bored."

"I know, but it would be great if you could build up longevity with the same employer," Rachel enthusiastically encouraged her. "Have you considered pursuing a promotion to a position in management?"

"I've never really liked the idea of managing, telling other people how to handle their responsibilities," replied Jill, again feeling like she had to justify herself. "I'd rather concentrate on carrying out my own responsibilities than telling other people how to handle theirs."

"Hey, what's with all the work talk?" Brooke teased. "We're supposed to be on vacation."

"Then what are you doing online so early this morning?" Rachel shot back.

"Not much—I keep losing the connection." Brooke lowered the lid to her laptop and crossed the room to join her sisters. "But I was trying to check on the availability of a block of rooms at a resort in the Columbia River Gorge."

"You planning another vacation?"

"No." Brooke smirked. "I was going to wait until Todd got here to tell you but he won't mind if I break the news myself… We're going to have a vow renewal ceremony on Labor Day weekend, before school starts up again."

Jill could hear the excitement in her sister's voice and as much as she wanted to share in it, the first thought that struck her was,

*I haven't even had* one *wedding yet and you're planning your second one—to the same guy?*

"A vow renewal ceremony? Is seventeen a special anniversary?" Rachel asked.

"This will be our *eighteenth*, and no, it's not a major milestone or anything. But one of the couples from our neighborhood renewed their vows beneath a waterfall in a park on Mount Hood and it was really beautiful. I thought it would be meaningful for us to proclaim our commitment to each other again, too."

There was an extended pause before Rachel replied, "It was meaningful the first time."

"Yes, it really was," Jill agreed, fondly recalling how Brooke and Todd were married on Dune Island in a 300-year-old church in Rockfield. The reception was outdoors at The Overlook Inn in Highland Hills, which had a gorgeous vista of the ocean. But Jill's favorite memory was of getting ready for the wedding here at Nana's house with her grandmother, mother and sisters. Brooke had worn a blush-white gown because she'd thought it was dreamier than traditional white and—*Hey! Maybe she's gotten so thin because she wants to fit into her wedding gown again*, Jill silently speculated.

"That's exactly why we're renewing our vows—they were so meaningful the first time that we want to demonstrate that we'd take them all over again." Brooke exasperatedly dropped onto the end of the sofa. "I know it's kind of short notice, but I thought you'd be excited about coming out to Oregon. Todd and I are going to cover the cost of all our guests' accommodations. So you'll only have to pay for airfare and you've both mentioned you wanted to visit us this year anyway."

"You're covering all of your guests' accommodations? Isn't that kind of lavish?" Rachel asked.

"We aren't inviting that many people. A few close friends, Todd's parents, Jill, you, Derek and the kids. It's worth it to have the people we care most about there with us."

"A mountainside ceremony sounds very romantic," Jill gushed, trying to move on from Rachel's comment about the lavishness of the event. Even though in this instance she agreed with Rachel about finances—Brooke's plans did seem a bit excessive—Jill selfishly didn't want her sisters to get into an argument.

Especially because she hoped that later this morning they could discuss their plans for Nana's estate.

"I've always wanted to see the Columbia River Gorge. Rachel and I won't have to wear frou-frou bridesmaids' dresses again, will we?"

"No, but the girls might," Brooke said with a smile, referring to her eleven and thirteen-year-old daughters, Kaylee and Ella. She also had a son, Zach, who was sixteen, but Jill knew he wouldn't be caught dead in a suit; the boy wore a T-shirt and shorts year-round. In fact, he probably wore the *same* T-shirt and pair of shorts year-round.

"You'll have to tell me all the details once Rachel and I are done with the grocery list," she suggested.

Brooke agreed to help them plan their menu for the next few days after all. As Rachel was jotting down ingredients, the room grew so dim she had to switch on a light so she could see what she was writing.

"It looks ominous out there," she said when they'd finished compiling the list. "I'd better wait till the storm passes before I go shopping."

"In the meantime, maybe the three of us should talk about what we want to do with Nana's house?" Jill suggested hopefully.

Rachel wrinkled her forehead. "Don't you want to wait until we have more time to discuss our options thoroughly?"

"Why would we need more time?" Jill could feel her shoulders tensing up. "Is it because you're still seriously considering selling the house?"

"I've given it a lot of thought and I believe that's what we should do, yes."

"But you know how much Nana loved it here. So do I and I thought you did, too!" Jill objected in astonishment.

"Of course I do. And I consider us very fortunate that we've been able to vacation on Dune Island all these years," Rachel asserted firmly. "But as grateful as I am for the past, I need to think about the future, too. Especially in regard to the children."

"Don't you want Sea Breeze Lane to be part of their future?" Jill implored, knitting her eyebrows.

"Ideally, yes. But practically speaking, I don't know how that's going to happen. It was different when the three of us were kids—we lived in New Hampshire. All we had to do was drive a couple of hours and then hop on a ferry. We weren't coming all the way from Maryland," Rachel rationalized matter-of-factly. "Besides, after this year, Grace and Noah will need to be involved in summer internships and volunteer activities if they intend to get into Ivy League schools."

Jill turned to Brooke, who wasn't bent on her children getting accepted by the most prestigious colleges in the country, the way Rachel was. "Don't you want Zach, Ella and Kaylee to be able to come here in the summer?"

Brooke's answer surprised her. "Yes, but I'm not sure *they* do. The girls love music camp and Zach's in his element on the lake, so they'll probably want to do something similar next summer. And as I've mentioned, we've really enjoyed vacationing in the mountains these past three years. It's become something of a family tradition."

Thunder growled in the distance as Jill began to lose hope. "What about *our* tradition? Our family has been coming to Hope Haven for over seventy years. I'm not suggesting you'd have to bring your children and stay for the duration of the summer, but couldn't you at least squeeze in a couple of weeks?"

"I suppose. But as Rachel said, it's a long trip to make for such a short vacation."

*And yet you expect us to make a cross-country weekend trip for your vow renewal ceremony?* Jill thought, but she kept the observation to herself. "I don't get it. You two have never complained about traveling to Hope Haven in the past."

"That's because we felt like it was a priority for the kids to spend time with Nana—and with Mom and Dad, when they were alive."

"Nice to know where *I* stand," Jill mumbled. "I've loved spending time with my nieces and nephews here, too. And it seemed like they've enjoyed being together with me and with their cousins."

Brooke almost rolled her eyes. "They *do* love spending time with you and with each other. But that doesn't have to happen on Dune Island. We all have a lot more flexibility than Nana did about where we get together," she said. "We'd be thrilled if everyone came to Oregon and went camping with us in the mountains next summer."

"That would be fun," Rachel enthused. "As long as the kids have a free week."

"You're willing to travel all the way to the West Coast but not to Dune Island?" Jill challenged her.

Rachel sidestepped the issue, saying, "It's not *just* the traveling that makes it prohibitive to keep Nana's estate, Jill. It's also the expense. In addition to property taxes, we'd have to pay for the upkeep of the house and the yard. It all adds up."

"I know that." Jill refrained from reminding her sisters that unlike both of them, she hadn't gotten married shortly after graduating college. She might not be a homeowner, but she'd lived alone and she'd been solely responsible for paying her household bills without the benefit of a dual income for a lot longer than either of her sisters ever did. "But those costs seem negligible compared to the benefit of owning a home on Dune Island. It's a luxury most people can't even dream of experiencing. Have you considered the big picture? Right now the kids might be involved in summer activities, but for all you know, after college they could wind up living in Boston or New York. If we keep the house, they could vacation here as adults. Eventually, they'd probably bring their own children to the island." Surely the thought of continuing their family tradition for generations to come would appeal to Brooke and Rachel?

"But for all *you* know, *you* might move to Chicago next year," challenged Rachel. "You wouldn't be able to pop in and enjoy Nana's place on the weekends. So then what? The house would sit unoccupied except for two weeks out of the year when you stayed here."

Jill had frequently touted her mobility as one of the advantages of being single and not owning a home. If she had to, she could relocate at a moment's notice to wherever she found the best career opportunity, which also allowed her to experience life in a new city.

But now, her sisters didn't know that she was potentially in danger of losing her current job, and that she might have to leave Massachusetts in order to secure a new one. So she decided to claim, "I'm *not* going to move out of Boston—especially not if I can visit Nana's house on weekends in the summer again."

A gust of wind rattled the screen doors in their frames and a long peal of thunder vibrated the floorboards beneath Jill's bare feet. When it stopped, she proposed, "If I pay all the taxes myself and you two could simply come here whenever you wanted, then would you agree to keep the house?"

"Even if you could afford it, we'd never let you do that," Brooke scoffed. "It wouldn't be right."

"Well, what if..." Jill stalled, desperately struggling to come up with an alternative solution. "What if we rented out the house on a weekly basis for half of the summer? This is prime real estate, so during peak season we could probably charge enough to cover the cost of upkeep and taxes for the entire year."

"That's only *if* we were able to get renters every week. But we'd also have to pay for a cleaning crew, which you yourself said is nearly impossible to find. And we'd probably need to purchase extra homeowner's insurance, too. In the end, we'd be lucky to break even," Rachel countered. "On the other hand, if we sell the estate, we're guaranteed to make a small fortune and we'd receive it in one lump sum."

"Pbft," Jill spluttered, offended that her sister was applying a simple risk analysis formula to an issue as personal as whether or not to sell their Nana's place. "Is that your objective—to turn a profit on our inheritance? Why would the three of us need that kind of money all at once anyway?"

Although Rachel was usually unflappable, her faced turned red as she replied, "It's not my *goal* to make money from the estate, but I don't want to go into debt over it, either. It doesn't make good financial sense to own a summer house on an exclusive island just so we can vacation here two weeks out of the year."

"This isn't *a* summer house—it's *Nana's* summer *home*." Jill was so frustrated her sister didn't seem to appreciate the distinction that her voice shook. "And I don't just want to own it so I can vacation here. I want to own it—to *keep* it—because it's *ours*. It belongs to us, to four generations of our family. This is where Dad taught me how to swim. It's where Mom and Nana soothed our sunburns with cool teabags the year we bicycled to Highland Hills in our bathing suits. It's where Gracie took her first steps and Zach caught his first fish, not to mention, Dune Island is where Brooke and Todd got married! To me, this isn't just a place—it's a part of us."

"I treasure what our family has shared here every bit as much as you do," Brooke said, her voice even more tremulous than Jill's. "But that's exactly why I'm leaning toward selling the house. The memories are everywhere. It was so painful coming to Dune Island without Mom at first and then without Dad. And now, Nana's gone, too. Not having them here makes remembering our joyful times together almost unbearable..."

Her sentence trailed off as she shook her head, obviously trying to keep herself from crying. The horizon flickered repeatedly with white light, followed closely by a menacing rumble. Stealing a peek at her sisters' shadowed faces, Jill realized Rachel had been right: they should have waited to talk about this subject. Jill still didn't agree with them about the house, but continuing to argue about it now would be counterproductive.

"Listen, Rachel and Brooke," she said gently. "We're all trying to come to terms with Nana not being here and you two are probably both still tired from traveling. I know it's important to discuss the estate, but I shouldn't have brought it up first thing this morning. I'm sorry."

"It's okay." Rachel conceded, "We're going to have to talk about it sooner or later anyway."

"Yeah, but we should take a few days to relax, first." *Maybe by then, something in Nana's letters will persuade you to change your minds*, Jill thought.

"That's a good idea."

"I agree," Brooke said. "Let's not talk about the house at all for a while. Let's just enjoy how beautiful and peaceful it is here."

No sooner were the words were out of her mouth than a barrage of raindrops pelted the glass panes so hard it sounded as if it would shatter them.

"Quick, the windows! The sliding doors!" Rachel leaped to her feet and so did Jill and Brooke. The sisters dashed around the house, battening down the hatches as lightning illuminated the sky and thunder reverberated directly overhead.

"Look at that," Jill marveled when they'd returned to the living room. The wind was bending the neighbor's pitch pines as easily as if they were beach grass and sheets of rain seemed to slice through the air horizontally. "I've never seen a storm like this on Dune Island. Do you think it's a tornado?"

"I don't know, but we should move away from the windows," Rachel suggested.

"Ha," Brooke chuckled. "That's impossible in this house."

"We could at least move into the hallway. We'll be safer there if a tree comes crashing through the glass."

As if on cue, a series of brilliant flashes lit the room and a sonorous *boom* simultaneously shook the house. It was instantly followed by the sound of splintering wood, a loud *whoosh* and then a dull thump, which set off the cars' alarms.

"Whoa. That was close," Jill remarked, a split second before the lights went out.

# CHAPTER THREE

*Sunday – June 19, continued*

"Look on the bright side—at least it didn't land *on* the cars," Brooke said half an hour later as the sisters stood in the front yard, surveying the fallen willow tree that had effectively blocked their cars from leaving the driveway.

"Or on the house," Jill added somberly, shielding her eyes against the rain. The storm had rolled across the island and out to sea but it was still lightly sprinkling out.

"Mm. We're very fortunate," Rachel acknowledged. "I hope no one else on the island was hurt in the storm, either. But now we have no electricity and no food."

"And since Nana's house has a well and the pump needs power in order to function, we don't have any drinking water and we can't flush the toilets or take a shower, either," Jill reminded her.

"I'm sure the electricity will be restored soon." Once again, Brooke's sanguine outlook bordered on fantasy. Hope Haven was notoriously ill-equipped to handle power outages; it was one of only two complaints their father had ever expressed about the island. The other was that the cost of living there year-round was so exorbitant that the communities had a difficult time attracting essential employees.

"How can utility workers and teachers and bus drivers afford to live here when food and housing are two or three times as expensive here as they are in the rest of the state, but the salaries are the same?" he'd rant whenever there was an outage.

The issue of low wages on the island meant the power company remained woefully understaffed. Which meant it likely would be a full day or more before Nana's house would have electricity again.

"We'll have to fill a few buckets with water from the bay so we can flush the toilets manually," Rachel said. "But we should ride bikes to the market to buy drinking water. We can get produce and other non-perishable food items, too."

Brooke held up a finger as if something just occurred to her. "Or, here's an idea… we could order takeout and have it delivered."

Rachel chuckled. "Nice try, but everyone in Lucy's Ham will probably be doing that tonight. Besides, we don't know how many other trees are down. The restaurants might suspend delivery services if the roads are impassable."

From what the sisters could tell, the willow tree hadn't been struck by lightning as they'd first suspected; it had snapped in the wind. It appeared the neighbor had lost three or four small scrub pines and a larger black locust tree. So it seemed likely the damage to the surrounding neighborhoods was extensive, too.

"All right, you win for now," Brooke answered. "But if the power's still out tomorrow, we're getting supper at The Clam Shack—even if we have to ride our bikes there like we did when we were kids."

"It's a deal," Rachel agreed.

As it turned out, three of the four bikes Nana stored in the detached garage for her great-grandkids' use had flat tires and the pump was nowhere in sight. So Rachel volunteered to make the first trip into town, while Jill researched tree removal services. The jet lag was finally hitting Brooke, so she needed to go back to bed for a couple hours.

The Wi-Fi connection on Sea Breeze Lane was spotty at best, especially after a storm like the one that had just rolled through. So when Jill couldn't get online inside the house, she ambled down the dirt road with an outdated business directory in hand, hoping her phone signal was stronger there. She was delighted when her call went through to the first company she called, Alexander's Tree Services.

After providing her contact info and address, Jill began to explain their tree situation, saying, "A large willow fell in our front yard, so we're trapped—" But her phone dropped the call before she could complete her sentence. She tried to reconnect several times without success, so she turned around, went back inside the house and plonked down in one of the swivel chairs.

Dingy gray clouds hung low over the flat, lusterless bay and Jill could see a thick swarm of gnats spinning above the beach grass near the trail leading to the stairs. The atmosphere felt muggier and even more oppressive than it had before the storm, a sensation emphasized by the moisture beading on the door screens and the water dripping from the eaves.

During bad weather at Hope Haven, Nana used to say, "It might be raining in paradise, but it's still paradise." That's how Jill felt about the location, too. But since her sisters apparently had grown less enamored of the estate than she was, she decided she'd do whatever she could to minimize the effects of the storm.

She began by locating Nana's various household buckets and carrying them down to the bay. After filling them with water, she lugged them back upstairs, one-by-one, and set them in the bathrooms so the three women would be able to flush the toilets.

Then she went into the front yard and collected stray branches, which she heaped on a tarp to bring to the waste drop-off center later. Not that it made much of a difference in the appearance of the lawn—the fallen willow was a huge eyesore. But it needed to be done and she hoped to demonstrate to her sisters that the upkeep of Nana's house and yard were manageable. After that, she swept the sand and other debris off the deck.

For some reason, the year-round tenants either hadn't used Nana's all-weather furniture or else they'd returned it to the garage before they moved. It was just as well, since the furniture could have smashed against the sliding doors or gone sailing across the yard if it had been left out during the storm. But it took Jill nearly half an hour to carry the wicker chairs, hassocks and side tables to the deck.

Later, her sisters would have to help her transport the larger dining table, because in good weather, they'd eat almost all of their meals outdoors, beneath the retractable turquoise blue awning. Jill giggled to herself, remembering the report about their summer vacation her niece Ella had delivered to her class at school when she was ten. Trying to sound sophisticated, she'd told them that every day her family had eaten breakfast *au naturel*—she'd meant *al fresco*—on the deck with her grandmother.

*Nana had gotten such a kick out of hearing Brooke tell that story,* Jill recalled, as she brought the beach chairs to the storage rack at the top of the dunes. Although she understood what her sister meant about memories being everywhere, she disagreed that it was unbearable to remember the joyful times, now that her parents and Nana were no longer there. Recalling Nana's amusement over such a small thing made Jill happier than she'd been since she first arrived on the island.

Her work finished, she trudged around to the other side of the house to close the garage door. By that time, the ends of her hair were dripping and her tank top was plastered to her back. *I'm going to go take a nice, cool outdoor shower*, she decided before remembering the house had no water supply. *The tide's too low to go for a swim and now the house has lost its only source of shade*, she thought, glancing toward the willow. Just as she turned to go back inside, a tall, brawny man wearing a navy T-shirt, jeans and a baseball cap came walking around the stump end of the fallen tree.

"Hello." He raised his hand in a small wave as he approached. Admittedly, Jill noticed right off that he wasn't wearing a wedding ring. "Ms. Sampson, right?"

How did he know her name? Then she realized, *He must be the courier—he's got Nana's letter!* Except he wasn't carrying anything. Then who was he? "Yes, I'm Jill Sampson," she said cautiously, crossing her arms over her chest when he came to a standstill in front of her.

"I'm Alex." He paused, as if waiting for her to recognize him.

There was something familiar about his eyes—they were a pale, iridescent, silvery blue. Their color reminded Jill of the eyes on a dogfish shark she'd found washed ashore during one of her morning excursions with her father and grandmother when she was a child. *Odd, that such an unlikely creature could have such beautiful-colored eyes*, Jill recalled. Those eyes were striking. Unforgettable. *I definitely would have remembered if I'd met him before*, she thought.

When she didn't say anything, he prompted, "You called me this morning."

Noticing the logo on his cap, Jill finally caught on. "Ohh, you're Alex from Alexander's Tree Service! I didn't make the connection." *Because I was too distracted by your eyes.* And by his biceps, which were almost as big as, well, as big as tree stumps.

"Yeah. I know it seems kind of conceited to name my business after myself, but I only called it *Alexander's* because I'm not very creative," he explained, self-consciously stroking his beard. Actually, the salt-and-pepper colored hair on his chin and above his upper lip wasn't a full beard and moustache; it was more like medium stubble. He had very full, dark brows and thick lashes, too, but from what Jill could tell, his head was bald. Or at least she didn't see any hair poking out from beneath his cap. "My last name is Short, so I couldn't use that or else potential customers might think I only provide service for short trees."

Jill chuckled. "Titling is my least favorite part of writing, so I understand the difficulty."

Alex raised his eyebrows. "Are you a novelist?"

"Hardly. I write instruction manuals for household appliances."

"Really? Have you written any I might have read?"

Jill grinned. No one she'd met had ever sounded that impressed by her profession—except for her father. He'd always been a stickler for referencing user manuals instead of employing a trial and error approach to operating new appliances and technology. So he'd been inordinately proud of Jill's profession, which had struck her as both touching and humorous, given that she didn't consider herself to be nearly as successful as her sisters.

"That depends," she answered. "Do you own a carpet cleaner?"

"No. I've got hardwood floors, so I just use a standard vacuum."

Jill couldn't help noticing that he'd said, "*I* just use a standard vacuum." Not, "*We* just use a standard vacuum." She interpreted that to mean he lived alone. Or did it only mean he cleaned alone?

"Unfortunately, I don't write about anything as glamorous as vacuums."

"Vacuums are considered glamorous in your line of work?"

"Yes, at least the robotic ones are. At my company, there's a team of hi-tech whiz kids who write the manuals for them. So they also write about the uprights, handhelds and sweepers. I cover the good ol' fashioned heavy-duty carpet cleaners. But I'm hopeful that one day soon, I'll be able to switch departments." Even as she facetiously held her crossed fingers in the air, Jill inwardly cringed. *Why am I blathering on about vacuum cleaners?*

Alex didn't seem to mind. His gaze lingered on her as a smile spread across his face. "Well, anyway, I'm glad you're not trapped."

"Oh, I definitely wouldn't say I'm trapped. I mean, there are days when I wish I could be doing something else to earn a living, but who doesn't have that thought once in a while?"

"No. I-I was referring to the message you left. You said a tree fell in your front yard and you were trapped." He made a sweeping motion toward the willow.

*Duh.* Jill's cheeks burned. "I meant our cars were trapped in the driveway. My phone lost the signal and I couldn't call you back to finish my message."

"I figured it was something like that, but I didn't want to take any chances." Alex stepped closer to the tree and looked it over. "Yeah, I should be able to cut you free in no time."

"Now?" She had expected they'd need to wait at least until tomorrow afternoon or the next day before anyone could remove the tree. "That's terrific!"

"No, not now. Sorry." Alex looked chagrined. "I don't usually work on Sundays—don't check voice mail, either. But I had to today because of the storm. Unfortunately, I already have several customers lined up ahead of you. It's just that when I heard your message, well, like I said, I thought I'd better come over and make sure everyone was safe."

"Oh. I really am sorry about the false alarm." Sort of. Jill was still glad he was here; at least she was making progress addressing the tree situation. "So when do you think you *can* remove it?"

"Well… If you don't mind us coming first thing in the morning, we can cut a path through it for you tomorrow. We won't be able to circle back here to section it and chip or haul away the wood until Tuesday or Wednesday, but at least you'll be able to move your vehicles out of the driveway. How does that sound?"

"Fantastic." Since Jill wanted to check the mailbox, she accompanied him as he meandered around the tree, heading toward where he'd parked his truck in the road. "Thanks again for coming out here to make sure everything was okay."

"No problem. I'm just glad your situation isn't as dire as it sounded."

"Oh, I wouldn't say it isn't dire. I mean, I've only had one cup of coffee this morning," she retorted, tongue-in-cheek. "But I'm sure plenty of other people in Hope Haven don't have food or water, either."

Alex stopped walking and turned to face her. "I can give you a ride to the grocery store, since it's only a couple of miles from here."

Jill didn't answer. She was too distracted by the way the pale blue irises of his eyes were rimmed with darker blue. It reminded her of the distinct line of color separating the sea and sky on a clear, sunny day. *Is that why I feel like I've seen his eyes before?* she wondered.

Stammering, he added, "There's—there's room for a third person if your husband wants to come, too. Or-or your child. Or a, uh, a friend."

*He's trying to find out if I'm single*, she realized. Flattered, she blurted out, "That's really nice of you, but I'm not with anyone." She immediately tried to gloss over her gaffe by speaking quickly, "I mean, I'm here with my sisters and one of them rode a bicycle to the store, so she'll be back any minute with food and water."

"You sure? Because we can swing by there real quick. My first customer isn't expecting me until noon."

Jill might have accepted his offer if Rachel hadn't already gone shopping, but she declined again. "No, we're good. Thanks for offering, though." As she pushed a lock of hair behind her ear, a large drop of sweat dripped onto her bare shoulder and trickled down beneath the front of her top, which she just noticed was already soggy with perspiration. *Real attractive.* She did an about-face and took off toward the house, calling, "See you bright and early tomorrow morning."

*

Brooke was awake and lounging in the great room, phone in hand, when Jill entered the kitchen from the deck. "Who was that guy you were talking to?" she asked.

"His name's Alex—he owns the tree service company I called."

"Is he going to remove the tree?"

"Yes. But not all at once. Tomorrow he's going to cut a path for our cars and then come later in the week to take the rest away."

"Nice." A mischievous smile animated Brooke's lips. "Did you notice how ripped he is?"

"It would have been difficult to miss," Jill admitted.

"Was he wearing a wedding ring?"

"I don't think so," she lied.

"Who are you kidding? I know you checked. Was he wearing one or not?"

"No, he wasn't." Jill grinned as she pulled a paper towel from the roll and squeezed the ends of her hair with it. "I wish I could take a shower. I'm grimy and sweaty. I feel gross."

"You don't *look* gross. You look sultry," Brooke said. "Or what was that other word Nana used to use to describe you? It wasn't voluptuous, but it started with a V, I think. It was one of those words that was popular when she was young…"

"Va-va-voom," Jill reluctantly answered. Although she knew her grandmother had meant it to be flattering, she'd never liked the expression. It reminded her of the sound a very large, very loud car would make.

Brooke snapped her fingers. "Yeah, that's it. I could tell Alex thought you were *va-va-voom* by the way he was leaning toward you while you were talking."

"You were spying on us?"

"I wasn't *spying*. I was admiring the scenery and you happened to be in it."

"The scenery is in the opposite direction." Jill gathered her hair onto the top of her head and patted the paper towel across the nape of her neck. Then she went over to sit down by Brooke. "I have to admit, though, he has very pretty eyes."

"I'm sure he thought the same thing about you," Brooke said. "You know, I'm really glad you aren't with Brandon any more—he didn't deserve a relationship with you. But how come you never told me that he broke up with you so he could make a pathetic attempt to relive his youth? Or the youth he *wished* he'd had?"

Jill chuckled; her sister had hit the nail on the head about Brandon's behavior. "It just seemed so petty compared to, you know, everything else that was going on at the time."

"Do you want to talk about it now?"

"Thanks, but I'm over him. I am *so* over him."

"Does that mean if Alex asked you out, you'd say yes?"

Jill shook her head. "I doubt he's going to, but even if he did, what would be the point? I'm only going to be here for two weeks."

"Does there have to be a point? Couldn't you just go out with him for the fun of it?"

"Fun is overrated," Jill scoffed, letting her hair fall back down around her shoulders. "Seriously, at this point in my life, I'm not interested in casual dating any more. I've sworn it off for good."

"Why?"

She thought for a second. It was hard to explain to her happily married sister why she might not want to put her energy into dating just for the sake of it. "Mostly because for me, there is no such thing as casual—somehow, my heart always gets involved. And more often than not, I wind up feeling hurt over someone I wasn't all that crazy about in the first place. Case in point—Brandon." Jill paused before confiding, "I hate it that I have to keep starting over again and again. I want permanence. I want to get married and build a life together with someone, the way you and Rachel have done. You have no idea how lucky you are you met Todd when you were young."

Brooke's face clouded. "Don't be so sure of that. Sometimes I wish I'd had gone out with more guys before I got married."

Jill was a little taken aback. Her sister had never voiced any doubts about Todd before. "But you've always said you knew right away that Todd was your soulmate. Your one and only."

"He is," she quickly assured her sister. "But sometimes I wish we hadn't met until we were older."

Jill chuckled wryly. "Why? So you could have gone through years and years of breakups?"

"If that meant I could have gained experience and grown and had some fun along the way until I met Todd, then yes."

She knew what Brooke meant, but when Jill compared their very different situations, she didn't see things the same way. The 'fun' she might have had in her twenties didn't seem worth her current loneliness and longing to find somebody. "Easy for you to say. You've been married for almost eighteen years. But if you were my age and still single with no end in sight, you wouldn't feel that way," Jill said, her voice cracking unexpectedly.

Brooke gave her sister's knee a love tap. "If I were your age and single, *I'd* ask the tree guy to go out with *me*. Or I'd at least say yes if he asked me out. You never know when or where you might meet The One."

"I'm just happy I met The-One-Who-Can-Saw-Us-Out-of-Here-Tomorrow," Jill said, forcing her voice back to normal. "But you have to support me when I tell Rachel I hired him on the spot. You know what she's like. She wanted me to go through a long, complicated, comparison shopping process."

"Hey, that might not be such a bad idea. You could meet all of the tree trimmers on the island." Brooke laughed at own suggestion. "Don't worry, I'll definitely back you up… Hey, you know what I need to do today? Take a drive to the surf shop in Port Newcomb so I can buy a new swimsuit ASAP. The elastic is so stretched out on mine that the fabric gapes around my thighs."

"Are you sure that it's the elastic that's the problem?" Jill tentatively asked. "Maybe you've just gone down a size."

"That's possible, but either way, I need a new suit. I've been thinking of surprising Todd by getting a bikini this year. I haven't worn one since before I was pregnant with Zach."

"Is that why you've lost so much weight?" Jill bit her lip. She had asked the question before she'd thought it through. "I wondered if it was because you were trying to fit into your gown again."

Brooke furrowed her brow. "What gown?"

"Your *wedding* gown. For the vow renewal ceremony."

"Oh, no." Brooke waved her hand. "That's in storage. And I actually think it would be too big on me now, not too small."

"Hey," Jill said with a smile. "No need to boast."

Brooke rolled her eyes. "I wasn't. I haven't been *trying* to lose this much weight. Look at how saggy I am." She pinched the skin right beneath her chin. "Talk about no elasticity—it drives me nuts."

"Do you think..." Jill hesitated to say it because she didn't want to alarm her sister if Brooke hadn't already considered it. "Do you think you might have a health issue going on?"

"No. Definitely not. I had my annual physical in January and everything checked out fine. I think I just need to eat better."

"No. You need to eat more. *I* need to eat better."

Just then, Rachel appeared at the screen, a thermal bag in each hand. "Did I hear someone say they wanted a fresh salad for lunch?"

As the three women washed and chopped the vegetables that Rachel had brought home from the farm stand, she told them about the damage she'd encountered on the way into town. "You should have seen all the trees down on the bike path. I took one look and realized I wasn't going to be able to lift my bike over them, so I turned around and cycled through the Bayview neighborhood, instead."

She reported that the metal roof canopy over the gas station on Bridge Road had collapsed and one of the arms had snapped off the island's historic windmill. "From what people in town were saying, the storm wasn't a tornado—supposedly it was a very localized microburst and Lucy's Ham bore the brunt of it. The grocery store was mobbed, so I went to the farm stand. Fortunately, they still had bottled water there. And produce, of course."

"Since you didn't pick up anything besides water and veggies, does this mean we're having salad for supper, too?" Brooke asked.

"No." Rachel smiled self-consciously. "I figured we could order take out. The pizza at Mario's isn't too expensive and they deliver."

"Ooh, pizza. Are you sure we can afford to splurge like that?" Brooke teased.

"It was just a suggestion. I'm fine with ordering from The Clam Shack or even from Captain Clark's in Port Newcomb, although the food will probably be cold by the time it gets here and we can't reheat it."

Seizing on her sister's change in attitude about the grocery budget, Jill decided to break the news that she had hired Alex. "Guess what, Rach? I found someone who's going to cut a path through the tree early tomorrow morning so we can get in and out of the driveway. But he won't be able to haul the wood away until later in the week."

"Really? You hired someone without even talking to me about it, first?"

"Well, yes. Since I'm not a child, I didn't think I needed permission," Jill retorted, annoyed by her sister's tone.

"It's not that you need permission, but I would have appreciated being included in the decision, since I'm going to be paying for the service, too."

Realizing that Rachel had made a fair point, Jill apologized. "I'm so used to making decisions on my own that I guess I didn't think that part through. It's just that it was nearly impossible to even get a phone connection to call around for estimates. I was only able to leave a single message at one company, so when the owner showed up here to assess our situation, it seemed like a no-brainer to hire him. He said he had a long list of customers ahead of us and I'm sure it's going to be the same for all of the other tree services on the island. I figured if I didn't pounce on the opportunity, we'd be stuck for at least a week. Maybe two."

When some women were upset, their voices went higher; Rachel's dropped so low it was barely audible. "How much is his fee?"

"I… I don't know."

"Jill! How could you agree to hire him without even getting an estimate?"

"It's not her fault. She was mesmerized by his eyes." If that was Brooke's idea of backing her up, Jill would have been better off without her support.

"For all you know, this guy charges double what the all the other tree services on the island charge," Rachel said, her voice even quieter now. "It could be the difference between hundreds of dollars."

"Oh, come on Rachel! He didn't strike me as someone who'd take advantage of his customers like that. For one thing, he came all the way over here in person because he was concerned we might be in danger. And for another, when I told him we didn't have any food or water, he offered to take me to the store himself."

Brooke harumphed. "I *told* you he thought you were va-va-voom!"

Jill shot her a silencing look, but she just laughed.

Rachel seemed even less amused than Jill was. "So are you going to call and tell him we need an estimate and then we'll have to consult a few more companies before we make our decision?" she asked as she aggressively tore a leaf of Romaine lettuce into small pieces. " Or would you feel more comfortable if I called him?"

"Neither, because I don't want to waste our vacation dithering about who we should hire to haul away the tree. I just want to get it *done.*" Jill set the peeler down on the cutting board, took a deep breath and let it out. "Listen, since I didn't consult you before I made the decision, I'll call around to other services and get estimates. If we find out Alex charges more, I'll pay the difference between his fee and the lowest quote anyone else offers. You, Brooke and I can split the remaining expense three ways until the insurance company reimburses us. But as I said, he's coming very early tomorrow morning as a favor. I'm afraid if we cancel his service, we're not going to get anyone else to come out for at least a week. Then we'll be stuck riding our bikes to the grocery store every day."

"But why would you be willing to squander your money like that? Is it so you won't offend him? Because this is a business decision, it's nothing personal."

"Or is it?" Brooke teased. As the middle sister, she frequently used humor as a conciliatory tactic, but in this instance, it wasn't helpful.

Jill ignored her and replied to Rachel, "I already told you—enjoying our time here is more valuable to me than saving a few dollars. Besides, if that's what I want to do, what do you care? It's *my* money."

"But Jill, don't you see? You've said you'd like to own a house one day, but you'll never be able to afford it if you keep squandering your money on unnecessary extravagances."

"The reason I can't afford a house of my own yet is because I'm underpaid and I live in one of the most expensive parts of the country," Jill railed. "It's also because I don't have a husband who shares my living expenses with me, like you do. So let's make a deal. I won't say anything about your nickel-and-diming if you don't say anything about my so-called squandering and extravagances."

"Okay," Rachel concurred quietly and continued shredding the lettuce. Jill noticed her nostrils were turning pink as if she was about to cry, something her oldest sister rarely did in front of anyone and never about something as seemingly trivial as a disagreement. A moment later, when Rachel pushed her glasses up and swiped a finger beneath her eye, Jill felt a jab of guilt.

Deep down, she recognized that her sister was trying to be helpful. She was looking out for Jill and trying to save them all a little money. Even before their mom died—actually, it was ever since they were girls—Rachel had acted as a mother hen to her two younger sisters. She had always protected, encouraged and guided them when they needed it—and sometimes when they didn't. As with most people, her strength was also her weakness. But Jill had benefitted from her oldest sister's wisdom and support more often than not. So, while she didn't want to back down about hiring Alex, she regretted hurting her feelings.

"Should we use all of these mushrooms in the salad?" Brooke asked, breaking the silence.

"No. Let's set some of them aside," Rachel suggested. "If we get pizza, we can toss them onto the crust so we won't have to pay for an extra topping."

Jill's mouth dropped open but then she caught Rachel winking at Brooke and realized her sister was making a joke at her own expense. Jill mocked herself, too, saying, "I realize this might sound indulgent, but I think we should order a pizza with *everything* on it. Then we'll pick off whatever we don't want and toss it out the window, along with our money."

Rachel threw back her head and laughed, but Jill noticed her eyes were watery. She sensed her sister was covering up something that was more worrisome to her than whether they overpaid for tree removal service or not. In time, Rachel would probably share what it was, but for now, Jill was just glad the tension between them had lifted. The storm had passed. And with any luck, they'd soon have another letter from Nana delivered to their mailbox.

# CHAPTER FOUR

*Monday – June 20*

Each of the bedrooms in Nana's house had woven wood shades and blinds on the windows and sliding doors, but Jill rarely closed them because she liked waking at first light. She'd languorously stretch out beneath the sheets, reveling in the dawn chorus of birds in the nearby trees and the waves lapping at the shore.

But this morning she stumbled out of bed and across the room before she'd fully opened her eyes. Even though her eldest sister had given in about hiring Alex, Rachel wanted a written contract for his services. Jill was positive he was going to give them one this morning anyway, since it was clearly in *his* best interest to do so. But just in case she was wrong, she wanted to be the one to discuss his fees with him.

Standing in front of the large, distressed driftwood-framed mirror, she lifted her brush from the bureau top and attempted to pull it through her hair. But cooling off in saltwater the past two days had made her roots gummy and her head was throbbing from caffeine withdrawal. She did her best to tousle her locks with her fingers instead. Then she exchanged her pajamas for a pair of frayed denim cut-off shorts and a white, breezy, peasant-style embroidered top.

Since it was so early, she didn't bother to apply sunscreen. Besides, the forecast called for more showers—it had rained off and on all day yesterday—and the sky was littered with dreary clouds. Jill hoped the precipitation wouldn't start before Alex and his crew arrived. Or at least that it wouldn't prevent them from sawing a path through the willow tree. She desperately needed to get coffee and later she wanted to swing by the library.

Unlike her sisters, who'd spent as much of the previous day online as the weak Wi-Fi signal would allow, Jill had sworn off technology during this vacation. The only exception was to use her phone for brief calls. And to check it for texts from her coworker, Erika, who'd promised to let her know immediately if there were any developments regarding the status of their jobs.

Yesterday, after lunch Jill had managed to go for a brief swim and an even briefer walk in between rain showers. But she'd whiled away most of the afternoon in her favorite swivel chair, alternately contemplating the sodden seascape and leafing through Nana's collection of bird guides. Today she intended to make a copy of the library's *New York Times* Sunday crossword puzzle, since she hadn't been able to purchase a newspaper yesterday.

Tiptoeing down the stairs, she wondered if the courier had come last night after they'd gone to bed. Yesterday, she had jogged out to the mailbox half a dozen times, only to be disappointed when she'd found it empty. But as Rachel had reminded her, Nana hadn't promised that they'd receive a letter *every* day; she'd said that they'd receive a letter most days, for a total of ten after the first one. It was also possible there was no courier service on Sundays. Or that the storm damage had prevented the delivery.

Even so, Jill was itching to find out more about their grandmother's secret and she slipped outside to check the mailbox at the end of the driveway. The fallen willow's branches blocked her view of the narrow, unpaved road, so she didn't see Alex's truck bouncing toward the house until she was on the other side of the tree. *Great. Now I'm going to seem like I'm one of those impatient, demanding customers, waiting for him to show up at the crack of dawn so I can micromanage his progress.*

"Morning," she called nonchalantly, as if it was perfectly normal for her to be checking the mailbox at sunrise. It was empty.

Alex returned her greeting and introduced her to the other guys. Diego and Logan both gave her a friendly hello. The young men appeared to be in their early or mid-twenties and Jill couldn't help but wonder, *Did they get that buff from doing their job, or did they get their job because they're so buff*?

"You can start unloading. I'll be with you in a sec," Alex said to them. They promptly strode to the back of the truck and began removing saws and other equipment. Opening a metal compartment on the side of the vehicle, Alex told Jill, "I have something for you."

*Good—it's the contract,* she guessed, swatting at a greenhead fly buzzing near her ear. The pesky insects were notoriously aggressive biters; she hoped the guys were wearing repellant.

Alex turned toward her, balancing four cups, along with multiple creamers and sugars, in a cardboard tray. "For you and your sisters," he announced, handing it to her. "I hope there aren't more than four of you or you'll have to share."

*I think I'm in love*, Jill rhapsodized to herself. She was only half kidding. "No, there are only three of us. This is awesome, thanks."

"It's the least I can do for coming at this hour and waking everyone up. Technically, we're not supposed to start sawing until seven a.m. per town ordinance. But I noticed your neighbors' house is still boarded up and since they're not around to complain about the noise, I figured I'd bend the rules and get an even earlier start, as long as your family doesn't mind the racket."

"Not at all. We're just relieved that—"

She was going to express how grateful they were that he was prioritizing their situation when Rachel came marching into view. She was carrying her ledger binder with a pen clipped to it. "Good morning," she said in the crisp, businesslike tone Jill had heard her use when she was on the phone with a difficult customer.

"Morning, Rachel. This is Alex Short—and look what he brought us." Jill held up the cardboard tray to show her sister the coffee, silently pleading, *So please don't insult him by recalculating his figures right in front of him.*

"Hey, that's great. I'm dying for coffee." Rachel smiled, but Jill wasn't fooled. Her sister hardly paused half a beat before asking Alex, "Did you bring a written estimate or a contract, too?"

"Absolutely. I was just about to discuss it with Jill." Alex pulled a tri-folded sheet of paper from his back pocket and opened it flat. Pointing to a number near the bottom of the page, he explained, "Here's the total, which includes stump removal. Since the tree was healthy, it's going to take longer to break it up than if it was rotted. I charge a flat fee for the stump, instead of charging by diameter—it works out to be cheaper for the customer that way."

Rachel lowered her glasses from the top of her head and adjusted them on her nose. "Hmm," she murmured as she studied the document.

"Oh, yeah, I should have mentioned that I realize your situation is kind of..." He glanced at Jill. "Kind of *dire* and you probably haven't had time to call around to get estimates from anyone else. So if you research other services and find out you could have gotten a better deal with someone else, I'll match their price."

If Jill didn't know better, she'd have sworn Rachel just fell a little in love with Alex, too. "Great. We appreciate that."

"*And* we appreciate the coffee, which is going to get cold. We should go inside to drink it, since we're all set with the contract now," Jill hinted to Rachel.

"Yeah," Alex agreed. "It's safer if you go inside. Quieter, too. It's going to get pretty noisy out here in a couple of minutes—if you want our service, that is?"

"Yes." Rachel nodded absently, still looking at the form. "We do."

Alex seemed to sense her hesitancy and he suggested, "How about this... you don't have to sign the contract yet. You can take it inside with you and review thoroughly. But in the interest of our schedule, we'll go ahead and get started. I'll check in to answer any questions after we finish clearing a path for your cars. If you decide you don't want us to haul the wood, too, you're not obligated."

His no-risk offer put a genuine smile on Rachel's face. "Sounds good—thank you," she said.

They'd barely made it to the back deck before the saws started revving. As the pair stepped inside the house, Jill cracked, "Let's hope the noise doesn't wake Brooke up. Then you and I can have two cups of coffee each."

"Brooke is already awake," their sister said from where she was lying flat on her back on the sectional, her legs dangling over the far end. "I was too hot to sleep."

"Does that mean you're too hot for coffee, too?"

"Never." She sat upright and Jill noticed her shirt was drenched with sweat. After handing Brooke a cup, she took a seat at the opposite end of the sofa so she wouldn't make them both feel even hotter by crowding together.

Rachel plunked down in a chair across from them, examining the estimate. "This is actually less expensive than the prices I saw quoted on the website of two other local companies."

*I should have known that's what she was doing online yesterday*, Jill thought. Not that she minded; it relieved her of the responsibility of calling other places for estimates, like she said she'd do. "Brooke should take a look at the contract, too."

Rachel slid it across the coffee table. Brooke perused it and said, "Prices are a lot different here than they are where we live in Oregon, but this looks good to me." She leaned over and handed it to Jill. "You should be the one to sign it since he's your boyfriend."

"Funny." Jill scrawled her name across the bottom. Leaning back against the cushions, she sipped her coffee, relishing the taste and waiting for the caffeine to kick in.

"Mmm, this is so good," Brooke crooned over the whine of the saws. She said something else but her sisters couldn't hear her, so she raised her voice louder. "I asked which one of you biked to the bakery this morning?"

"Neither of us did. Alex brought it," Rachel shouted back. "Wasn't that thoughtful?"

"Oh, so now you're on a first name basis with him, too?" Brooke needled her. "I can't wait to meet this guy who has managed to charm *both* of my sisters."

"Shh." Jill held a finger to her lips.

"If he can hear me over that noise, his ears are even more impressive than his muscles," Brooke yelled, finishing her sentence just as the sawing stopped. She clapped her hand over her mouth and all three women momentarily froze, wide-eyed.

Their instinctive, collective reaction reminded Jill of when they were young girls. Often on summer nights when they were supposed to be sleeping, she and Brooke would sneak into Rachel's room so she could tell them one of the stories she liked making up. If they heard their parents' footsteps pausing in the hallway, they'd hold so still that they'd practically forget to breathe. Which was as silly then as it was now, since it wasn't as if they'd get into any real trouble if someone had overheard them talking.

"How come they stopped sawing?" Jill whispered after a minute.

"I don't know," Rachel whispered back.

"Why are we whispering?" Brooke asked in a hushed tone.

An abrupt rap on the front door followed her question, causing Jill to flinch so violently she nearly bounced off the couch. Brooke burst out laughing. Clutching her stomach, she began to stand up.

"*I'll* get it." Jill elbowed past her. With the mood her sister was in, there was no telling what she might say to Alex.

But it was Diego who was standing on the doorstep. Extending an envelope, he explained that the courier wanted to hand-deliver it to the house, but Alex said it wasn't safe for her to pass by the tree without a helmet on. "She said to tell you she was sorry she couldn't bring it to you yesterday because of the storm, and that you shouldn't expect a second letter today."

Jill thanked him and returned to the living room area. Aware her sisters had been straining to hear every word, she didn't bother repeating what Diego had said. She held up the envelope and asked, "Since it's not raining yet and it's too noisy up here, do you want to read this down on the beach?"

"Yes," Brooke immediately agreed. "We can stick our feet in the water to cool off."

So they carried their coffee and beach chairs outside to the bottom of the dunes. Jill cherished the familiar, post-storm messiness of the shore, where scallop, jingle and slipper shells were scattered across the damp sand. The wrack zone was also strewn with tangles of seaweed, mermaid's purses and horseshoe crab exoskeletons. *Maybe we'll go beachcombing later if the rain holds off,* she thought, glancing across the rumpled water at the low-slung ashen clouds drooping in the distance.

After they'd situated their chairs at the edge of the bay, she volunteered to read. She was barely able to contain her anticipation as she tore open the envelope.

*Hello again, girls,* she began. *I hope good weather is in the forecast—* Jill chuckled at the irony and then started over again:

*I hope good weather is in the forecast and that you've already adjusted to the pace of island living. I assume the children and your spouses are vacationing with you. As I write this letter on a wintry day in January, it tickles me to imagine a full house at Lucinda's Hamlet again.*

"It's not as full as she thinks," Brooke mumbled.

*Before I can get to the heart of the matter, I need to fill you in on my family background. Some of this your father may have told you, but most of it, even he didn't know.*

*When I think about my past now, it seems so long ago it's almost as if it happened to someone else. That's how I prefer to tell this story, too. Like those books I used to read to your father and then to you and your children, I'll begin with "Once upon a time, there lived…"*

*… two sisters, who were identical twins. Hattie and Rose Coleman. The sisters had exactly the same wavy brunette hair, big brown eyes and pointy-tipped noses. Yet they couldn't have been more different, even from an early age.*

*On their first day of school, when the teacher fretted that she wasn't going to able to tell them apart, their mother advised her to observe the girls' behavior for the telltale clue. "You can associate Rose's name with how she acts. She's my gentle wallflower."*

*Hattie was known for being bolder. Willful. Dramatic. She was considered "the beautiful twin," even though the sisters were identical.*

*The girls were the only children in the family; they'd had a younger baby brother, Theodore, but he'd died when he was eight days old.*

"Aww," Brooke mewled. "That's so sad. I wonder what happened to him."

"Me, too, but Nana doesn't say," Jill replied, scanning the page. She went on:

*Their father, Paul, was a physician and their mother, Audrey, a homemaker. The family lived in West Hartford, Connecticut, and while they weren't especially wealthy, they enjoyed certain privileges, such as summers on Dune Island when they were young. Every year their parents rented a sea captain's large home in Benjamin's Manor overlooking the water. Throughout the season, Audrey and Paul invited friends to stay with them for the weekends, sometimes longer.*

*If the guests brought their children, all the kids would tramp down to the bay and spend hours upon hours making sandcastles, swimming, and splashing through the tidal pools in pursuit of minnows and hermit crabs.*

*On rainy days, Hattie would corral the others into performing plays that Rose had written. Hattie always acted in the lead roles and often she'd improvise with song and dance numbers. She wanted to be an actress since she was very young, whereas Rose's dream was to become a wife and a mother.*

"No wonder Nana always found it so funny when I'd put on skits with the kids when they were little. It must have reminded her of her sister," Jill said. "Remember how we'd hang blankets on the clothesline and then we'd 'raise the curtain' at showtime? I'll never forget the one we did about the people who were shipwrecked. That was so corny."

"No it wasn't," Brooke countered. "It was hilarious. You were such a creative auntie."

"I think it was as much fun for me as it was for the kids." Jill cleared her throat and got back to the letter.

*When the girls were alone, Rose would plead with Hattie to play house and Hattie would indulge her, but eventually she'd get restless pretending to host tea parties, dressing up their dolls and cooking dinner for their make-believe husbands. So she'd create melodramatic characters and storylines, such as that she was a trapeze artist who only spoke French or that she was Rose's dying mother-in-law. Yet despite their differences, the girls were inseparable and they got along exceptionally well.*

*Don't misunderstand; jealousy occasionally arose when Rose was praised for being so much like their mother or when Hattie's theatrics earned her an inordinate amount of attention. But mostly, each twin appreciated the other's personality and delighted in her sister's achievements almost as much as she did in her own.*

*Theirs was a happy, healthy childhood, until the War broke out during their later youth. With it came many changes and hardships, but even then, the Colemans were exceptionally blessed in that they and their extended family remained relatively safe and healthy for the duration. However, after serving as a navy physician, Rose and Hattie's father returned home very depressed: he rarely came out of his study and he wouldn't practice medicine for months and months.*

*So the summer after the War ended, the girls' mother insisted they resume their vacations on Dune Island because she thought the solitude and fresh ocean air would do their father good. The large home they'd rented before the War was no longer available, but that was just as well, since they didn't intend to host guests or throw parties.*

*Back then, the island was far less populated than it is now, but Audrey wanted her husband to take a respite somewhere even remoter than Benjamin's Manor. So she rented two cottages on the bayside dunes in Lucinda's Hamlet. One cottage was for the four of them and Audrey's parents stayed in the other.*

Jill stopped to marvel, "There were *two* cottages on this property? I never knew that, did you?"

"No. Dad only mentioned that there was one," Brooke recalled. "He said it was lost in a winter storm when he was a boy."

"Shh, keep reading," Rachel urged, so Jill did.

*Like the twins, the tiny houses were identical. Both had typical weathered gray shingles and their doors were painted yellow, with white trim. Although the boxy structures were primitive, with exposed interior walls and cramped quarters, the cottages provided all the essentials; electricity, a gas stove and an indoor toilet. More importantly, they afforded uninterrupted privacy, proximity to the water and awe-inspiring views.*

*It turned out that Audrey was right; Paul benefitted greatly from the peace and quiet and long oceanside walks with his wife and daughters. By the summer's end, he returned to Connecticut and immediately began seeing patients again.*

*The next summer the family vacationed on Sea Breeze Lane again. The year after that, in 1948, the girls graduated high school. Their parents surprised them by announcing they'd purchased the cottages and the three-plus acres of land they were situated on. They paid less than $950 total.*

*It was tacitly understood the cottages were a kind of dowry, a place where the young women could vacation with their husbands and children someday. There was no question as to which twin would inherit which cottage. Rose would get the one nestled within two dunes, almost as if it was hiding. The one closer to the edge of the cliff and plainly visible from land and sea would be Hattie's.*

Brooke cut in to say, "This is incredible. It really does seem like you're reading a novel or something."

Rachel added, "It's sweet to picture those two little cottages so close together, yet so different, just like the sisters were. I'm glad Nana decided to share this with us."

"Especially since it must have taken her forever to write this by hand. Look how many pages I still have left." Jill held up the stack for her sisters to see before she continued:

*That year, Paul and Audrey only stayed on Dune Island with their daughters for two weeks. As a graduation gift, Rose and Hattie were permitted to remain there on their own for the rest of the summer, financially supported by their parents. The season was intended to be a time for them to experience a taste of independence, without any of the worries or responsibilities that came with adulthood.*

*Rose was delighted by the opportunity to "keep house" in a cottage of her own. Hattie auditioned for—and was awarded—the part of Laurey Williams in the play,* Oklahoma!, *which was performed at the Hope Haven Playhouse in Port Newcomb.*

Rachel snapped her fingers. "Hey, we went there once when we were kids. Jill, you were too young, but Mom took Brooke and me to see *Fiddler on the Roof* the summer it rained for ten days straight."

"I remember that!" Brooke exclaimed. "But didn't they convert the theater into a restaurant about ten years ago?"

"No. Now it's a very exclusive B&B—as if the island needed another one of those," Rachel replied sardonically before Jill returned to the letter.

*While Hattie was at rehearsals, Rose would read and experiment with new recipes. When together, the twins would spend their time swimming and beachcombing, or else they'd bicycle all over the island.*

*That was the year after construction had begun on the boardwalk and new shops were still being built right and left. Rose always wanted to stroll down the beach to that part of town, hoping to attract the attention of the young construction workers and carpenters. However, she was too shy to go alone and when she went with Hattie, she felt she might as well have been invisible, since the men were only drawn to her sister.*

*But no matter how many times they whooped and wolf-whistled or offered to buy Hattie lemonade or ice cream, she didn't give them a second glance. As she told Rose, acting was her passion. She couldn't imagine ever being as interested in a man as she was in performing in the theater. However, just like Rose eagerly helped Hattie rehearse her lines, Hattie accompanied Rose to the boardwalk as often as possible. Whenever they went, she tried to shine the spotlight on her introverted sister, but her efforts were to no avail.*

*One afternoon, trying to be helpful, Hattie suggested they attend a beach party at a waterfront mansion on the oceanside of the island. The young man summering there was named George Rutherford and the residence belonged to his great-uncle, one of the theater's wealthiest patrons. George played Curly McLain opposite Hattie's character in* Oklahoma!, *and he'd confided that he was smitten with her. If she hadn't been so committed to pursuing acting, she might have returned his affections. As it was, she'd gently turned him down, but they still enjoyed being friends and co-stars.*

*So when George invited her to the party at his relative's house, Hattie jumped at the chance to bring Rose. Her sister was such a strong, skillful swimmer that their parents often called her Mermaid Rose. Hattie was certain that any young man who saw how confident and graceful her sister appeared in the rolling surf would trip over his feet trying to get to know her.*

*But when they arrived at the party, Rose refused to remove the shorts she wore over her swimming suit. She felt too self-conscious about people seeing the patch of scarred, shiny skin on her upper left thigh where she'd burned herself with a cup of her mother's tea when she was a child. So she remained on the beach blanket the entire afternoon, no matter how Hattie tried to coax her into the water for a swim.*

"I always wondered why Nana never wore shorts," Rachel interjected. "I thought it was a generational thing."

Brooke agreed. "I assumed she had varicose veins she didn't want anyone to see."

"I didn't particularly notice that she didn't wear shorts, but I used to think it was strange she didn't ever come swimming with us since she clearly loved the water," Jill admitted.

She finished reading the final page of Nana's letter:

*Rose never did get a boyfriend—or even a date—that summer. But she said she didn't really mind. She rationalized that at the end of the season, she would have had to break up with a boyfriend anyway when she and Hattie returned to Connecticut. "When I fall in love, I want it to last forever," she'd claimed.*

*"And I want my next role to make me into a Broadway star," Hattie had declared, echoing her twin's youthful naiveté.*

*Then they promised that no matter how many children Rose had after she fell in love and got married and no matter how famous Hattie became, the sisters would always find a way to reunite for at least two weeks of vacation on Dune Island ...*

*I think I'll close my letter here, with what I call "The Sweet Summer of '48" so vivid in my mind that I only need to close my eyes and I can see my sister's shining, hopeful expression as she spoke about our futures.*

*My darling girls, how quickly the future has become the past.* Jill's voice caught a little. *Make the most of the time you have—and especially of the time you have together.* She ended by saying, "It's signed, *With love, Nana.*"

"Oh," Rachel sighed and Brooke wiped her eyes with the back of her hand, obviously as moved as Jill was by their grandmother's letter. She pondered its contents as a solitary great black-backed gull flew low over the bay on its way toward the marsh, followed a few moments later by four or five herring gulls. The tide gently nudged her ankles and Jill absently wiggled her toes in response, stirring up flecks of mica.

"I wish I could have met Nana's sister," she finally said aloud.

"Me, too. It sounds like Nana and Hattie were so different, yet so close. The way she wrote about their relationship reminds me of ours," Brooke reflected aloud. Then she chuckled and asked, "Can you believe Nana and her sister went to the boardwalk to see if the boys would notice them, just like we used to do when we were in high school?"

"*I* never did that," Rachel retorted. As a teenager, she'd been a serious, overachieving student who preferred to spend her spare time reading or playing the piano. "You're the one who sounds most similar to Nana when she was young, Brooke. You loved playing with dolls when we were little. And you were so boy-crazy as a teenager I'm surprised Mom and Dad ever let you go to the boardwalk alone."

Brooke acted offended, but couldn't deny the truth in Rachel's words. "I didn't go alone—Jill always came, too."

"I was so proud you let me tag along," Jill recalled. "But I know exactly how Nana felt around Hattie, because the boys didn't pay any attention to me." She nudged Brooke. "They only flirted with you."

"My, how times have changed." Brooke exaggerated a sigh. "No one flirts with me any more. It's because I look so haggard."

"It's because you look so *married.* Your wedding ring, remember?"

"What wedding ring?" Brooke held up her left hand and wiggled her fingers beside her face. "I can't wear it any more. It's too loose. Seriously, I haven't worn it for over a month and no one has given me a second glance."

Jill cocked her head. "Are you *trying* to get a second glance from someone other than Todd?"

"Not trying, no. But if it happened, I wouldn't mind. At least then I wouldn't feel so invisible."

Ignoring their chit-chat about guys, just as she'd done when they were young, Rachel switched the subject. "What's fascinating to me is what Nana wrote about our family's background within the context of global history. Like about how her father recuperated in Hope Haven after the War."

*That's why we can't sell our ancestors' estate*, Jill felt like saying. *This place was literally life-saving to them. It's obvious they expected to keep the cottages in the family for generations to come.*

She also felt like emphasizing what Nana had written about pledging to get together with Hattie on Dune Island, no matter what else happened in their lives. Jill wished that she and her sisters could make that kind of promise to each other, too.

But she resisted the urge to express what she was thinking. She had the sense that if she waited it out, her grandmother's words would be far more effective than anything Jill could say to persuade her sisters to change their minds about Nana's estate.

However, she didn't stop herself from hinting, "I wonder if George Rutherford's great-uncle passed his mansion down to him or to his other relatives. Maybe his descendants are summering in Highland Hills right now, just like we are."

Rachel reached for her phone. "Maybe. We could look them up online."

"No, don't do that," Brooke objected sharply. "Nana waited all these years to tell us about this part of her life in her own words. You can't start researching people she knew to find out what happened to them—it's cheating. It's like reading the last page of a novel before you've read everything that comes before it."

"Okay, okay, I won't. I promise," Rachel said.

"Me, neither," Jill agreed.

"Um, excuse me?" a man's deep voice cut into their conversation. The three sisters twisted their necks to see Alex standing at the top landing of the staircase, cupping his hands around his mouth. Jill had been so consumed by her grandmother's letter she hadn't realized until now that the sawing sound had stopped.

Leaping to her feet, she called, "I'll be right up." She handed Nana's letter to Rachel and jogged up the stairs with the contract. When she reached the top, she held it out to him. "Sorry, it looks like I got it a little wet but I think my signature's still legible."

"Thanks," he said, but he didn't take the document. "I-I'm afraid one of my staff members had a little accident."

"Oh, no!" Jill reflexively touched his forearm. "What can I do to help? Should I call an ambulance? Do you need first aid supplies?"

"No, no. Sorry. Not that kind of accident. No one's injured. But Logan was moving a limb and he scratched one of the cars."

"Is that all? I'm just glad no one's hurt. A scratched car is nothing to get upset about."

Alex's expression remained grim. "You'd better come see the damage before you say that. The scratch runs almost the entire length of the driver's side."

"I'm not worried about it," she reassured him as they headed toward the front of the house. *Although I can't promise Rachel will feel the same way.* "So, um, which car was it?"

"The green one."

Jill exhaled. "Phew!"

"I take it the green one isn't yours?"

"No. The green one *is* mine," she said.

Shaking his head, Alex gave her an appreciative, sidelong grin. "Most people would have had the opposite reaction."

Jill shrugged. "A scratch doesn't interfere with how well it drives."

"It goes without saying that I'll pay for you to take it into a shop," he told her when they'd reached the car. The scratch was definitely noticeable and long, but Jill could see it wasn't deep. It hadn't even penetrated the primer level of the paint job.

"This is nothing I can't fix with a good repair kit," she told him.

"But the car is only, what? Two or three years old? You really should take it in to a shop and have it professionally corrected or repainted."

Jill thrust her hands on her hips, pretending to be more indignant than she felt. "For your information, eight years ago I happened to revise the instruction manual for one of the best car scratch repair kits on the market. I've also successfully used that same kit on two of my friends' cars and they look as good as new. So I like to think of *myself* as a professional."

Covering his eyes with his hand, Alex tipped back his head and groaned. Then he dropped his arm and looked at her, red-faced. "I'm sorry. I was only trying to underscore that I'll pay whatever it costs to restore the paint job to its original condition. I didn't mean to sound condescending or sexist or something."

Jill smiled; she had a soft spot for any man who blushed in her presence. "It's fine. I wasn't really offended."

"I still hope you'll take it in to a shop. Not because you can't do it yourself, but because why should you have to deal with that hassle when I'm the one who ruined it?"

"I thought you said Logan scratched my car."

"Right, but I'm responsible for his work."

"That's why I'm glad I'm not in management—or a business owner. I couldn't handle the pressure of being responsible for what other people do," Jill empathized.

"Well, to be fair, the scratch was probably more my fault than his," Alex admitted. "Logan's part of a summer vocational training program, so I should have provided more detailed instruction, but I bungled our communication."

A man who owned his mistakes was every bit as attractive to Jill as a man who blushed in her presence. *I'd better be careful*, she thought, remembering her resolution not to fall for someone if they had no future together. She caught a glimpse of Logan and Diego loading equipment into Alex's truck. Maybe he was just preoccupied with what he was doing, but it seemed to her Logan was keeping his back turned on purpose. "Could you let Logan know I'm not upset about the scratch?"

"Sure. I'll pass along the message." As the guys banged the doors shut, Alex said he'd better get going.

"Don't forget this." Jill held out the contract and this time he took it.

"Thanks. I'll see you tomorrow around three or three-thirty."

*Looking forward to it*, she thought. "See you then."

Jill came around the house just as her sisters were going inside. After she told them about the scratch on the car and what she intended to do about it, Rachel immediately said, "You really should take it into an autobody shop and have the paint job restored, Jill. Someday you might want to sell or trade in your car and a scratch will affect its value. I'm sure Alex has insurance to cover accidents like this."

*Funny how Rachel is usually in favor of DIY projects, unless someone else is footing the bill*, Jill thought. But she didn't want to hurt Rachel's feelings again by retorting the way she'd done the day before, so she said, "I'm not worried about it."

Rachel seemed to get the hint that she shouldn't worry about Jill's car, either, and she let the subject drop. Surprisingly, however, Brooke piped up, "Rachel's right. You shouldn't let him get by with scratching your car just because he brought us coffee."

*Where is* that *coming from?* Jill wondered. "I'm not letting him *get by* with anything," she replied. *A superficial scratch on an inanimate object apparently doesn't mean as much to me as it means to you*, is what she wanted to say, but didn't.

Brooke combed her fingers through her hair and frowned. Depositing the loose strands into the garbage bin, she said, "I wouldn't want him to take advantage of your easy-going nature, that's all."

*Like Brandon did, is that what you mean?* Jill thought, regretting that she'd told her sister about why they'd broken up. "I wasn't born yesterday, you know—and I wasn't born sixteen years ago, either. So you might want to save your relationship advice for Kaylee and Ella."

"My *relationship* advice? I thought we were talking business."

Rachel intervened with an abrupt change of subject. "Brooke and I decided to go to Port Newcomb. Do you want to come with us?"

"Now?" Jill was disappointed. "Does this mean we're done discussing Nana's story?"

"Well, Brooke wants to shop for a swimsuit and I need to pop into the pharmacy before we head to the grocery store. But we could talk about the letter in the car."

That didn't seem as if it would be worthwhile; there'd be too many distractions. And Jill didn't particularly care to drive to town with her sisters just for the purpose of running errands. She didn't even feel like going to the library any longer. All she wanted to do was give Nana's correspondence the attention she felt it deserved. So after Brook and Rachel had left, she settled into the scallop-shaped swivel chair to reread her grandmother's letter.

There was so much to take in, but what particularly struck Jill after a second reading was how different Nana Rose was from her sister. Hattie knew from the time she was young that she didn't want to get married or become a mother. *It couldn't have been very common for a woman back then to deliberately choose a career over marriage and motherhood,* she thought. *She must have* really *loved acting.* Jill wondered what it would be like to be that passionate about her vocation and it saddened her to realize that Hattie had died before her aspirations were fulfilled.

She was equally sorry that Nana's wish to fall in love and have it last forever didn't come true, either. Her *husband's* love hadn't lasted forever, anyway. The girls had grown up never knowing their grandfather. But now that she thought about it, Jill realized she'd never heard her grandmother speak a word against him, nor had she ever remarried. As far as she knew, Nana had never even dated again after her divorce, years before the girls were born, when their father was just a little boy. Was it possible that was because she'd never stopped loving her husband, even though he'd left her to marry another woman? Were Nana's feelings about him somehow related to her secret?

*I'm getting ahead of the story*, Jill realized, recalling what Brooke had said about not flipping to the last page in a book before reading what came before it. Although it frustrated her, Jill was just going to have to wait to learn more about her grandmother's past. She was also going to have to wait to find out what would happen with the estate. As well as with her job. She was even going to have to wait for the power to come back on.

Yet as she refolded the letter and slid it back into its envelope, Jill could almost hear Nana reminding her, "My darling girl, you're on Dune Island time now. The tide will come in when it comes in. So stop worrying about the future and go enjoy a long, leisurely stroll down the beach."

A tear trickling from the corner of her eye, Jill silently replied, *I'll try, Nana.* But she knew it wasn't going to be nearly as pleasurable without her grandmother or sisters there to walk along beside her.

# CHAPTER FIVE

## *Tuesday – June 21*

Because the power still hadn't been restored to Nana's house, on Tuesday morning Jill charged her phone in the car as she drove to pick up coffee and almond croissants from the bakery.

It was forecasted to be another sticky, sunless day. White sky and moist air. Jill preferred storm clouds and downpours to this in-between kind of weather that made it difficult to tell what time of day it was, and if it was misting or she was just sweating. So when she returned, she idled in the driveway, her eyes closed as she relished the cool, dry, air-conditioned interior for a few luscious minutes longer.

Finally, she turned off the ignition and checked her phone for a text from her coworker, Erika. There wasn't one. "No news is good news," she said aloud, right before someone rapped on her window.

Jill didn't know what surprised her more—that it was Alex or that he wasn't wearing his cap. This was the first time she'd seen him without it. She noticed that although he had a receding hairline, the rest of his skull wasn't balding; it was shaved. In contrast to his speckled scalp, his brows and beard appeared heavier and darker than they'd looked when his head was covered. They framed his face and turned his eyes an electrifying shade of blue. Peering into them, Jill felt as if she couldn't move. It was like Brooke had said: she was mesmerized.

"Hi, Jill," he greeted her through the glass.

"Hi, Alex." She fumbled with her seatbelt and he stepped back so she could get out. "I didn't expect to see you here until later this afternoon."

"I had to reshuffle my schedule, so I thought we'd clear away most of the tree this morning and then finish up the rest tomorrow afternoon, if that's okay with you." When she agreed, Alex turned toward his truck and gave the thumbs-up sign. Diego and another man got out and began unloading equipment.

"I notice Logan isn't here today." She joked, "You didn't fire him, did you?"

"No, nothing like that." Alex rocked back on his heels, his thumbs hooked in his pockets. Jill liked how he always made it seem as if he had plenty of time to chat, even though she knew he was actually really busy. "He only works for me part-time. On Tuesdays and Thursdays he takes classes at the vocational school in—oops, watch out, a greenhead just landed on your shoulder."

Jill turned her head to the left and squinted. "Where?"

"Other side. Here." He whisked his fingers over her right shoulder and down her bare arm to her elbow. Talk about electrifying; his eyes paled in comparison to his touch. Jill shivered noticeably in response. "Sorry, but he was ready to bite. Although it looks like his friends beat him to it."

Jill stuck her elbow out to the side, examining the length of her arm. It was spotted with half a dozen pink welts. "Supposedly, they're attracted to the scent of salt. Since the power's still out and our well pump runs on electricity, I haven't been able to rinse off after I've gone swimming."

"That's rough." Alex's cheeks slowly widened with a grin. "But here's an idea… You could swing by my place for a shower."

Jill had realized there was a spark between them, but all of a sudden he was coming on a little too strong for her comfort. It was a turn-off. And unprofessional. "No, thanks," she said, her shoulders tensing.

He must have noticed the change in her tone and body language, because he clarified, "I meant you could swing by my house now, when I'm not there. It's-it's an outdoor shower."

"An outdoor shower?" she repeated, looking askance at him.

"Yes, but don't worry, it's got hot water. I also let my little sister and her housemates use it though, so you might have to get in line."

"There's a *queue* of young women showering at your house?" Jill uttered in disbelief. "In that case, definitely no thanks."

"That came out wrong." Alex was blushing again. Most of the creeps she'd encountered weren't usually that embarrassed by their behavior, so she decided to hear him out. "My sister, Sydney, lives a couple of streets over from me in a home for women with intellectual disabilities. I let her and her housemates rinse off at my place after they go to the beach because they don't have an outdoor shower at theirs, and the sand can wreak havoc on indoor plumbing. Their home manager always accompanies them and they never shower there when I'm home. If my truck is in the driveway, they aren't allowed to stop in—that's the rule. No exceptions."

"Oh." Now that she had a better understanding, Jill relaxed her stance. "At our place, the rule is that we have to latch the shower door when we're done, otherwise it will bang against the frame in the wind." She'd hoped to put Alex at ease, too, but her comment didn't elicit a smile.

He stammered, "I-I really appreciated how calmly you reacted after I told you Logan scratched your car and I wanted to do something helpful to make your day a little easier, too. That's why I suggested the shower. But I'm sorry if I came across as unprofessional or if I offended you. I hope you'll accept my apology."

"Of course, I do," she said, nodding decisively. She could practically see the relief washing over Alex's features and to be honest, she was relieved, too. She'd felt awfully disappointed when it seemed as if he might have been a letch toward his sisters' friends. "And I appreciate the offer, but I'm hopeful our electricity will come on any second now."

"Okay. But if doesn't, I live at 15 Driftwood Ave. It's off Main Street, four blocks north of The Clam Shack. If you can smell fried food, you know you're getting close."

"Thanks. I'll remember that," Jill said with a smile, just as a delivery truck pulled to a stop parallel with the driveway. She went to greet the courier as Alex rejoined his crew.

"Special delivery," Jill announced in a sing-song voice when she entered the house, holding up the envelope. "Another letter from Nana."

"Great, but where's our coffee?" Rachel asked, prompting Jill to remember she'd left it in the car.

By the time she'd retrieved it and the trio had settled onto the sofa in the great room, the coffee was lukewarm, much to her sisters' dismay.

"Next time you go to the bakery, could you please bring our coffee inside *before* you spend half an hour flirting with Alex? Or at least remember to take our thermal cups with you?" Brooke shouted. It was difficult to tell whether she was genuinely irked or if she was only raising her voice to be heard over the din of the saws and woodchipper.

Jill couldn't deny that the coffee had grown cold while she'd been talking to Alex, although cranking up the A/C in the car hadn't helped, either. Mumbling an apology, she got up and closed the sliding doors. Since there wasn't a breeze blowing through anyway, Jill figured she might as well block out some of the noise.

"I hope there's not going to *be* a next time," Rachel said. "The utility company had better restore our power by this afternoon, or else we're going to blow our entire grocery budget buying takeout coffee."

"I don't mind not having a coffee maker, but what I really can't wait to do is wash my hair. I'm shedding like a cat and I think it's because I've got so much salt and sand on my scalp," Brooke complained. "If the power doesn't come on by noon, I'm going to go wash it in one of the town beach showers in Rockland or Highland Hills."

"You can't," Rachel objected. "Shampoo use is prohibited in the town beach showers."

"So let a park ranger fine me, then. It will be worth every penny to have clean hair again."

"But is clean hair worth disturbing the ecosystem?"

Although Rachel was right about the need to consider the environment, Jill anticipated her know-it-all tone was going to tick Brooke off and she already seemed highly agitated. So she interrupted her sisters' quibbling to suggest, "We could go over to Alex's house and use his outdoor shower while he's here working on the tree."

Brooke guffawed, as if Jill had been joking and Rachel cracked, "Sure thing, Goldilocks. When we're done using his shower, we can eat up all his porridge, too."

"I didn't mean we should *sneak* over to his house and use his shower without him knowing about it," Jill clarified indignantly. "He *told* me I could use it. I'm sure he wouldn't care if you did, too."

Brooke and Rachel exchanged one of those raised-eyebrow looks that aggravated Jill as much at thirty-nine as it had when she'd been thirteen. Even after she fully elaborated on her conversation with Alex, Rachel said she was going to have to pass.

"I'm going to pass, too, so it looks like you're on your own, Jill." Brooke said. "But, just to be clear… aren't you the same woman who sat here on Sunday and claimed she wasn't interested in casual dating any more?"

"I'm *not* interested in casual dating any more."

"Does Alex know that?"

Rather than answer Brooke's question, Jill came back with, "Are you almost done eating that croissant? Because I'm happy to take your turn reading Nana's letter if you're going to be chewing for a while." She reached for the envelope on the table, but Brooke snatched it up first.

After swallowing the last bite of her croissant, Brooke took a sip of coffee, scowled into the cup and set it aside. Finally, she opened the envelope and began reading their grandmother's words:

*Hello, Rachel, Brooke and Jill,*

*I like to imagine myself in a lounge chair near the edge of the dune, watching all of you swimming and diving and playing games down below in the bay. I know you and your children will stay in the water until your lips turn blue and the skin on your fingertips and toes wrinkle, just as my sister and I used to do.*

"We would if we had better weather, but it's been raining off and on for days," Rachel said conversationally, as if Nana was speaking on the phone to them.

Brooke lowered the letter to her lap. "No kidding. Can you believe we still haven't seen a single sunset since we got here?"

Because Nana's house was located on the western side of the island and it had an unimpeded view of the horizon, watching the magnificent sunsets together was a cherished family tradition, something even the children learned to appreciate from a young age. It didn't matter what else was going on; if it was time for the sun to set, everyone stopped whatever they were doing and went out to the deck to witness it.

Jill counted those evenings among her favorite experiences on Dune Island, but Brooke looked forward to them even more than she did. In fact, she'd often said that her only regret about her wedding was that she'd held the reception at a venue facing east, instead of west. She thought it would have been more romantic if her first dance with her husband had been against the backdrop of the setting sun.

So Jill understood how disappointed she was that there had been heavy cloud cover for the past four evenings. But she was impatient to hear more of Nana's letter. She pressed her sister to keep reading and Brooke obliged.

*Anyway, I'll pick up where I left off in my previous letter, with the twins returning home after spending the summer in the cottages. Despite being bright young women, they had no interest in going to college since they didn't believe it would foster their ultimate goals. Rose enrolled in secretarial school, whereas Hattie wanted to continue to pursue acting, much to her parents' dismay. While they appreciated her talent during her youth, in their circles, acting wasn't considered a respectable profession for a grown woman. They'd hoped after performing in* Oklahoma!, *she would have gotten the acting bug out of her system and settled down to do something sensible until she got married and started a family, like her sister planned to do.*

*On the contrary, performing only increased Hattie's interest in the theater. The topic of her future was the source of much friction between her and her parents. Rose was often in the middle of their disagreements, trying to smooth things over or help each side see the other's perspective. Despite her twin's best negotiation tactics, at the end of September, Hattie and her parents had such a heated argument it resulted in Hattie moving to New York City against their wishes.*

*Drawing from a small inheritance the twins' paternal grandparents had left the girls, she was able to pay rent on an apartment she shared with three other young ladies until she secured employment as a hotel switchboard operator. She worked the overnight shift so she could spend as much of the day and evening as she could watching rehearsals and going to plays, which was how she studied and learned from leading actresses.*

*It was very, very difficult for the twins to be separated. But of the two, Hattie probably had it worse, because she wasn't just lonely for Rose; she missed her parents and she was homesick for the slower pace of Connecticut. She'd use the phone at work to call her sister twice per shift—when it began at night and again just before it ended in the morning. By November, Hattie couldn't stand being away any longer so the twins made plans for her to surprise their parents by coming home for a visit at Thanksgiving.*

*However, two days before her arrival, the girls' parents were killed—*

Brooke stopped reading, waited, and tried again, her voice wobbling. *When a truck hit their automobile as they pulled out of an intersection.*

"I can't do this." Brooke wiped her cheek with one hand and extended the letter with the other. One of you has to read it."

Despite her earlier offer to take Brooke's turn, Jill didn't think she'd be able to keep her voice steady, either. Rachel took the letter and carried on.

*The young women were beyond devastated; they were traumatized to the point of despondency. (Even as I write this now, I have absolutely no recollection of what happened during the several weeks following Thanksgiving.) If the sisters hadn't had each other to cling to, they surely would have drowned.*

That strange line made Jill choke up because it resonated with how she'd felt when her mother and then her father had died. But at least Jill and her sisters weren't as young as Nana and Hattie had been when they'd lost their parents—and they hadn't lost both parents at the same time, either. *It's no wonder Nana knew just how to comfort me after Mom passed away suddenly… and then when Dad died, too,* she thought.

Wiping her eyes with her fingertips, she realized she'd missed what Rachel had just said, so she asked her to repeat it. Rachel read:

*The girls' maternal grandparents, who lived on the opposite side of the river in East Hartford, took them in and ushered them through their initial bereavement. That winter was every bit as bitter for Rose and Hattie as the summer had been sweet. But by early March, when Hattie heard about an audition for a role she really wanted in New York, she decided it was time to pick up the pieces of her shattered life and return to acting.*

*Consequently, Rose's grief was compounded by loneliness for her twin. She had dropped out of secretarial classes when her parents died, but she felt too lost and listless to re-enroll after Hattie left. Instead, she helped their grandparents attend to the details of Audrey and Paul's will and sell the house, since she had no desire to live there on her own.*

*The family's long-term accountant, Robert Sampson, helped her out. A divorcé without any children, he was twelve years older than Rose. But that didn't stop him from becoming interested in her, while he worked on her parents' financials. He was clever enough to seek her grandparents' permission to date her before he asked Rose out. They were taken in by his charming manners and the honorable intentions he expressed toward their granddaughter, who appeared to reciprocate his affections.*

*Hattie, however, was skeptical. She suggested Robert was too old and questioned whether he was more interested in Rose's trust fund than in Rose herself. Especially since he was the one who knew his way around the paperwork.*

*Profoundly hurt, Rose told her sister she was selfish for not supporting her desire to become a wife and mother, especially since Rose had always fostered Hattie's dream of becoming an actress.*

*Because the girls rarely argued, the emotional distance between them proved even more difficult to bear than the physical separation. The rift was so intense and painful that they considered forgoing their vacation together on Dune Island. However, both of them were aware that if Rose got married soon, the vacation might be their last opportunity to spend two weeks alone, so they kept their promise to reunite at the cottages.*

*At first, their interactions were polite, yet strained, and both of them were on the defensive. But the ocean has a way of uncovering hidden things and bringing them to the surface. Not just shipwrecks, but a person's fondest longings and deepest hurts…*

*After a few days of living alongside the ocean—and alongside each other—the girls both broke down in tears. Rose confided how abandoned she'd felt when Hattie left her alone after their parents' death. Hattie, in turn, confessed that there had never been any audition in New York that past March. She'd fled to the city because she couldn't stand the shame and guilt of knowing the last words she'd spoken to her parents were in anger.*

*There were many more tears after that, but in the days that followed there was healing, too. As Rose said when it came time for the sisters to part, "I'm so glad we had this time together. It feels as if we're opposite halves of the same heart again."*

Although Brooke and Jill had both become tearful several paragraphs earlier, stoic Rachel had managed to carry on dry-eyed. Now, however, she paused, lifted her glasses and pressed her palms against her eyelids before reading any further.

*The following November, when Rose married Robert in a civil ceremony at the courthouse—they didn't even exchange rings—Hattie stood proudly beside her as her maid of honor. And when Hattie earned her first bit part in January as a substitute dancer in what would now be called an off-Broadway play, Rose caught a train to New York by herself during a snowstorm so she could watch her sister's two-minute performance.*

*... Speaking of snow, my arthritis is flaring up in my fingers, which means the weather's about to change, so I need to stop writing now. Strange to imagine that as you read this, you'll be wearing T-shirts and swimming suits. Don't forget to use sunscreen.*

"She signs it, *With love, Nana*," Rachel reported, before setting the letter on the table. She rose and wordlessly crossed the room to retrieve a box of tissues. After removing one, she passed the box to Jill, who helped herself before handing it over to Brooke. Years ago, Rachel and Jill had learned that once they surrendered the box to Brooke, they'd never get it back, so they'd better take what they needed first.

"No wonder Nana never wanted to talk about her history," Brooke cried, yanking six tissues from the box in rapid succession. "We don't know what her upsetting secret is yet and we haven't even gotten to the part of her life when her sister dies, but Nana's past is already heartbreaking."

"It is heartbreaking," Jill somberly agreed. "But it's also inspiring that Nana was so strong. That she got through it."

"I admire her for that, too," Rachel said. "The tragedies in her life didn't break her. They didn't make her bitter, either. Nana was one of the most loving, hopeful and encouraging—" Her voice broke off and she dropped her head into her hands, her shoulders convulsing as she sobbed.

Jill and Brooke caught each other's eyes. It was alarming to see Rachel cry so openly. They simultaneously got up and went to sit beside her.

"I miss Nana a lot, too." Brooke wrapped an arm around her elder sister's back and rested her head against her shoulder. "I keep thinking I hear her humming in the kitchen the way she used to do when she was preparing meals for all of us."

Jill enveloped Rachel from the opposite direction. "When I look outside, I can almost see her standing perfectly still on the deck, resting her morning cup of coffee on the railing. She's tipping her face to the sky and smiling because she always said that was the best way to greet the day…" Jill's voice faltered and she broke down in tears, just like her sisters.

It was the first time since arriving at their grandmother's house that the three of them shared a good, hard cry about her absence, and they wept even harder than when they'd first found out that she had passed away. Maybe they felt freer to express their grief because no one else was there to see them. Or perhaps being in the place where Nana had always seemed most alive had intensified their awareness of her death. It also might have been that the letter reminded them of losing their own parents, which added to their bereavement.

In any case, the way they held onto each other made Jill think again of Nana's line, *If the sisters hadn't had each other to cling to, they surely would have drowned.* The trio cried for so long that when they finally parted, Jill and Brooke literally had to peel their arms apart from each other's, and Rachel's back was damp with sweat. It provided a moment of much-needed comic relief.

"Maybe we should go with Jill to take a shower at Alex's house after all, Rach," Brooke joked, sniffling as she gathered the wads of tissues littered around her feet. "We're pretty sticky."

"Still no," Rachel replied. "But I *will* go to Rockfield or Highland Hills with you to shower, as long as you don't use shampoo or conditioner."

"I won't use soap, either," Brooke promised. "If you want, we can even wait until after five o'clock, so we won't have to pay to park in the lot."

"That's a good idea. We'll go after supper and on the way back, we can stop at Bleecker's and get cones for dessert," Jill suggested. "It's been three years since I've had chocolate-cranberry ice cream and I'm ordering a triple scoop. One for each year I missed."

Brooke arched an eyebrow at her. "I thought you were planning to shower at Alex's house."

She shrugged. "I only thought that was an option for the three of us because you were complaining about your hair. I never had any intention of going there alone." *Although I* did *consider it.*

"Good. I'm glad you're coming with us," Rachel remarked.

"I am, too. But poor Alex is going to be disappointed," Brooke remarked. It was difficult to gauge whether she was serious or not, so Jill gave her a lighthearted response.

"I doubt that's true. But even if it is, he'll have to deal with it. You, Rachel and I are only together on Dune Island for two weeks out of the year. And hanging out with my sisters is a lot more important to me than… than being able to wash my hair with shampoo."

Shortly after Alex and his crew left for the day, the sky erupted with a drenching downpour. Within fifteen minutes, it had tapered off to a steady rain, but just as abruptly it came down in torrents again. Ordinarily, Jill appreciated the contrast of bright green beach grass with the bleached dunes and drab gray sky. But the raindrops that beaded on the windows and sliding doors blurred her view almost completely and the sound they made hitting the panes and deck reminded her of someone thrumming their fingers on a table. The harder she tried to ignore it, the more it bothered her.

Which was also how she felt when she tried to put her worries about Nana's estate out of her mind. She was tempted to bring up the subject with her sisters, but she knew they were too emotional from reading today's letter. Jill doubted she could have engaged them in a conversation anyway, considering how busy they quickly became. Brooke had scheduled two back-to-back video meetings with caterers in Oregon, so she needed to drive to a nearby park where there was a stronger satellite signal. And whenever Rachel wasn't trying to reach Derek by phone, she was poring over data on her laptop.

So while her sisters were occupied, Jill made lunch, slogged down to the bay to fill their "flushing buckets," and then went into town to purchase propane for the grill, since their renters had left it empty. Afterward, she considered visiting the library, but on a rainy day like this the lot would be full and she'd have to spend half an hour circling the neighborhood in search of a place to park.

On her return trip she encountered three detours—likely the result of storm damage—and the stop-and-go traffic made her feel even more frazzled by the time she got home than when she'd first set out. After storing the propane tank in the garage, she began prepping the vegetables for salad for supper.

"Maybe instead of dragging the grill out to the deck where we usually put it, we should just set it up near the entrance to the garage," she suggested to her sisters who were both now sitting in the great room, absorbed in their separate projects.

Rachel was suddenly all ears. "Absolutely not. I hope you've never tried that, Jill, because even with the doors open, there might not be enough ventilation. You could get carbon monoxide poisoning."

"No joke," Jill snapped. Sometimes it felt like Rachel acted as if she was still a young child. "I didn't say we should set it up *inside* the garage. Just close enough to the entrance so we can stand inside while we're waiting for our food to cook."

"I still don't like that idea. All it takes is for a single drop of fat or chicken juice to fall on the flame. It could flare up and—"

"Okay, you're right." Jill agreed emphatically in order to put an end to Rachel's lecture. "But you two will have to haul the grill—*and* the propane tank—to the deck by yourselves because I've done my share to prepare supper tonight."

Brooke proposed, "Maybe we should skip the chicken and just have salad. Or better yet, we could order out. I'd be happy to treat all of us to supper from The Shack."

Rachel twisted her mouth to one side and made a clicking sound, the way she always did when she was vacillating. "It *is* raining pretty hard. Maybe ordering out isn't such a bad idea."

Jill silently balked at that. *After everything I did today—picking up the propane, schlepping the tank into the garage in the rain, running around for chicken and vegetables—so we could have grilled chicken like they said they wanted and now they're not even going to make it?* Peevishly assuming the same tone Rachel had used to lecture her about using the grill inside, Jill said, "I'm not surprised you'd suggest that, Brooke, because you've been craving a clam roll ever since we got here. But I can't believe you'd go along with her plan, Rachel. Talk about wasting our grocery money. You're willing to chuck a pound of expensive organic chicken just because you don't want to get wet?"

"Ack—I keep forgetting that we don't have any way to preserve our food. You're right, we definitely shouldn't just toss it or let it spoil." Rachel paused and glanced out the slider. "Did either of you happen to bring a rain jacket I can borrow?"

"No, but I have a golf umbrella in my car. Or you could use the beach umbrella. It's even wider."

"But it doesn't stand up on its own and it's too big to hold the entire time," Brooke said. "I think we should put on our swimsuits to grill the meat, Rach. Then it won't matter if we get wet."

"I don't know..." Rachel hesitated.

"Can you think of a more practical solution?"

"No," she admitted reluctantly. "Okay, let's do it."

"I'm coming, too," Jill decided, following them toward the stairs.

"I thought you said you've already done enough work for today," Brooke commented over her shoulder.

"I have. That's why I don't plan to help—I'm going to supervise." There was an edge to her retort. "We'll see how the two of you like being bossed around by me for a change."

"Oh, boo-hoo. It's so hard being our baby sister," Brooke ridiculed.

But Rachel came to a halt, causing Brooke to knock into her and nearly making Jill lose her balance, too. Twisting halfway around,

Rachel asked, "You know why Brooke and I sometimes offer you unsolicited advice, don't you?"

"Yes. It's because your daughters aren't around, so I'm the next easiest target," Jill quipped.

"No. It's that we don't want you to make the kind of mistakes we've made." Rachel's tone was sober. Or was she only deadpanning? "Right, Brooke?"

"Right." Brooke sighed heavily before adding, "It's too late for us, but there's still time for you, Jill."

"Oh, sure. Because I'm in danger of making a mess of my life by experiencing smashing career success or marrying my dream guy, the way you two did," she replied facetiously and gave them each a playful nudge to keep them moving up the stairs.

Five minutes later, Jill and Rachel returned to the kitchen. As they waited for their middle sister, Rachel took out the grilling utensils and prepped the chicken and Jill set the table. Remembering they'd need towels after they came in off the deck, Rachel retrieved three from the linen closet and put them by the sliding door. Brooke finally came downstairs, her eyes pink-rimmed, as if she'd been crying.

"You okay?" Jill asked.

"I'm fine." She was a lousy faker, but it was obvious she didn't want to talk about whatever was upsetting her.

Rachel and Jill exchanged discreet shrugs before Rachel asked, "How come you're not wearing your new swimsuit, Brooke?"

"I don't want to take the tags off yet. It feels too, I don't know, too revealing. I might return it."

"You shouldn't—you look great in it," Jill told her. "It accentuates your long legs."

"Thanks." A tiny smile returned to Brooke's lips. Gesturing toward the deck, she asked, "Are we ready?"

Rachel wavered. "This seems like something our kids would do."

"It is." Brooke slid the door open. "But why should they have all the fun?" she asked, before stepping outside, with Jill close on her heels. Rachel wasn't far behind.

Even though the temperature of the rain and air felt nearly tropical, there was something about the force of the downpour that made all three women shriek and squeal. They pattered across the yard and by the time they'd reached the back door to the garage, their swimsuits were sopping wet and their hair was slicked against their heads.

The sisters had to squint their eyes to see through the rain as they maneuvered the heavy grill to the deck and up the stairs. While the burners were heating up, Brooke realized they'd left the plate of chicken breasts on the breakfast bar, so she went back inside to get it. On her way back out, she stubbed her toe and tripped. She steadied herself before she fell, but her lopsided motion caused the raw poultry to slide off the plate. It sailed through the air and landed in a puddle at Jill's feet.

"Hold on—don't move," Rachel cautioned, making a dive for one of the pieces. She lifted it to eye level to examine it. It was sandy and there was a pine needle poking out from one side, but the meat was otherwise clean. "I think we can salvage this if we wring it out first," she announced.

Her assessment struck Brooke and Jill as hilarious and they doubled over, stamping their feet with laughter.

"Stop doing that. Stop it, you two," Rachel scolded. "You're going to step on our supper!"

Her warning made Brooke and Jill howl even louder. Pretty soon Rachel was cracking up, too. Reaching out, the sisters clutched each other's arms to steady themselves. And as the rain washed the last traces of salt from their skin, they laughed harder at the end of the day than they had cried at its beginning.

# CHAPTER SIX

## *Wednesday – June 22*

Although it was raining again and the electricity was still out, Nana's house seemed noticeably brighter on Wednesday morning. At least, it *felt* brighter, a change Jill attributed to the levity she and her sisters had shared the previous evening.

She decided she'd take advantage of their collective good mood and bring up the subject of Nana's estate after they'd finished reading her letter. Since she was the first one awake and dressed, Jill went to the bakery for coffee. When she returned, balancing three thermal cups on top of a cardboard box, she announced, "The coffee's piping hot this morning, just the way you like it, Brooke."

"What's in the box?" Brooke asked blearily.

"Half a dozen muffins."

"Only six?" Brooke joked. Or maybe she was serious.

"How is it that you're eating more food than ever, yet you're losing weight? Where are all those calories going?" Rachel asked bluntly.

Last night, they'd ultimately decided not to save the chicken that had fallen on the deck. Instead the sisters had eaten salad and then gone to Bleecker's for ice cream. Despite boasting that she was going to buy a triple scoop cone, Jill only got a double. Rachel had a small dish, but Brooke ordered a large banana split, with extra fudge topping. Then on the way back, she'd made Rachel stop so she could buy pita chips, an avocado and salsa to eat once she got home.

"I don't know. I can't understand it, either. But I don't have an eating disorder, if that's what you're worried about," Brooke assured her sisters. Lifting the lid to the box, she complained, "We should have gone to the beach last night to use the showers after all. The rain made my hair even gluier than ever."

"I doubt plain tap water without shampoo is going to work any better than the rain did," Rachel said. "But I suppose if the power's not on by five o'clock we could go give it a try."

"We'd *better* have our power back on by five o'clock. If I don't get a shower today, the herons are going to start nesting on my head instead of on the utility pole at the end of our road."

"Those are ospreys, not herons." Impatient to get to Nana's letter—although she wondered if her sisters were trying to avoid a repeat of yesterday's emotions—Jill asked, "Whose turn is it to read?"

"Brooke's. She only read a few paragraphs yesterday."

"I can't. My mouf if full," Brooke mumbled through a mouthful of cranberry muffin.

"*I'll* read it." Jill tore open the envelope and unfolded the letter.

*Dear Rachel, Brooke and Jill…*

*It's been three days since I last picked up my pen. As I'm waiting for one of the aides to come and take me to the doctor's office, I thought I'd add a few lines to what I last wrote about Rose getting married and Hattie performing in an off-Broadway play. It really seemed as if their dreams were coming true; however, life is rarely all sunny skies and smooth sailing.*

"That's for sure." Brooke nodded her chin toward the window.

*Sadly, the honeymoon phase of Rose's marriage to Robert barely lasted until Christmas. That's when the girls' grandparents informed Rose and Hattie they'd reallocated the profits from the sale of their parents' house, as well as all of Paul and Audrey's other savings, into a trust fund. The money was to be awarded in equal amounts to both girls on their twenty-fifth birthday.*

*Apparently, Robert had anticipated having immediate access to the finances as soon as all the legalities were ironed out and he was disgruntled about the way the trust was set up. For someone who worked as an accountant, he was surprisingly inept at noticing the small details and handling money.*

*Prior to getting remarried, he'd lived in an apartment. But after the wedding, he and Rose rented a house, as young married couples often did. The rent was beyond their means and they'd come up short almost every week. Since Robert didn't want Rose to work (married women were expected to be full-time homemakers then), they had to ask for money from Rose's grandfather to buy groceries or pay other bills.*

Rachel cleared her throat. "That seems really irresponsible of Nana's husband. He should have known how to anticipate their living expenses better than Nana, since he was older, he had more experience and he was an accountant. Why didn't they just live in his apartment until they could afford something else? It must have been embarrassing for her to have to ask her retired grandparents for money every week."

"Nana wrote that he was counting on her inheritance money to come through." Brooke speculated, "Maybe when it didn't, he figured Nana's grandfather owed it to them to help pay their bills."

"Do you think the way he handled money is somehow related to Nana's shameful secret from her past?" Jill asked.

"I've been so absorbed in the emotional aspects of Nana's story, I forgot that it's supposed to include a secret," Brooke admitted. "Why do you think it might have to do with money?"

"I wonder if it's possible that maybe Robert—our grandfather—ended up wasting Nana's entire inheritance," Jill suggested. "After all, this is the first time we've really ever heard any details about him, except that he was unfaithful. For all we know, he could have had a gambling problem."

"Well, keep reading so we can find out more," Rachel urged her.

*Hattie wasn't faring much better financially. Even though she shared an apartment with three other young women, after depleting her childhood account, she could barely cover the cost of rent and groceries, much less attend performances. So she decided to only eat one meal a day and she took a second job as a costume seamstress, hoping to gain free access to the theater.*

Rachel interrupted again to praise Hattie, saying, "Becoming a costume seamstress was a very resourceful way for her to study acting."

"Yes, it was." Jill was impressed by the level of dedication her great-aunt had shown toward achieving her goal. Yet she couldn't help but add, "But deciding to skip all those meals… poor girl."

She continued.

*However, she was disillusioned by how the laborers were treated in comparison with the actors and actresses and she also became disheartened by her lack of success auditioning.*

*Still, the girls viewed their circumstances as a grand adventure and took their obstacles and setbacks in stride. The following summer, the twins relished spending two weeks vacationing together on Dune Island. Robert didn't accompany his wife; he said he couldn't take the time off from work, but Hattie suspected he found island life too boring. That suited her just fine and Rose didn't seem to mind very much, either. The twins drew strength from the sea and from each other's presence and afterward they returned to their daily lives invigorated and ready to face any challenges head on.*

"That's how I always feel after I've been on Dune Island with both of you," Brooke said.

"You took the words right out of my mouth." Jill reflected quietly for a moment before admitting, "I never would have said this to Nana, but during the past three years, I haven't felt as resilient as I usually do. I haven't had as much clarity or been as grounded, either. And I know that's mostly because we haven't been able to get together here."

She knew her remark might make it seem as if she was trying to pressure her sisters into keeping the estate. And maybe on some level, she was. But more importantly, Jill wanted Rachel and Brooke to understand how much she valued their relationships as sisters. And how much she relied on them for support, even if they sometimes crossed over the line into bossiness.

They nodded in acknowledgement of what she'd said and she continued reading:

*Yet after a couple more years passed, the twins began to question their choices. It wasn't their financial struggles that caused them to lose confidence; it was that Hattie hadn't landed anything approaching the prestige of her tiny off-Broadway role and Rose couldn't get pregnant. Their grandmother's death, followed by their grandfather's stroke and subsequent nursing home confinement, deepened their sorrow and left them feeling even more vulnerable and uncertain.*

*"Maybe I should quit acting, return to Connecticut and get married," Hattie said that summer toward the end of their stay on Sea Breeze Lane.*

*"You can't do that!" Rose vehemently objected. "Acting is your vocation. It's your calling. You don't want to be a wife and mother any more than I want to be a Broadway star. We've got to keep trying. It will happen for both of us. I can feel it."*

Rachel told her sisters, "That's almost exactly like what Nana said to me when I was considering dropping out of business school."

"You were going to drop out of business school?" Brooke sounded as surprised as Jill was. "Why?"

"It was so expensive. I was afraid that after I earned my degree I wouldn't be able to put it to good use, so I'd have wasted all that money for nothing. Right before I began my second semester, someone offered me a good job as a legal secretary and I almost took it. But Nana encouraged me not to give up on achieving my goal. She said that we don't always get to choose our paths in life, but in this case, I did. And that I'd be dissatisfied if I settled for doing something else just because it was a safer road."

Even though Jill felt a twinge of envy because she didn't have the kind of passion about her own career that her sisters had about theirs, she said, "Good for you for sticking with it, Rach. I know how much you love owning and running your business and I'm glad the risk was worth it."

"I've always been proud of your success, too," Brooke remarked.

Blushing, Rachel modestly waved away their compliments, urging Jill to continue their grandmother's story.

*Sure enough, that December, Rose became pregnant. Hattie said she'd never seen her so luminous and self-assured—it was as if she should have been dazzling audiences on Broadway.*

*But Rose's pregnancy glow was only a flicker compared to how radiant she appeared after giving birth to a son, James Robert Sampson—*

At this point, Brooke cheered, "Yay, Dad!"

The three of them spontaneously applauded their father's birthday and then Jill reread the same sentence before continuing:

*Rose's pregnancy glow was only a flicker compared to how radiant she appeared after giving birth to a son, James Robert Sampson, the following September. Hattie was amazed by how blissful her sister was, despite her lack of sleep.*

"I remember that feeling, don't you, Brooke?" Rachel asked; her voice dreamy.

"Like it was yesterday."

Jill paused to allow them a moment of nostalgia before reading further:

*Robert, on the other hand, seemed remote, almost indifferent, and he rarely touched or paid attention to the baby.*

"Dad's father didn't pick him up when he was a newborn?" Brooke repeated disdainfully. "What was wrong with the guy?"

"I don't know, but I used to feel kind of short-changed because we didn't have a paternal grandfather in our lives," Rachel said. "Now that I'm learning more about him, I realize it was probably a good thing that we never met him."

Jill kept reading to see what else Nana had to say about their father's babyhood.

*One evening when Jimmy was about two or three months old and Hattie was visiting, Rose asked whether it seemed strange that her husband didn't want to hold their son.*

*"Maybe he's afraid he'll drop him," Hattie suggested. Then she teased, "Besides, when would he have a chance to pick Jimmy up? You and I are always holding him."*

*It was true; as someone who never wanted to play dolls as a child, Hattie seemed to love cradling the baby in her arms almost as much as Rose did. She'd inhale the scent of his downy-fine hair, claiming nothing except the ocean had ever smelled so good. And if he cried, she'd pat him on the back, serenading him with the latest Broadway songs until he was cooing again, which she claimed was even better than receiving a standing ovation.*

"Aww, I love that." Jill was touched by how accurately Hattie had described the bond between her and her nephew. As an auntie who didn't have children of her own, Jill had felt the same way about her sisters' children.

She read Nana's closing lines:

*... Oh dear, the aide is here, time to go. I'll write a longer letter next time. Give your children and husbands a hug from me—and give each other one, too. With love from Nana.*

Jill turned the page over to see if she added a postscript, but the back of the sheet was blank. Disappointed, she said, "That was a short one today."

"It's a good thing it was," Brooke's eyes were ablaze, a marked difference from her usual tearful reactions to Nana's correspondence.

"I wouldn't have wanted to hear more about Robert. Not that I blame Nana for writing about him, but it tears me up inside to know that Dad's own father—our grandfather—neglected him when he was a newborn."

"It's painful to imagine a parent—*any* parent—neglecting their baby," Rachel agreed. "But it's comforting to know that Nana was so nurturing and loving toward him. It sounds as if Hattie was, too."

"That doesn't excuse his lazy bum of a father from paying attention to him," Brooke muttered.

"No, it doesn't. But I'm still happy that Dad had Nana as his mother."

"I'm happy that *Nana* had *Dad* as her son," Jill said. "He was her dream come true, the baby she'd longed to have. According to Hattie, giving birth to him made Nana more radiant and self-assured than she'd ever been. Considering all the other tragedies she endured in her lifetime, I'm really glad her dream of motherhood was fulfilled."

Rachel and Brooke nodded in unison. The three of them finished sipping their coffee without speaking, lost in their thoughts. Jill was just about to bring up the subject of Nana's estate, when Rachel's phone vibrated.

"Oh, I've been waiting for this call." She grabbed it off the table and hurried upstairs.

"I'd better go see if I can reach Todd before he starts his workday." Brooke wrapped a second muffin in a napkin to take with her. "I've narrowed down our appetizer options for the ceremony and I want to get his opinion."

Since the rain had diminished to a drizzle and Jill's plans to talk about the estate were foiled, she decided to take a walk so she could contemplate what she'd just read in Nana's letter. The tide was at its highest, which meant she had to pick her way across the soft, uneven mounds and hollows of damp sand near the dunes instead of roaming the wide, hard flats. It was slow going and the greenheads were in attack mode. Since Jill had forgotten to apply repellant, she kept flapping her arms around her head to fend them off. Even so, within a hundred yards, she'd been bitten four times, which made her so cranky she turned around and headed back.

Stamping the sand from her feet at the top of the stairs, she spied Alex coming around the corner of the house, smiling. He was wearing denim jeans and a black T-shirt and when he raised his hand in a wave, the first thought that ran through Jill's mind was that she'd never been embraced by a man with arms like his. Her next thought was that she wished she could be.

"Morning, Alex," she said as she neared him. "Looks like another beautiful day, huh?"

"Maybe not for the beach, but it's good working weather." He'd come close enough that Jill caught a whiff of his soap. "I hope it doesn't interfere with your schedule to have us back here a little early today."

"We don't have a schedule—we're on Dune Island time." Jill explained, "That was my nana's motto. I think she learned it from the utility company."

"Still no power, huh?" Alex sympathized. "My offer stands if you need to take a—"

"Hello," Brooke interrupted, zooming across the yard toward them. "I heard someone knocking on the other door a minute ago, but I was on the phone. Is everything okay?"

*Your timing is terrible*, Jill thought, but she started to make introductions. "Alex, I'd like you to meet—"

He cut her off, smiling. "We've already met… Hi, Brooke."

Brooke looked as utterly confounded as Jill felt. "I'm sorry… we've already met?"

"Yes, a long time ago. It was back when I still had hair on my head." He sheepishly ran his hand over his scalp. "Although I didn't have much of a beard yet. I was fifteen."

Brooke squinted at him for a moment before her mouth dropped open. "I don't believe it! Jill didn't tell me you were *that* Alex."

"Apparently, she didn't remember."

"I didn't tell you he was *which* Alex?" Jill asked, starting to feel like a third wheel.

"You know who he is," Brooke insisted, despite all evidence to the contrary. "Alex was Shane Davids's friend. They followed us home from the boardwalk when we teenagers."

Alex ruefully elaborated for Jill's benefit, "Shane and I noticed you and your sister a couple of times at the arcade. He wanted to ask Brooke out for ice cream or something and he finally managed to work up the courage, but you two left before he could talk to her. So we followed you down the beach but he chickened out again. He didn't want Brooke to see him and we tried to hide up by the dunes. But Jill, you happened to notice us and you chewed us out because you said we were trespassing on—"

"The piping plovers' nesting area!" Brooke shrieked, helping Alex finish his sentence.

In a flash, Jill remembered. That was the first summer the bird sanctuary staff had roped off sections of the island's beaches in order to protect the small, sensitive birds. During one of their early morning treks, Nana and Jill's dad had explained the plovers were on the endangered species list. From a safe distance, they'd pointed out a shallow depression in the sand that was lined with bits of shells and served as a nest for the well-camouflaged creatures. Jill had been appalled to realize how easy it would have been to accidentally step on a chick and crush it, which would have been sad, as well as illegal.

While it was only natural for her to want to protect the birds, the day Alex and Shane followed the girls home, Jill had stood with her hands on her hips and shouted like a fishwife at the boys, "What's the matter—can't you two read? The sign says not to enter that area. How would *you* like it if someone trampled on *your* home with their enormous, smelly feet?!" Then she'd delivered a self-righteous diatribe about birds and trespassing that made her wince with embarrassment just to think about it now.

Brooke had been livid that Jill's rebuke had supposedly ruined her chance of being asked out. The following day, she wouldn't let her younger sister come with her to the boardwalk. But Jill's tirade about the birds had served as an ice-breaker and Brooke ended up going out with Shane for pizza or ice cream three or four times before the Sampsons's vacation ended.

"Piping plovers blend in with the sand," Jill said feebly, repeating in her defense the same thing she'd told Alex over two decades ago.

"That's true. And we were being careless," he acknowledged. "I never forgot how concerned you were about those birds."

*And I never forgot your eyes*, Jill realized, looking squarely into them now. *I just didn't associate them with your face, probably because I was so upset that afternoon.*

"How *is* Shane, anyway?" Brooke butted in and Alex broke eye contact with Jill to answer her.

"He's doing well, I think. I don't really keep in touch with him—he moved to Florida a long time ago, but last I heard he was married, with three sons. He's a pilot for a major airline now."

"A pilot, huh? That's impressive," Brooke said. "I'm an occupational therapist. I have three children now, too. And a husband. I mean, I've been married for almost eighteen years. In fact, we're celebrating our anniversary this year by having a vow renewal ceremony at a resort in the Columbia River Gorge. That's in Oregon, where we live."

"Oregon, huh? Your state tree is the Douglas fir," Alex replied, because what else was he supposed to say? Jill didn't know why her sister was rambling on about her vow renewal ceremony, but she kind of wished she'd leave. Instead, it was Alex who shuffled his feet and said, "Speaking of trees, I'd better get to work. Could you move your car into the road again, Jill? The other one is fine where it is."

"Sure," Jill said although she wished she could have chatted with him in private for a while longer. She headed toward the house, with Brooke following her.

"It was great seeing you, Alex. If you ever talk to Shane, tell him I said hi," she called, sounding more like her teenage daughter than like a middle-aged mother of three.

A few minutes later as she was approaching the deck after moving the car, Jill heard Brooke and Rachel's voices emanating from the great room. Although she couldn't quite make out what they were saying, she didn't want Alex or his crew to overhear them, too, before the sawing started. So when she stepped inside, she pushed the slider shut behind her.

"Seeing Alex brought back some really fun memories of how excited I felt when I was allowed to go on a real date," Brooke was reminiscing aloud to Rachel. "Shane Davids. It seems like it was ages ago when he asked me out…"

"It was. You were only in high school," Rachel reminded her.

Her sister's remark seemed to snap Brooke out of her reverie. "Oh! I forgot to ask. Was that someone from Densmore Prep who'd called you earlier?"

Jill turned from the kitchen counter, where she'd been cutting an apple, to spy Rachel with her finger pressed to her lips. It was obvious she was signaling Brooke to keep quiet, so of course Jill inquired, "Densmore Prep?"

Caught, Rachel explained that Noah and Grace were on the waiting list for enrollment at the elite high school. She'd been expecting to hear whether they'd been accepted, but the call she'd received was from a business associate, not from the school's admissions department. "I didn't want to say too much about them going to a private school until I heard if they've been accepted."

"Oh." Jill chewed a slice of apple. Thinking aloud, she asked, "Is that what's been on your mind lately—you're worried they won't get in? Because Noah and Grace are brilliant, talented students. I'm surprised they were wait-listed in the first place."

Rachel took a piece of the apple Jill extended to her before replying, "That's probably because by the time they applied this spring, virtually all of the offers of admission had already been awarded to students who'd applied last fall."

"They missed the autumn application deadline? But you're so organized. How did—" Jill stopped mid-sentence. Suddenly, everything clicked: the twins hadn't applied until spring because that's when Nana died and Rachel was named a beneficiary of her estate, along with Jill and Brooke. "So *that's* why you want to sell the house. You want the money so you can pay for them to go to private school, right?"

"That would be one use for it, yes," Rachel confirmed. "But Noah and Grace both applied for merit-based scholarships, which would cover their tuition in full."

"So let's say that they're accepted and they receive scholarships—or that they don't get in at all, which is unlikely—then would you change your mind about selling Nana's house?" Jill asked hopefully.

"Well..." Stalling, Rachel grimaced and tipped her head from side to side, working a kink out of her neck. "I suppose it's possible."

Jill's heart turned handsprings and she couldn't stop herself from cheering. "Yes!"

Holding up her hand, Rachel cautioned, "Wait a second. I have to be honest, Jill. I've been going over our finances with a fine-toothed comb. Even if the kids get scholarships to Densmore, Derek and I can't afford to contribute a full one-third of what it's going to cost to keep the house. So if you, Brooke and I end up deciding we don't want to sell the estate, you'd have to make up a few hundred dollars' difference of my share every month unless things change for us financially. I feel bad about that, but since you're the one who really wants to—"

"It wouldn't be a problem," Jill interrupted, without stopping to consider that if she lost her job, she'd struggle to cover her own third of the costs, much less Rachel's. Nor did she say that Rachel and Derek made five times the salary she did, so she was baffled about why Rachel was acting as if they were barely scraping by. All that mattered to Jill was that there was still a possibility that they could keep Nana's place—provided her middle sister was also open to that option. Appealing to Brooke's sentimentality, she asked, "Have you given any more thought to what we should do with our inheritance, now that we know more about the two little cottages and the time Nana spent here with Dad and Hattie?"

"It's almost *all* I've thought about," Brooke said, picking at her thumbnail instead of meeting Jill's eyes. "I know how much you want to keep it, but I'm still on the fence. As I mentioned, we've really come to love camping in the mountains in the summertime. Also, I can tell from the photos I've seen online that Ella and Kaylee are having a great time at music camp. Next year they might want to go for an even longer session. And Zach texted a message to Todd saying how much he loves being at the lake."

"But does that absolutely mean you wouldn't have time to come here for a couple of weeks? It seems like taking two family vacations—one on the west coast and a second one on the east coast—might be the best of both worlds." Jill knew it was up to her sister to decide where she spent her family vacations. But she just couldn't help defending their nana's house to the end. How could anybody want to go anywhere else?

"That's true. But my other hesitation is still that this place stirs up so many memories of when Mom and Dad and Nana were alive. I thought once I got some rest, being here wouldn't make me feel so lonely. But if anything, I'm even lonelier now than I was when we first arrived."

"That could be the weather affecting your perspective. Once the sun comes out—"

"It's not about the weather, Jill. It's about…" Brooke bit her lip and blinked repeatedly. She wiped her eyes with the back of her wrists but she didn't finish her thought. Jill knew her sister was holding something back.

"What's really bothering you, Brooke?" she quietly prompted. "If you tell us, I'll just shut up and listen, I promise. I won't try to convince you to keep the house."

She was serious, but Brooke laughed. "You know me. I'm always weepy." She took a tissue from the box and blew her nose before answering. "The only thing that's wrong is that I'm getting hungry—*again.* I need something more substantial than salad for lunch. Anyone want to go to the store with me?"

"I will," Rachel volunteered.

"So you don't want to discuss this any more?" Jill asked, concerned that she hadn't found out what was truly upsetting her middle sister, but Rachel must have thought she'd been referring to the estate.

"Well, since Brooke is still ambivalent and I can't make any decisions until I hear the outcome of the twins' applications, there's not much more to talk about for now," she said. "Besides, that sawing noise is grating on my nerves. I'll be really glad when they're done and gone."

*I won't be glad*, Jill thought. *Talking to Alex has been the highlight of my vacation—which is usually how I feel about talking to you and Brooke.*

After her sisters left, Jill went upstairs to flop onto her bed, where she reflected on the morning's conversations. Although she was relieved that neither Rachel nor Brooke had definitively decided against keeping the house, she'd never expected the decision to be such a point of contention between her and them. Frankly, it was exhausting.

The next thing she knew, Jill was waking from a nap and it was after three o'clock. The sawing noise had stopped and the rest of the willow tree was gone. If it weren't for a scattering of woodchips and the circle of dirt where the stump had been dug up, Jill might have believed she'd only met Alex in her dreams.

*Bye-bye, summer flirtation*, she thought dolefully. *It was fun but it never would have lasted.*

Stretching, she glanced out the window. The otherwise white sky was blotted with pewter-colored clouds, but at least it wasn't raining. *Maybe Brooke and Rachel will take a walk with me down to the marsh. We can talk about Nana's letters and maybe take a swim.* But when Jill headed for the stairs, she noticed Brooke in her room, video chatting with someone she assumed was from the resort in Oregon. The Wi-Fi connection must have been strong today, because downstairs Rachel was also on the phone, discussing tariff hikes with Derek.

*So much for making the most of our time together*, Jill brooded, recalling what Nana had advised in an earlier letter.

Not that she could really blame her sisters for being so preoccupied: she knew Brooke wanted the vow renewal ceremony to be just perfect and she could imagine how demanding it was for Rachel to co-manage her business from a distance. And now Jill was aware of her worries about Noah and Grace's education, too. Besides, the weather wasn't exactly conducive to enjoying the outdoor activities they usually engaged in when they came to Dune Island. But still, Jill felt at a loss. She was used to being independent, so she had no problems doing things by herself, but that was just the point: she was tired of being alone. She wanted to be with her family.

*Maybe I should start researching employment opportunities, just in case*, she thought. It was a dreadful idea, but a few seconds later, she was struck by a better one: she knew a place where she could take a nice, long, hot shower.

Set far back on a sandy, wooded lot, Alex's house was surrounded by a surprising number of scrappy scrub oak and crooked pitch pine for someone who tended trees for a living. Jill grabbed her bag from the car and tentatively tiptoed over the carpet of pine needles and pine cones. Even though she had a standing invitation, using Alex's shower while he wasn't there actually did make her feel a bit like Goldilocks approaching the three bears' cabin in the woods.

The large shower was located in the back of the house beside an equally expansive deck, where she also noticed an impressive dual-chamber gas grill, an all-weather table and matching chairs, and a couple of comfortable-looking loungers.

When she opened the door to the wooden stall, she was delighted to see it had a changing room that was separate from the bathing compartment; an exorbitance compared to most outdoor showers on houses this size. The second feature she especially appreciated was that the water got hot almost immediately and stayed warm the entire time it was running.

*I* love *modern plumbing*, Jill raved silently, tipping her head back as she lathered her hair a second time. The extravagantly steamy shower released all the tension from her muscles and she emerged from the enclosure relaxed to the point of lethargy. Lingering on the deck to finger-comb her hair, she half-hoped that if she stayed there long enough, she might bump into Alex's sister, Sydney.

However, while she'd left a note for her sisters saying she'd gone for a ride and not to wait for her for supper, she was actually getting really hungry. So Jill reluctantly headed back to the driveway, where she found Alex sitting in his truck with the windows open and the stereo on. He immediately hopped out, with a sheepish look on his face and a large brown paper bag in his hand.

"Hi, Alex. Did you lock yourself out of the house or something?"

"No. I, uh, saw your car and figured you were showering, so I thought I'd go grab dinner and hang out here until you were done."

*Aww, that's so sweet—he was so eager to make sure I didn't feel uncomfortable, he waited outside his own house*, she realized. "You didn't have to do that, but I appreciate the privacy. I hope I left you enough hot water. It was so refreshing to finally take a shower that I couldn't seem to make myself get out. I love the changing room. It's much better than hanging your dry clothes or towel over the wall and then having them slip into a puddle."

She was rambling, feeling awkward that she'd kept him waiting. But he didn't seem to mind.

He laughed. "I actually built that extra compartment for Sydney—she complained about the same thing."

Okay. It was becoming more and more difficult not to really like this guy. So when he asked if Jill was hungry and held up the paper bag of takeout from The Clam Shack, saying he'd bought enough for two, she wavered. "I'd love to—it smells delicious."

He invited her in and showed her around the house, which was sparsely but tastefully decorated and filled with lots of western light, even on this cloudy evening. After he washed up and got them drinks, they took their meal out to the deck, because the forecast had promised a glimpse of sun that evening. There wasn't one, but that hardly mattered to Jill.

"That food tasted as amazing as my shower felt," she said when they were almost finished eating.

"Mm. It's not the healthiest meal in the world, but on occasion, nothing hits the spot on a summer day like fried clams from The Shack."

"That's for sure. We tried ordering clams there a couple of times this week, but the wait time has been too long. How is it you were served so quickly? Is there a secret password that only year-round residents know?"

"Kind of—I have connections. I bussed tables one summer there during high school."

"That must have been hectic during tourist season."

"Yeah, but they let us eat as much as we wanted at the end of our shift, so that was a great perk for a teenager. Although I've got to admit, the experience taught me I never wanted another indoor job again."

"So that's how you became a…?" Jill didn't exactly know what his title was.

"Tree guy?" Alex laughed. Brooke must not have been the only one who'd ever referred to him like that. "I'm actually a certified arborist, I'll have you know. But along the way, I had a string of other jobs. If it was outdoors, I did it. Lifeguard. Deckhand. Construction worker. Surf instructor. It took a while to find the sweet spot of what I wanted to do. I had to eliminate a lot of other things, first. But now I wouldn't trade my occupation for anything."

"Lucky you," Jill said earnestly. "I envy people who've found their life's calling."

"Oh, yeah, that's right… You're not trapped but you're not happy in your vocation."

"What?" Even if that was exactly how she felt, Jill didn't ever remember telling him that.

"The other day when I said I was glad you weren't trapped, your mind immediately associated the question with your job as a tech writer."

Jill wasn't about to ruin their time together by complaining about her job—especially since she knew she should be grateful that she still had a job to complain about. "Yes, that is where my mind went. But I also said I still had hope that one day I'll get to write about robotic vacuum cleaners. And when I do, that will make all the tedium worth it," she joked before changing the subject. "So, have you always lived and worked on the island?"

"Yeah, except a brief stint during college. And then one awful summer when I took a job as a landscaper in Greenwich."

Jill wrinkled her nose, trying to picture Alex working in what was considered Connecticut's Gold Coast. "What made you choose to do that?"

"To be blunt, I was trying to make my fiancée happy. She grew up in Hope Haven, just like I did. But she didn't love it here enough to stay and as I found out, I didn't love her enough to leave."

"There's no place quite like Dune Island," Jill said wistfully.

"My sentiment exactly. Plus, my family's here. Well, now it's just my sister and me." A tone of sadness had entered his voice. "My father died when I was in my early twenties and my mother died about ten years after that."

"Oh, I'm sorry for your loss… I know how hard it can be—my parents have both passed away, too," Jill said. Alex returned her condolences, but she sensed he needed to talk about his own experience, so she questioned, "If you don't mind my asking, had your parents been ill for a long time before they passed, or…?"

"My father died from complications of intestinal surgery. So, he'd had some health challenges, but nothing critical and his death was unexpected—which is putting it mildly," Alex confided, his eyes momentarily downcast. Then he looked up and continued, "My mother had cancer for two years before she died. Sydney had been living with her, but when my mom was diagnosed, the first thing she did was to begin transitioning her into the home where she lives now. She knew I had to work so I couldn't give Syd the kind of support she needed during the day and she wanted my sister to be as independent as possible."

"It sounds like good planning on your mother's part," Jill remarked, pleased that Alex was opening up to her.

"Yeah, but Sydney wasn't too happy about moving into a new place. It takes her a really long time to adjust to change, but now she loves where she lives." Alex's expression brightened as he spoke about his sister's contentment. "She considers the women there to be the sisters she never had and the home manager is like her second mom. But I know she'd go to pieces if I moved off-island, so I'm staying put. Besides, why would I ever want to leave with all of this around me?"

Jill grinned. "My nana used to say almost the same thing about Hope Haven and I'm really close to my family, too, so I understand completely."

"Most women don't." He held her gaze without blinking. "A relationship is the only thing I'm missing. That's the one drawback of living here."

This conversation was moving in the wrong direction. Jill didn't want Alex to ask her out, because she didn't want to have to turn him down. So she teased, "Oh, c'mon. It's not as if this is a *deserted* island. There are new women arriving every summer—every *week.* I'm sure Brooke and I weren't the last girls you and your buddies ever followed down the beach."

He didn't deny it, but he said, "I have a confession to make about that summer."

"Don't tell me—it wasn't Shane who was interested in Brooke first. It was you, right?"

"Actually… I was interested in *you.*"

Okay, now he was really laying it on thick. "You were not."

"I was. Really," he insisted. "I hoped to see you the next day at the arcade, but your sister came alone and when we all got to talking, she told us you were still in middle school. Being the very cool high school sophomore that I was, I was mortified I had a crush on an eighth-grader. I assumed you were Brooke's friend, not her sister."

"Yeah, people often thought that I was older than Brooke was when we were teenagers. I sort of… went through an early growth spurt." Nana hadn't called Jill va-va-voom for nothing.

"No one would mistake you for being the older sister now." Leaning forward, Alex looked straight into her eyes and she was magnetized, in spite of herself. "I honestly planned to look for you the next summer, but that was the year I worked at The Shack, so I didn't get to the arcade very often. The following year I was a lifeguard over in Rockfield… Anyway, it's not often someone gets a second chance twenty-five years later. So, can I take you out this weekend?"

*No, no, no, don't ask me that.* "To the arcade or the bowling alley?" she jested.

"To anywhere you want to go." He sounded serious. And those eyes…

Somehow, Jill managed to decline. "I'd love to say yes but I'm only here for two weeks and then I'm going back to Boston, and, you know…" She allowed her sentence to trail off, assuming he'd understand the implication.

"You're seeing someone there?"

"No. I'm not seeing anyone anywhere." Jill didn't want to explain that she'd sworn off casual dating and since he definitely wasn't moving off-island, there was no chance that she could fall for him. That would sound presumptuous.

Besides, she'd already fallen for him, at least a little bit.

"See, the thing is, my sisters and I came here to try to decide what to do with my Nana's house. She recently... she passed away and I'm not in a great place emotionally. I just sort of need to stay focused."

Alex solemnly stroked his chin and once again offered his condolences. "I remember trying to make those kinds of decisions about my parents' house after my mother died. It was very stressful and overwhelming," he sympathized. "But maybe instead of focusing on it, what you might need is something to distract you. It doesn't have to be a date. For instance, this Friday I'm taking my sister and her housemates to the outdoor concert at the pavilion. It's sort of our summer weekend ritual. They need me to drive them there, but then they won't let me sit anywhere near them. It's a no-men-allowed kind of situation. If you came, too—as a friend from my youth—I wouldn't have to sit by myself. You'd be doing me a favor and it might be a good break for you, too."

Jill hesitated. She was familiar with the outdoor concerts that were performed every Friday or Saturday evening throughout the season. Faint strains of the music carried down the boardwalk to Nana's deck. But Jill hadn't attended one of the concerts in person since she was a young girl. It occurred to her that this might be her last opportunity, if she and her sisters ended up selling Nana's house. "You're right. Going to a concert with a friend could be a pleasant distraction from everything that's been on my mind," she said, emphasizing the word *friend* more for her own benefit than for his.

"Great. We'll pick you up at six-thirty. I always treat Sydney and her housemates to cones from Bleecker's before they abandon me, so don't eat dessert," he said with a wink.

*

When Jill walked into Nana's kitchen fifteen minutes later, Rachel said, "Oh, hi, I'm glad you're back. I was just going to have to toss this piece of grilled haddock, but if you haven't eaten, you can have it. It's delicious and I think it's still warm."

Before Jill could answer, Brooke squealed, "Look—she took a shower! You went to Alex's house, didn't you, Jill?"

"Yup. It felt splendiferous to wash my hair. *Twice*," she boasted. "Alex came home just after I got out and he shared his supper with me. Clams from The Shack."

Brooke groaned. "I am literally drooling with envy," she said. "I so wish *I* was the single sister right now. Want to trade places with me?"

Ordinarily, Jill would have said, *If only I could.* But tonight her answer was, "Not especially, thanks."

# CHAPTER SEVEN

*Thursday – June 23*

"Remember how Dad used to call this weather *fizzling*, because it's a cross between foggy and drizzling?" Jill asked her sisters as they sipped their coffee on Thursday morning.

"I thought when he said it was *fizzling*, he meant the rain was dwindling. That it was dying down. Fizzling out, like a romance," Brooke said.

"I *wish* the rain would fizzle out," Rachel grumbled.

"I do, too. But remember what Nana used to say," Jill cheerfully reminded her sisters. "It might be raining in paradise, but it's still paradise."

"If this weather keeps up one more day, we're going to have to change the adage to, 'It might be paradise, but it's still raining,'" Rachel drolly replied.

"We've had a few breaks in the rain. It isn't that bad."

"We may have had breaks in the rain, but that's not the same thing as having sunshine. I think even Nana would be sick of this by now." Brooke added, "But there is one bright spot on the horizon—I've found a gym where we can pay to take a seven-minute shower."

"How much does it cost?" Rachel asked.

"Who cares? I'm so salty and sandy that I can't afford *not* to take a shower. It's up to you if you want to come with me or not, but as soon as we finish Nana's letter, I'm out of here," Brooke warned. "Someone else is going to have to read unless you want to wait for me to finish eating my breakfast."

So Rachel said she'd do it. The letter began with their grandmother's usual warm salutation, but almost immediately, her tone took an ominous turn.

*I hope you can decipher my penmanship today. My hand seems shakier than usual and I don't know if it's because my body is winding down or if it's because I dread what I'm about to write. Either way, I'd better cut to the chase while I still can.*

A sour taste rose on Jill's tongue and she set her bowl of yogurt on the coffee table.

"Uh-oh," Brooke said. "I knew this was coming sooner or later."

"We all knew it. The question is, are we ready for it?" Rachel asked. Since they didn't have any way of knowing how Nana's words would affect them, they decided they might as well continue reading.

*I'll fast forward to the summer of 1955, when Jimmy was almost two and the twins were nearing twenty-five.*

*That year, Hattie won a small dancing and singing role in a Broadway revue. Rose was every bit as thrilled for her as Hattie had been when Rose had the baby. Rehearsals were scheduled to begin in early July, which was when the twins usually met at the cottages. They didn't want to miss their vacation together, so they decided to meet on Dune Island in late June, instead.*

If Jill hadn't been so apprehensive about the rest of Nana's letter, she might have pointed out to her sisters how important it was for Hattie and Nana to get together in Hope Haven. But she was on the edge of her seat, caught between wanting Rachel to hurry up and read whatever the secret was and wanting to delay finding out what it was for as long as possible.

*Oddly, Robert decided he wanted to come, too. He said a client of his was summering nearby and he'd promised to get Robert into the golf club any time he wanted. "I'll be gone so often it will be as if I'm not even on vacation with you," he told the twins. And to be honest, they preferred it that way; they'd come to think of their vacation in Lucinda's Hamlet as their "sister time."*

*Hattie was floating on air because of her upcoming role. However, Rose was uncharacteristically weepy and she wouldn't say why. Assuming her twin was overly tired, on the third morning of vacation, Hattie offered to take the baby down to the tidal flats so his parents could sleep in a while longer.*

*Jimmy had learned to walk the previous year and he loved to stomp through the squishy area where the little rivulets run in and out from the bay when the tide is changing.*

"That's funny. Zach liked to do that, too," Brooke commented. "I never knew Dad was the same way."

*Hattie would have preferred to cross the damp sandbars where the surface was firmer. She didn't like the sensation of the terrain giving way beneath her and she was bothered by a sense of foreboding.*

*But Jimmy kept indicating he wanted to splash in the tiny stream, demanding, "Pash. Pash, Mama." Hattie knew he only called her "mama" because he couldn't say "auntie," but she loved it that he associ-*

*ated her with his mother and she indulged his whim to slog through the squishy sand.*

"Aw, that reminds me of when Ella used to call you mommy, too. Remember that?" Brooke asked and Jill nodded. Like Hattie, she'd considered it a high compliment even if it was simply a matter of a limited vocabulary.

*They were halfway out to the bay when Jimmy abruptly stopped and shrieked at the top of his lungs. The puddle where he'd been standing was tinged with pink: he'd sliced his toe on a razor clam embedded just below the surface.*

"Aw, Dad had a boo-boo," Rachel said, making a concerned face as if one of her own children had just gotten a cut.

*Hattie scooped him up and ran with him all the way back to shore, which was no small feat, considering what a pudgy little boy he was.*

*His screams carried across the flats and by the time Hattie reached the stairs, Rose was running down them to see what happened. The sisters charged up to Hattie's cottage, because it was closer than Rose's. As they were rinsing the baby's foot, Robert sauntered in, freshly showered and shaven.*

*"I told you not to get hysterical. The kid's fine," he said to Rose after Hattie explained what had happened. Then he left for the club, complaining that Jimmy's crying was getting on his nerves.*

"What a loser," Brooke growled under her breath.

"It seems like Hattie thought that about him, too. Listen to what she says…" Rachel continued.

*His dismissive, condescending attitude angered Hattie but she didn't want to further upset her sister, who looked even more miserable than Jimmy did. So she held her tongue and distracted the baby with a vanilla wafer while Rose bandaged his toe. Afterward, Jimmy was as cheerful as ever and they gave him a pail and shovel so he could dig in the sand beside the patio while the sisters sunned themselves in the Adirondack chairs.*

*They'd barely sat down before Rose burst into tears, confiding that she suspected Robert had been having an affair for some time. Worse, Rose figured the woman was summering on the island, which would have explained his sudden willingness to join the twins at the cottages. Hattie tried to calm her by suggesting maybe he just needed a vacation, but her sister was resolute that he'd been unfaithful. She detailed his other behaviors that admittedly sounded fishy. Hattie asked whether she'd ever confronted him about the subject.*

*"Yes, several times. But he accused me of being paranoid or hysterical, just like he did about the baby's toe. And maybe I am overreacting—I'm so exhausted I can't think straight. I feel like I'm losing my mind because I keep second-guessing myself."*

*She said she'd been so distressed that she'd had insomnia for months. The doctor even prescribed sleeping pills but she wouldn't take them. She was afraid they'd make her so sleepy she wouldn't hear the baby fussing during the night. As she was speaking, Rose wept so hard that little Jimmy came over and patted her bare knee, saying, "No cry, Mama. No cry," which made her sob even more.*

Brooke cut in, "I don't know if I can bear to listen to any more of this part of Nana's life story. I didn't expect it to be so upsetting."

"You didn't? Even though Dad told us a long time ago that his father left Nana for another woman?" Rachel questioned.

"That's different—we only knew about it in general. We didn't know any of the details." Brooke's face was red and she appeared more angered than sorrowful. "I don't understand why Nana would want to share them with us now."

"I don't understand either. But she must have had a good reason and she obviously trusted us a lot to tell us," Jill reasoned. "You don't have to listen if you don't want to, Brooke. We can summarize it for you later. But Nana was always very sympathetic when I confided in her about my heartaches, so I feel like I owe it to her to listen to her story."

Brooke huffed, causing her bangs to lift off her forehead. "I'm going to listen, too. Go ahead, Rachel."

"Are you sure? Because—"

"I said keep reading," Brooke snapped, so Rachel did.

*Alarmed by how distraught her sister was, Hattie suggested she take a nap there, where the sea breeze was stronger and the bedrooms cooler than at the other cottage. She figured Rose would be able to think more clearly after she'd had some rest and then they'd come up with a plan together. Rose agreed and she even asked Hattie to retrieve a sleeping pill from the other cottage, so she could take half of it to make her drowsy.*

*"Jimmy and I will go next door so we won't disturb you," Hattie said. "Sleep as long as you need to. Don't worry about a thing—I know what he eats, when he naps and which toys he likes best. I'll take good care of him while you're resting."*

*"I know you will." Rose smiled wanly; she had such dark circles beneath her eyes. She hefted the toddler to kiss his cheek and embrace him. "I love you, Jimmy. Be a good boy for your other mama."*

*Jimmy leaned his head against her shoulder and patted her back. "Yove—oo," he murmured, which was his way of repeating, "I love you."*

*Because it appeared Rose might start weeping again, Hattie light-heartedly echoed, "I yove-oo, too, Rose."*

*"And I yove-oo, Hattie," her twin replied with such gravity it made Hattie shiver.*

*But then Jimmy urgently announced, "Potty."*

The three sisters chuckled when Rachel reported what their father had said as a little boy. Jill welcomed the humor after hearing about such a poignant exchange between Rose, Jimmy and Hattie. But she almost immediately felt uptight when her sister started reading again.

*So Rose set him down and Hattie took him over to the other cottage so he could use the potty chair. Just before going inside, they turned to see Rose watching them from her patio and they blew each other kisses.*

*While the toddler was in the bathroom, Hattie absently-mindedly paced from room to room, giving him his privacy until he needed her help. She happened to notice Robert's golf cap hanging from a peg near the door, which struck her as strange. His hair was thinning and he was so concerned about his scalp getting sunburned that she couldn't imagine him playing golf without covering his head.*

*At first Hattie tried to tell herself that Robert had forgotten the cap because he was so agitated by the baby crying. But as she helped Jimmy wash his hands and then sliced a banana to give to him as a snack, she was tormented by a niggling doubt. The more she tried to push it from her mind, the more it vexed her. "This must be how Rose <u>always</u> feels," she thought. "No wonder she's a wreck."*

*Suddenly, all the anger she'd been suppressing ever since the day her sister voiced concern about Robert's apathy toward the baby bubbled up inside of Hattie. She made up her mind that she was going to find out if he'd really gone where he'd said he was going. Women and children weren't allowed at the club, but Hattie had no intention of entering the building: all she needed to do was to check whether Robert's car was parked there or not.*

Rachel stopped reading to ask, "You don't think that Nana's going to tell us that her sister Hattie… that she somehow *hurt* Robert, do you? Because if she did, I don't think I want to know about it."

"No, of course she didn't hurt him," Jill exclaimed.

At the same time, Brooke said, "If she did, he had it coming."

"Brooke!" Rachel sounded appalled. "That's a terrible thing to say."

"Why? I don't *really* think she hurt him. I'm just expressing that after the way he treated Dad and Nana, I don't have any sympathy for the guy."

"I still don't think that—"

"Oh, stop being so sanctimonious and give me the letter." She snatched the pages from Rachel and continued where her sister had left off:

*Since she had no transportation except her bicycle, she knew she'd have to walk nearly three miles each way. But Hattie figured the medication her sister had taken would keep Rose asleep at least until suppertime. Jimmy would probably nap in the stroller and Hattie decided to pack a lunch so they could have a little picnic in the park on the way back.*

*As she made sandwiches and filled a small jug with water, Hattie schemed about what she'd do if Robert spotted her and questioned why she was in that part of town instead of at the beach with her sister. It dawned on her that she could tell him Rose was worried about his scalp getting sunburned, so Hattie offered to bring him his cap while her sister rested. It seemed a likely excuse, since the day was especially hot. Hattie donned her sister's sunglasses and a straw hat to make her concern seem even more credible.*

*She found a piece of paper and scribbled a note just in case Rose woke up and came looking for her and the baby. "Jimmy and I went for a walk. Hope you had a good nap. Be back soon, XX," it said. Hattie placed the message beneath the salt shaker on the table.*

*She and Jimmy were almost out the door when she noticed her shirt and shorts were splattered with blood from the baby's cut. So she had to stop and exchange her clothes for one of Rose's dresses, rinse the garments in the sink and hang them out to dry on the clothesline.*

*Then Hattie and the baby set out toward the golf club—the local one on the other end of the boardwalk, not the one in Benjamin's Manor, which was far more exclusive.*

"Oh yeah, I know which one that is. It's where the Presidents go golfing when they're vacationing in Hope—"

"Rachel, quit interrupting for something that's not important," Brooke complained, barely pausing before she continued:

*Because Hattie was pushing the stroller, she couldn't walk straight down the beach to where the boardwalk began. Instead, they traveled the maze of sandy back roads. Despite the bumpy terrain and bright sunshine, the baby fell asleep within minutes.*

*As Hattie walked, she grew increasingly anxious. What had seemed like a good idea when she was angry suddenly felt rather foolish. Suppose she did find out Robert wasn't at the golf club? What would that prove? He might claim he was giving someone a ride home or running an errand. Whether he actually was or not, the twins would have no way of knowing. Rose might become even more unsettled about the issue of his fidelity than if Hattie hadn't spied on him.*

*And although Hattie was going to the golf club with the intention of being helpful, Rose hadn't consented to the plan and she might not approve. Hattie didn't want to create any conflict between her sister and herself. Plus, if she learned Robert wasn't there, she'd have to be the bearer of bad news, a responsibility she felt should rest squarely on* <u>*his*</u> *shoulders.*

*On the other hand, if Robert's car* <u>*was*</u> *at the club, Hattie would be able to reassure Rose he'd been telling the truth. The possibility she might be able to offer her sister peace of mind seemed to make any negative consequences worth the risk. "Maybe I should only tell Rose what I find out if it's good news," she thought. Yet if she discovered Robert wasn't at the club, Hattie wasn't sure she'd be capable of keeping a secret like that from her twin.*

*She had less than half a mile to go when the toddler woke and began to whine. Hattie offered him a cool drink but he wanted to get out of the stroller. Since they were only a short distance from the ice cream parlor, she decided to stop for a treat now, instead of after lunch. After all, it was an auntie's prerogative to spoil her nephew, wasn't it?*

*She bought a small vanilla cone for Jimmy and they sat on a bench facing the wide span of open lawn bordering the park. As they watched a couple playing fetch with their dog, the blazing sun burned right through Hattie's straw hat and she felt a headache coming on. Her stomach fluttered and her breathing grew tighter and tighter, as if she had a severe case of stage fright. "Going to the club was a terrible idea," she thought and resolved to return to the cottages as soon as Jimmy finished eating his treat.*

"Thank goodness," Rachel uttered as she leaned back against the sofa. "I've been on pins and needles, worrying about how this was going to turn out."

"Me, too," Jill admitted. Her eldest sister's anxiety was contagious and against her better judgment, she'd begun to worry that Hattie might have done something to harm Robert, too.

"But it's not over yet," Brooke remarked, reading a few lines ahead. "Here, listen to this…"

*She was tipping the small jug of water to her lips when she noticed a car exactly like Robert and Rose's powder blue, two-door Studebaker sedan pull parallel with the curb some thirty yards away. The driver got out, strode across the grass and paced in circles around the small fountain in the middle of the lawn. Woozy, Hattie had the sense of imagining a mirage: could it really be Robert she was seeing?*

*Another car pulled up behind his and a short, bosomy woman with red curls exited it, calling, "Bobby, over here!" He turned and hurried toward her, smiling. When he reached the woman, he touched her waist and drew her toward him for a long, passionate kiss on the lips.*

"The lousy little…" Brooke uttered a rare expletive.

*Unaware she'd been holding her breath, Hattie gasped, trying to take in more air. Then Robert opened the back door and a little boy, maybe three or four years old, hopped out and threw his arms around Robert's legs in a gleeful embrace. He tousled the child's hair before lifting him onto his shoulders. The woman retrieved a kite from the back seat and took Robert's hand. As the three of them started across the lawn, Hattie felt as if she were suffocating.*

*She closed her eyes and tried to concentrate on breathing, but all she could think was that Robert wasn't only being unfaithful to his wife; he being unfaithful to his son. He was betraying Rose's most treasured hope for her family.*

"Ohh," Jill whimpered and pressed her hand against her chest.

Brooke muttered, "Poor Nana."

"And poor Dad," Rachel echoed.

Jill added, "I feel sorry for Hattie, too."

"Hattie?"

"Yes. She was so close to her sister and I can imagine how crushing it must have been for her to discover that Robert truly had been unfaithful to Rose," Jill explained. "If I found out that one of your husbands was having an affair, I'd be crushed on your behalf, too—not that Todd or Derek would ever do that."

"They'd *better* not," Rachel muttered.

"Okay, enough talking," Brooke said impatiently. "I'm going to keep reading."

*"Aw gone," Jimmy announced a moment later and Hattie opened her eyes. He spread his sticky fingers to show her he'd finished his cone.*

*"All gone," Hattie repeated absently, wiping his hands with a napkin before she dabbed the moisture from her cheeks. She set the toddler back in the stroller, intending for them to slip away unnoticed, but it was as if every muscle in her body revolted and she made a beeline for the trio across the lawn.*

*By the time she reached them, the boy was standing beside Robert, who had crouched down on one knee to untangle a loop of string while the child held the kite. The woman was paying them both rapt attention. Hattie cleared her throat, causing Robert to glance up. He did a double take, nearly toppling over sideways at the sight of her.*

*In a low, controlled voice, Hattie said, "Hello, Robert. I was on my way to the club to bring you your cap." Then she turned to the woman and pointed out, "As you can see, his crown is balding and his scalp gets sunburned easily." She dropped the cap on the grass at their feet and twirled the stroller around, without another word.*

"Yes!" Jill triumphantly thrust a fist above her head. "I *knew* Hattie would let him have it!"

"He deserved a lot worse than that." Brooke's tone was venomous. She turned to Rachel, "And don't you dare tell me that's not a nice thing to say."

"I wasn't going to!" Rachel said. "What happened next?"

Brooke traced her finger down the page to find her place and picked up from there.

*Hattie had only walked a few yards before the woman asked Robert, "Was that your wife?"*

*"Yes, it was."*

*His mistake might have made Hattie laugh if she hadn't been so livid. Her anger propelled her forward and she was several blocks away before she heard him behind her demanding, "Rose, wait! Rose!"*

"Oh, nooo." Rachel groaned, covering her face with her hands. "This is what I was afraid would happen."

*Hattie walked even faster, her heartbeat throbbing in her ears. Partly, she was furious at Robert and partly she was frightened by what she'd just done. Should she tell him who she was or would that only humiliate him more and make the situation even worse? And how would all of this affect her sister?*

*A few paces later, Robert grabbed her arm and jerked her and the stroller to a stop. The baby fell back, bumping his head against the seat. He let out a startled squawk, which caused a passerby to look their way. Robert immediately released Hattie's arm.*

*"That woman was only a client," he lied. "I can explain everything, but not here. Be reasonable, Rose, and come with me to the car."*

"Unbelievable! He's gaslighting her," Brooke said, tossing the letter down on the table. "I can't stand to read this. She had better not get in the car with him. A man who plays mind games like that is dangerous."

"Do you think *that's* Nana's secret? That Robert did something to *Hattie*, instead of the other way around?" Rachel questioned.

"Hold on," Jill said. "Let's not jump to conclusions." She picked up the pages and continued from where Brooke had left off.

*Although she loathed the thought of riding with him, Hattie felt desperate to reach her sister before he did. If Rose was still sleeping in Hattie's cottage, Hattie could wake her and tell her the full story. Rose could put on the dress Hattie was wearing before she spoke to Robert, so he wouldn't find out about her ruse and get angry.*

"Smart thinking," Rachel mumbled.

*Besides, Hattie felt parched and her legs were tired. So she reluctantly ambled with him back to where he'd parked beside the curb. When they got there, Hattie noticed the other woman's car was gone.*

*"Listen," Robert said once they were driving down the road. "Daisy's husband left her earlier this year, so she asked me to come with her to—"*

*"I don't want to talk about it," Hattie interrupted. She was embittered by the irony of him being unfaithful with a woman named Daisy, such a common flower, when he had an elegant, classic Rose for a wife. Thinking quickly, she added, "When we get to the cottages, I'll go ask my sister to watch the baby so we can have the privacy to discuss this after I've cooled off a little."*

Despite what she'd said about speculating, Jill pressed her hand against her abdomen to quell the jittery feeling in the pit of her stomach. This wasn't going to end well, but she couldn't predict whether it was Hattie or Robert who was going to wind up getting hurt.

*They traveled a couple of blocks in silence and even Jimmy was quiet, as if he was aware of the tension between them. Fearful that at any second Robert would recognize her, Hattie turned her face way from him, toward the open window. She wasn't as concerned about him getting angry at her as she was about him lashing out at Rose, who was completely innocent in this charade. Nor did Hattie want him to try to intimidate her into keeping what she'd seen a secret from his wife.*

*"Roll the window up," Robert gruffly instructed her. "Something smells awful."*

*"No. I'm hot," she countered, even though an acrid stench of what smelled like burned wood and rotten eggs filled her nostrils, intensifying her nausea. As they neared the turn-off to the road leading to the cottages, they passed an ambulance—the same kind of car they used for hearses back then, except ambulances were orange and white—pulling out from the intersection.*

*"It didn't have its siren on. Whoever's inside it must have already died," Robert pointed out matter-of-factly, as if commenting about the weather instead of about a life lost.*

Brooke uttered something about Robert's insensitivity that Jill couldn't hear but she could guess what it was and she nodded her agreement.

*By contrast, Hattie wrung her hands and her voice quavered as she asked, "What if he was coming from our area of the beach? I hope my sister's okay. Hurry, Robert. Please hurry home."*

*Shaking his head, he sneered, "See? This is exactly what your problem is. You overreact to everything. You're always imagining trouble where there isn't any."*

Brooke snickered disdainfully. "Again with the mind games."

*But when they turned down their lane and saw the fire engine parked in front of the cottages, Robert's tone turned grim. "I'll go find out what's going on. You stay in the car with the baby," he ordered.*

Jill's fingers trembled as she tried to flip to the next page, but the sheets were stuck together. She tried to lick her finger to separate them but her mouth was too dry, so she shook the papers and that did the trick. In her peripheral vision, she noticed Rachel covering her mouth and Brooke sitting at attention. Jill raced through the rest of the letter without stopping or even remembering to breathe, just repeating what Nana had written as quickly as she could.

*Yet even before the car had rolled to a stop, Hattie jumped out and ran toward the driveway, where the red truck was obscuring her view of the dunes. A man in a uniform—it must have been the fire captain—stepped toward her and blocked her path. "You can't come any closer, ma'am."*

*"But we're vacationing here. We own the cottages on this land."*

*"Both of them?"*

*Suddenly beside her, Robert answered, "The one to the south is ours. The northern one, closer to the edge, is my sister-in-law's."*

*"What's her name?"*

*"Hattie—Hattie Coleman. Why? What happened?"*

*"I'm sorry to inform you there was a fire in her cottage. It burned to the ground. Your sister-in-law appeared to be sleeping at the time. She didn't survive."*

*But of course, the fire captain was wrong. It wasn't Hattie who had died.*

*It was Rose, the mild twin. Mermaid Rose, the wallflower daughter. Jimmy's mother and Robert's wife.*

*It was Rose, the other half of my heart.*

# CHAPTER EIGHT

*Thursday – June 23, continued*

Jill didn't know which one of them gasped and who choked back a sob or covered her mouth and uttered, "No. No way. That can't be true." Maybe all three of those reactions came from inside *her* and not from her sisters. She was vaguely aware that she'd had this experience before; it was when the cardiologist had ushered the three sisters from the family waiting lounge into a private room and told them their father hadn't survived open-heart surgery. Now, like then, Jill couldn't quite take in what she'd heard, even though she'd been the one speaking the words Nana had written.

She vacantly stared at the sliding door, which was too blurred with moisture for her to see through it. Or were those tears obscuring Jill's vision? A mix of emotions was causing her eyes to fill. Sadness about the circumstances of Nana's sister's death. Empathy that Nana had to experience that kind of trauma, especially since she'd already been through something similar when her parents passed. But also shocked confusion and—she hated to even acknowledge it—a bit of anger at discovering Nana wasn't the person Jill had always thought she was.

After a while of shared silence, Rachel softly asked. "You want me to finish reading it?"

"There's nothing else to read—that was the end. Nana didn't even sign it this time. She probably became so upset writing about her sister's death that she just stopped writing."

Brooke leaned forward to tug several tissues from the box. She patted her cheeks with one of them and said, "I can't believe her sister died here, on this property, when they were supposed to be enjoying their vacation together. It must have been right around this time in June."

The parallel to their own lives was too close for comfort and Jill tried not to imagine the anguish Nana experienced after losing her sister, but she couldn't stop herself. Judging from the looks on her sisters' faces, they were plagued by similar thoughts.

After more silence, Rachel shook her head and said, "I can't believe Nana wasn't really Dad's mother. And that she wasn't really our grandmother, either—she was our great-aunt."

"She was still our Nana. She was the only grandmother we ever had," Jill insisted in Nana's defense, even though she felt as stupefied as Rachel. "And we couldn't have asked for a better one."

"No, I know. But I can't wrap my head around the fact that Nana… that she wasn't Rose Sampson. That she was Hattie Coleman. I wonder who else knew. And if Robert ever found out. I just… I don't understand why she wouldn't have told Dad. He died without ever knowing that she wasn't his mother. It doesn't seem right."

"What isn't right is that Dad's father was such a manipulative, unconscionable cheat. If it wasn't for him, Nana's sister wouldn't have had insomnia and she wouldn't have taken the sleeping pills and died in that fire," Brooke said.

"I don't just mean it wasn't right like that. I mean it wasn't… it wasn't very emotionally balanced of her to pretend to be someone else for all—"

"Stop making it sound as if Nana had lost touch with reality," Jill interrupted.

"It's not a judgment," Rachel clarified. "I think she deserves a lot of compassion. She'd already suffered the trauma of her parents' accidental death. Maybe losing everyone in her immediate family at such a young age was too much to bear and she couldn't internalize it. She might have subconsciously felt so guilty about her sister's death that she assumed her identity…"

"It wasn't as if she was *unaware* she was pretending to be her sister," Jill argued. "She knew and she deliberately kept it a secret. Furthermore, everyone has secrets and that doesn't mean they're emotionally unbalanced. I'm sure there are things you keep from *your* children."

"Nothing this big." Rachel jiggled her head in disbelief. "I really suspected Nana's secret was going to be that Hattie had hurt Robert or that Robert had hurt Hattie or Nana. I never saw *this* coming."

"Neither did I. I was afraid Hattie had died in a drowning accident and that was the real reason Nana never went swimming," Brooke admitted. "That would have been distressing enough to hear, but this is a lot worse. Not just because of the way Nana's sister died, but because of how it affected her entire life. Dad's, too—and ours, as well. I still don't understand why she's telling us this now."

"Well, in her first letter she wrote that it was because she wanted to die with a clean conscience," Rachel reminded her.

"I'm sure that's a big part of it," Jill said. "But I think Nana might be about to tell us something else that she wanted us to know before we decide what to do with her estate." At least, that's what Jill was still trying to believe.

"I think she *did* just tell us. I think she confessed that her sister died on this property because she understood we might not want to keep it if we knew."

"That's ridiculous. It's not as if the estate is haunted or something," Jill scoffed. "Besides, it was Nana's sister who died, not ours. So if anyone would have wanted to sell the estate, it would have been her, but she loved this place. If she had any qualms about coming here because of her sister's death, we would have picked up on it."

"I don't know about that. We never noticed any signs that she wasn't really our grandmother," Rachel said. "And Dad never knew she wasn't his mother."

"That's because she *was* his mother in all the ways that mattered," Jill shouted, startling both her sisters and herself.

"Rachel isn't criticizing Nana, Jill. She's just saying how much of a shock it is to learn her true identity."

"I *know* it's a shock. Don't you think I'm shocked, too? It's as if my entire world has been turned upside down and inside out." Jill covered her eyes and finally admitted aloud, "I feel like I've been duped. And I hate feeling that way about someone I love as much as I love Nana."

Her sisters got up and sat beside her. Brooke patted her back. "Nana would never do anything to deliberately hurt us, Jill. Or to hurt Dad. So she must have had a good reason for keeping her secret all these years—and a good reason for telling it to us now."

"That's right," Rachel agreed, changing her tune a little. Maybe she was reassuring herself as much as she was comforting Jill when she added, "We haven't heard Nana's full story yet. We still have five or six more letters to read. I'm sure the next one will shed some light on the subject."

At that exact moment, the power came back on. Jill and Rachel gaped at each other in astonishment, and Brooke exclaimed, "What timing!" She jumped up and moved toward the staircase. "I'm sorry, but we can talk about this more later. I have *got* to go take a shower."

"I'll use the one outside—unless you want to use it first?" Rachel asked Jill.

"No, that's fine. I showered yesterday. You go ahead."

Besides, Jill wanted time to reread and reflect on Nana's letter in private. She took it upstairs to her room and lay down on the bed, perusing it three more times. It never got any easier to read about what Nana had endured on the day her sister died. In fact, Jill noticed two things she'd missed the first time that made her weep even harder than she had at first.

One was that Rose's last words to her son included, *Be a good boy for your other mama.* She'd also said *I love you*, to both her son and sister, who'd repeated the sentiment back to her. It made Jill wonder if Rose had had a sense she was saying a final goodbye.

The second thing Jill realized was that at the same time Rose was dying, Nana was growing thirstier and hotter, and she was struggling to breathe. Almost as if *she* were the one being overtaken by the flames and fumes. *Was that because they were twins or was it only a coincidence?* Jill asked herself as a shiver racked her body.

She wondered how many times these same questions had run through Nana's mind over the years. It hurt to think that Nana had carried this horrible burden by herself for almost her entire life. *Was a clean conscience* really *the reason she decided to share the secret now*? Until they'd read today's letter, Jill had been relatively certain that Nana was going to share something that would help convince her sisters to keep the estate. Now it seemed as if the opposite might be true; as Brooke suggested, maybe Nana's secret was meant to motivate them to sell it.

*We still have more letters to come. Only time will tell,* she reminded herself, but that didn't help her feel any more patient. She got up and went into Brooke's room, where her sister was sitting on the bed, a comb in her hand, her wet hair hanging to her shoulders. She was staring at the watery window, clearly lost in thought.

"Feel better?" Jill asked, referring to the fact she'd finally been able to take a shower.

"Not really. I keep thinking about Nana's sister dying right over there." She gestured in the direction of the dune to the right of the house. "We've been tramping past that spot thousands of times and we never knew."

"It's not as if she's *buried* there," Jill said. "Besides, in Nana's letter, she mentioned the cottage was located right on the lip of the dune. A good section of that area was probably eroded at the same time the other cottage was washed away in the storm when Dad was a boy."

"I meant it figuratively. In the sense that all these years we've been obliviously enjoying running right by the place where our grandmother's wish for her adulthood began—and where it ended. Rose's dream to get married and have a family was so similar to mine…" Brooke's eyes watered and she sniffled. "I don't know how Nana could have ever come back here after her sister died."

"For one thing, Nana was really strong. And for another, I think this place contained her happiest memories, too. Like the ones she had of her parents and grandparents coming here together after the War, before Robert came into their lives. Maybe the happier memories outweighed the devastating ones."

"Maybe." Brooke didn't sound convinced. She absently combed the ends of her hair. "Remember that guy I dated senior year in college? His name was Ken."

"The one whose summer job was coaching golf?"

"No, tennis. Remember his tennis tan? His torso and upper arms were so white compared to the rest of his skin, it looked as if he was wearing a shirt." Brooke said. "At the time, I was actually contemplating the idea of marrying him."

Jill hadn't been aware that Brooke had ever considered marrying anyone except Todd. "Why did you decide not to?"

"Mostly, it was something Nana said. I'd invited him to visit me here and he liked it well enough, but he wouldn't come into the water even though he knew how to swim. Rachel was dating Derek by then, so they were both here and you were here, too. The four of us were having a blast—we'd made up some kind of aquatic obstacle course—but he just stood on shore, waiting for me to come out. Nana remarked that he literally seemed like a fish out of water."

Jill snorted a laugh. "He *really* did—especially because he had such a white belly, like a gigantic cod."

Brooke hardly smiled. "Nana said there's nothing wrong with wanting to get married and have children, but she wondered if I was rushing into it. She said that she wouldn't want me or my children to suffer because I was lonely and married the wrong man." Brooke lifted her comb to eye level and removed the nest of hair interwoven between its teeth. "At the time, I thought that was the closest she ever came to telling me she regretted her choice in a husband. I thought she was referring to divorce. That she was warning me because of her own experience. I never would have guessed that she'd been referring to her sister…"

"How could you have guessed? None of us knew she was keeping a secret like that." Jill felt as if she might start crying again, so she segued to Brooke's favorite topic. "I'm glad you married Todd instead of Ken. That reminds me, I haven't seen photos of the venue for your vow renewal ceremony. Want to show me?"

"Maybe later. I just want to sit here and think about things for a while."

Jill took the hint and left to look for her older sister, but Rachel was talking on the phone in the great room. Jill brought one of the bird guides back upstairs and stretched out on her bed. She briefly leafed through the book but the blanched sky created a glare that made reading difficult, so she closed her eyes instead. Suddenly, she was so enervated that she wished she could sleep until the following morning. By then they'd receive another letter and maybe it would help her feel as if Nana was still the person Jill had always thought she was.

Right before dozing off, it occurred to her that this was the first time in her life she'd ever wanted her time on Dune Island to pass quicker, rather than slower. It was also the first time that Nana's place didn't feel like paradise—and the rain had nothing to do with it.

# CHAPTER NINE

*Friday – June 24*

"Any luck?" Rachel asked as Jill pulled the slider open and stepped inside.

It was almost eleven o'clock on Friday morning and they still hadn't received a letter from Nana yet, so Jill had gone outside to try to get a strong enough connection to call the courier service. She'd walked nearly half a mile down the road in the rain.

"I finally got through, but the guy who answered said there weren't any deliveries scheduled for us today." Jill slipped out of her sandals by the door and trod over to the overstuffed armchair across from her sister. Dropping into it with a disgusted sigh, she said, "He told me they'll keep an eye out for it and that I can keep checking every hour, just in case it shows up. Somehow, that doesn't give me a lot of confidence that they haven't misplaced it."

"It's possible there isn't one," Rachel suggested. "Maybe Nana wanted to give us a little time to process yesterday's bombshell."

Brooke scuffed into the kitchen, sniffing the air. This was the first time she'd been downstairs all morning and she was still wearing her pajamas. "Are you seriously baking something *again*?" she asked Rachel.

"I can't help seem to help myself—I'm so happy to have the oven working. It was crazy to pay as much as we were paying for prepared food when I can make something five times healthier for a fraction of the cost."

"Yeah, but the oven's making it feel really hot down here," Brooke complained, even as she pressed the button on the coffee maker. "And you're wasting energy, since we still have leftovers from yesterday."

No one had eaten much the previous afternoon or evening; they'd been so out of sorts they'd lost their appetites. A couple of times they'd tried talking about Nana's letter, but their discussions had ended with one or more of them in tears over what they'd learned about her life. Ultimately, the three sisters had retreated to separate parts of the house to manage their emotions by themselves.

"You should talk about wasting energy," Rachel said. "What are you on, like, your fourth shower since yesterday?"

"I *didn't* shower yet this morning. My hair's just wet because it's so muggy in here." Brooke lifted her wilted locks from the nape of her neck with one hand and fixed herself a cup of coffee with the other. "Why do you look so glum, Jill? Has the concert already been called off because of the forecast?"

Jill had completely forgotten about going out with Alex tonight. But now that Brooke mentioned it, she hoped the event would be canceled so she wouldn't have to make up an excuse for not going. The last thing she felt like doing this evening was attending a public concert; there was already too much racket in her brain. "No, I'm annoyed because the courier service can't find Nana's letter."

"It's not that they can't find it—they said there isn't one today," Rachel clarified and her verbal hair-splitting adding to Jill's irritation.

"That makes sense." Brooke sank into a couch cushion, almost sloshing coffee onto her lap. "Nana always did like to build up a sense of suspense—remember when she'd read us bedtime stories and she'd close the book at the most exciting part? She'd say, 'You'll have to show up at the same time and place tomorrow to find out what happens next.'"

Jill remembered that, too. But she'd figured out a long time ago that Nana hadn't actually always stopped reading at the most suspenseful part of the story. Rather, the stories had *seemed* suspenseful no matter where she'd stopped because she'd had such an animated reading style. In light of yesterday's letter, it just occurred to Jill that Nana's amazing narration skills were probably the result of her theatrical experience.

"When I got older and had children of my own, she told me that was the only way she could be sure we'd come to bed when we were supposed to the next night," Rachel recalled. "She always did the same thing with my kids when she read to them here. I tried copying her trick at home, but those two little monkeys would find the book and finish reading it on their own."

Brooke chuckled. "Grace and Noah have always been so clever. No wonder they got into Densmore."

"They got into Densmore?" Jill asked.

Brooke cringed. "Oops. Sorry. I thought you told her, Rach."

"No. I didn't get the chance." Rachel said, glowering at her before turning to Jill. "I found out yesterday and I was going to tell you, but you were taking a nap and then we had another upsetting conversation about Nana's letter, so..."

"That's great, congratulations." Jill forced herself to pause for a second before asking, "Did they get scholarships?"

"We won't find that out until early next week."

*Talk about keeping someone in suspense,* Jill thought. "Okay, so, just to be sure we're on the same page... if they don't get full scholarships, you'll still definitely want to sell the estate?"

"I'll *need* to sell it, yes. Otherwise, they won't be able to attend. But as I mentioned, if they *do* get full scholarships, then I'd be willing to keep the estate as long as you can cover the portion of expenses I can't afford," Rachel said, recapping their earlier agreement. "Of course, all of this is dependent on whether or not Brooke wants to sell the estate."

Jill raised an eyebrow at her middle sister, as if to ask what she thought.

"After hearing yesterday's letter from Nana, I'm leaning even more toward selling," Brooke admitted regretfully. "I suppose her letters could contain something in the next few days that would make me reconsider, but I highly doubt it."

If her apologetic tone was meant to soothe Jill's feelings, it had the opposite effect. Why was it *she* had to acquiesce to her sisters' decisions, as if they had all the power? "What would happen if I didn't accept that?" she asked.

"What do you mean?"

"I mean, what would happen legally if I refused to agree to sell the house? This decision is supposed to be unanimous, isn't it?"

"Well, as the attorney explained, Nana's request wasn't legally binding," Rachel iterated. "But she trusted the three of us to work this out and come to a unanimous decision."

"I understand. But what if we couldn't agree? What if I absolutely didn't want to sell the house no matter what?"

"Well, if Brooke and I—or just one of us—absolutely *did* want to sell it, you'd have the option to buy us out. If you couldn't afford that, there are ways we could force the sale and divide the assets. But of course that would take time and money and legal action. We'd never want it to come to that."

*So in other words, I really* don't *have any say in the matter*, Jill thought, defeated. "I wouldn't want it to come to that, either," she said. "But it doesn't seem fair that—"

Before she could complete her thought, the oven timer went off and Rachel jumped up and hurried into the kitchen to check on her apple scones.

"Oh, that timer reminds me—I've got to call Todd and remind him to put the deposit down so we can reserve the rooms at the resort. He insisted on doing it from home because he doesn't trust the security of the internet connection here." In a flash, Brooke disappeared up the stairs.

*Of course, you go right ahead, that's fine. What I was saying wasn't important anyway*, Jill thought sarcastically. She got up and grabbed her keys from the hook by the door. Pushing her feet into her sandals, she told Rachel she'd be back in a while. Jill didn't know where she was going, but she had to get out of the house before she said something she'd regret later.

The rainy-day vacation traffic crawled past the boardwalk near the center of town, but just beyond the golf course it thinned out and picked up speed. Without deliberately thinking about it, Jill turned onto the scenic, meandering road to Highland Hills, where the residences were fewer and scattered farther apart than those in Lucinda's Hamlet.

She crested the incline that led to her favorite ocean overlook, pulled onto the sandy shoulder and turned off the car's engine. In the distance below, the high tide and stormy weather combined to form wind-lashed waves that pounded the shore with chaotic ferocity; a perfect match for Jill's mood.

She'd barely had a moment to unbuckle her seatbelt when her phone chimed. It was a number she didn't recognize. *The courier! They must have found Nana's letter.*

"Jill?" The caller sounded familiar.

"Yes?"

"It's me. Erika. I tried texting, but my message wouldn't go through. You said you wanted to hear any updates about work, even if it was bad news…"

Jill's stomach churned as her coworker explained that their entire department had been laid off, including their manager. Apparently, there was too much overlap between their roles and the roles of staff already employed by the corporation that had recently acquired their company. "They escorted all of us out of the building a couple hours ago. I felt like a common criminal instead of like someone who has devoted twelve and a half years of my career to their service. Consider yourself fortunate you weren't here to go through that kind of humiliation."

Jill hardly felt fortunate at the moment, but she commiserated with her colleague and promised to keep in touch about potential job leads and networking opportunities.

Toward the end of their conversation, Erika asked her not to let anyone else know she was the one who had tipped Jill off about their entire department being let go. "It's probably not considered very professional of me to give you a heads-up about the situation before someone from HR officially notifies you. They've probably been trying to call you, too."

"I won't let on that I have any clue," Jill promised. "Thank you for making such an effort to let me know about it, even though you couldn't get through right away."

"I wish I'd had better news—I'm sorry if I ruined your vacation."

*My vacation was already ruined*, Jill thought bitterly. "No, it's fine, really. I appreciate the call."

"Well, I know how much you love Dune Island. So on the bright side, at least now you don't have to hurry back to Boston, right? You could stay there all summer if you wanted to."

*If only*, Jill thought. She said goodbye to Erika and before she had time to process what she'd just heard, she received another call. It was Alex, phoning to tell her the concert had been canceled because of the weather.

"Sydney and her friends are staying in and having a movie night at home. But you and I could do something else. Like go out to for dinner some place healthier than The Shack? No pressure—I know we'd just be going as childhood friends from the arcade."

"Thanks, but…" There were so many legitimate excuses Jill could have given him for not wanting to go out that she couldn't narrow it down to just one. And with the news she'd just heard about her job, plus the conversation with her sisters, she didn't have the energy to explain them all. So she joked, "I'm not allowed to go out alone with boys who are so much older than I am."

He chuckled. "How about next Friday's concert, then? My sister and her housemates will be there, too."

"Next weekend will be my last weekend on the island," she reminded him. "Trust me, I'm not good company right before I have to leave." *Especially not if it's my last weekend on the island forever.*

"Okay. But, hey, you're still welcome to use my shower any time you want."

"Thanks, but our power finally came on."

"Oh, that's good." His sigh told her he meant the opposite. "How about if we go to the concert on this Friday of next year?"

"Sure, why not?" *Other than that I probably won't be here next year.*

"Great. It's a date. I-I mean it's a deal," he stammered and Jill imagined he was blushing. She could picture his blue eyes, too, and suddenly her own eyes began to swim with tears.

As soon as she'd hung up, she hollered, "Arg!" and pressed her car's horn in frustration, scaring away the gull that had been perched on the split rail fence post in front of her. Then she leaned her head against the steering wheel and broke down in tears.

She'd lost her nana. She'd lost her job. And she'd lost whatever miniscule hope she'd had of ever sharing a future with a man like Alex. As soon as her sisters found out she was unemployed, that would cinch it: Jill would also lose the place she loved more than anywhere else in the world.

Which was exactly why she decided she wasn't going to tell them.

# CHAPTER TEN

## *Saturday – June 25*

"Good morning, sleepyhead," Brooke greeted her when Jill ambled into the great room at some time after nine-thirty on Saturday morning.

Jill hadn't actually been asleep; she'd purposely been secluding herself in her room for two reasons. The first was that after she'd come home from her drive the previous afternoon, her sisters had commented about how keyed up she'd seemed. She'd told them she was disappointed because the concert had been canceled so she wasn't going out with Alex. Which wasn't entirely a lie—the more time that had passed, the more she regretted not saying yes to going somewhere else with him. After all, she'd needed a pleasant distraction from her problems yesterday even more than she'd needed it the first time he'd asked her out.

But disappointment wasn't the main thing that was putting Jill on edge. The real truth was that she'd felt guilty about not telling her sisters she'd lost her job. Not guilty enough to actually *tell* them, but guilty enough that she'd been avoiding being in their presence.

The other reason she'd been isolating herself was that she'd been researching job opportunities online on her phone. And when she couldn't get a connection, she'd been trying to come up with a way to pay her rent and one third of the cost of the upkeep on Nana's house, in addition to whatever Rachel couldn't afford. It would have been a challenge on the salary she'd been earning, but now that she was unemployed it would be next to impossible.

Jill supposed she could withdraw money from her retirement account, although then it would be subject to a tax penalty. She also considered moving somewhere cheaper than Boston, since she didn't necessarily need to be so close to the city now. But neither of those options seemed to be an adequate long-term solution to the financial hurdles she'd have to overcome *if* her sisters agreed to keep Nana's estate. Which they probably wouldn't anyway.

In any case, mulling over the predicament had given her a whopper of a headache. In the end, she'd been driven from her room by her need for caffeine, as well as by the realization that she couldn't avoid her sisters' company for the rest of their vacation.

"You'll be happy to know another letter arrived this morning from Nana." Rachel told her as Jill served herself a cup of coffee.

*I won't be happy unless it says that she expressly forbids us to sell the house*, Jill thought. "Whose turn is it to read?"

"I'll do it," Brooke volunteered.

With the way Jill was feeling, she didn't think she could tolerate any of her sister's blubbering this morning. "Do you think we could just try to read straight through it, without so many interruptions today?" she suggested as she sat down with them.

"Fine," Brooke snapped. Jill's head hurt too much to care if her sister was insulted by her request.

*Dearest Rachel, Brooke and Jill,*

*I'm sorry I ended the last letter so abruptly. I was overcome with emotion. Also, it occurred to me I shouldn't sign the letter "Nana." But "Your great-aunt Hattie" doesn't seem right either.*

"No, it doesn't," Jill agreed, thinking aloud. "I could never call her any name other than Nana."

"Is this the kind of interruption you don't want us to make?" Brooke gibed. "Or is it only that I'm not allowed to cry?"

"Just read."

*I imagine you were quite upset to discover I'm not your biological grandmother. You probably feel betrayed, as if I've been playing some sort of twisted trick on you your entire lives. That's one of the reasons I wanted you to be together when you found out—so you could comfort each other.*

*It seems almost laughable for me to say it now, but I truly never meant to live a life of deception. I know I can't justify what I did by posing as my sister all these years, but I at least want to explain it to you girls.*

*The moment after the fire captain told us Rose hadn't survived, I fainted dead away. The next thing I remember was coming to in a bright, white room. At first, I thought—I may have even wished it—that I was the one who had died after all. But then a doctor told me I was in the hospital and he asked me to say my name and the date.*

*"Hattie," I croaked, my throat so dry I could hardly get the word out. "Hattie!" I repeated as loudly as I could.*

*You see, I tried, I really did try, to set the record straight. But the doctor must have thought I was calling hysterically for my sister and he medicated me. The next time I woke, I was lying in a narrow bed in a dimly lit room, cuddling Jimmy.*

*When I was more coherent, I would realize I was in the summer mansion of Lawrence Rutherford—the waterfront residence where I'd gone to George's beach party with my sister the summer we were eighteen. Like everyone else on the island, Mr. Rutherford had heard about the fire almost immediately after it happened. Believing I was Hattie's sister, he invited us to stay in his home so I wouldn't have to return to the cottage.*

*Robert reportedly had details to sort out with the fire department for insurance purposes, so we couldn't leave the island for a couple of days. I was in a complete stupor; someone must have been giving me Rose's sleeping pills. In any case, Mr. Rutherford's housekeeper, Christina, watched Jimmy during the day, but at night he wouldn't go to sleep unless he was in my arms. Or maybe it was the other way around, I don't know. Regardless, I slept with him in a twin bed and Robert slept in the room next door.*

*If he ever expressed sympathy about my sister, I can't remember what he said. I do vaguely recall, however, that he told me the fire had started on the kitchen stovetop and that my sister was apparently sleeping. They figured she'd gotten up to make tea and then went back to sleep before she'd finished making it. That made sense to me. Rose always said that tea calmed her nerves, no matter how hot the weather. Perhaps before the water was ready, her medication took effect and she fell asleep. Maybe she'd set a napkin or a pot holder too near the flame. It's even possible a breeze blew the window curtain across the stove and it caught fire.*

*Again, I have no way of knowing; they didn't investigate these matters then the way they do now, especially on a small island. But judging from how the sleeping pills affected me, I can understand why my sister never roused. And once the propane tank exploded... well, it would have been too late.*

Brooke stopped reading here and shuddered, but she didn't say anything before picking up where she'd left off.

*Since our grandfather, my only surviving relative, was incapacitated by his stroke, planning a funeral should have fallen to Robert and me. However, I was too traumatized and Robert wasn't adept at managing such matters. So, some of my friends from New York and Connecticut, as well as a few acquaintances from Dune Island, volunteered to make the arrangements. Because of the manner in which my sister died, there wasn't the usual urgency for a burial, and they scheduled the service for a few weeks after the fire. I think they wanted to give me—the person they thought was Rose, I mean—time to recover so I could attend it.*

*The day Christina informed me of their plans was the first day I hadn't taken any medication. It was the first time I had the presence of mind to realize that everyone, including Robert, still thought I was my sister. Initially, I was appalled he couldn't tell the difference between Rose and me. Had he always been that inattentive to his wife? Then I caught sight of my reflection in a mirror: it appeared so anguished and aged—so vacant—I hardly recognized my own face.*

*I realized I urgently needed to confess to him what I'd done before informing anyone else. Not only was I mourning, but I was terrified, guilt-ridden and ashamed of the situation I had unintentionally created. But mostly, I was genuinely worried about Robert. As incensed as I'd been about his affair, I would have given almost anything to spare him the reality of Rose's death, made crueler by my impersonation of her. Afraid he'd fall to pieces the way I had, I thought it best to speak to him in private.*

*So when he came back to the house late that afternoon, I told him I was ready to go pack my belongings at the cottage and return to Connecticut the following morning. He seemed surprised and tried to talk me out of it for some reason, but I insisted. I suppose he didn't want to make a scene, so he gave in.*

*We thanked our gracious host and said goodbye and then the three of us—Robert, Jimmy and I—went back to Sea Breeze Lane. As we turned into the sandy driveway, my head started to spin and my mouth felt cottony. So I focused my attention on placating the baby, who was whimpering as if he, too, remembered what had happened the last time we drove down that road.*

*My first glimpse of the cottage—rather, of its charred remains—nearly buckled my knees. But then Robert pointed to the patch of scorched earth and blackened rubble and offhandedly remarked, "If it weren't for the sand, the fire might have swept across the grass and we would have lost our cottage, too." His shocking callousness was oddly helpful, in that it momentarily made me too angry to break down at the sight of the devastation.*

*I hurried down the path ahead of him, carrying Jimmy until we got to the door of the cottage. As soon as I set him down inside, he trotted to his parents' bedroom, his hands raised above his head.*

*"Mama! Mama!" he exclaimed, clearly believing Rose was waiting for him there. When he didn't find her, his cries turned plaintive. "Ma-maa. Ma-maa," he bleated, like a lost, motherless lamb.*

Brooke's face contorted into a red gnarl. "Don't even," she warned Jill, holding up a finger and wiping her eyes with her other hand.

"I wasn't going to say anything," Jill assured her. She was misty-eyed by this description of her father as an infant, too.

Brooke extended the sheets of paper in front of her. "Somebody else has to take over. I'm done."

"I can give it a try." Rachel said. She dabbed her eyes and adjusted her glasses.

*I rushed to pick him up, but he made his body go limp and we fell backward onto the bed, both of us sobbing.*

*A few moments later, Robert appeared in the doorway. "I knew this would happen. That's why I tried to tell you not to come back here," he said quietly. In fairness, I do believe he was being as compassionate as he could. But the man simply had no tolerance for crying and he said he was going for a drive until I calmed down.*

*I rocked Jimmy in my arms and eventually he drifted off to sleep. I tucked him into bed and went to the kitchen. As I was filling my glass, I noticed two mugs in the sink. The only reason they caught my eye was because one had lipstick on the rim. The shade was too bright to have been my sister's—she only wore coral or pink. This shade was red; it was garish. I knew right away it was Daisy's.*

*Robert had allowed his mistress to come to the cottage while he believed Rose was mourning her twin's death? I can't say I was completely surprised by his lack of sentimentality toward me, but I was astounded by his lack of respect for his wife's suffering. I sat down at the table—the note I'd written to Rose was still there, beneath the salt shaker—and set the mug in front of me. Staring at it, I realized it was just one more indication that my sister's marriage was as disintegrated as the cottage.*

*Yet for Jimmy's sake, I knew I was somehow going to have to put things right between Robert and me. I was going to have to confess I was Hattie. So when my brother-in-law came back, I took a deep breath and began, "Sit down, Robert. We need to talk."*

*His eyes darted to the crimson, accusatory stain on the rim of the mug and he immediately got his hackles up. "I told you, Daisy's just a client. She's separated from her husband and that day in the park she asked me to help her son fly a kite, since his father obviously isn't here to do it with him. When she heard about the fire, she stopped by to see if there was anything she could do for you. She was trying to be helpful."*

*As galling as his lie was, I shook my head. "I don't want to hear about it," I replied, because I didn't. All that mattered now was saying what I had to say before I lost my nerve. My head was swimming and I forgot the carefully worded explanation I'd been rehearsing. I forgot my apology and words of comfort. And I forgot my promise to help him raise Jimmy. Instead, I heard myself blurt out, "I'm not your wife, Robert. I—"*

*He abruptly leaned forward and banged his palms on the table, startling me and making the mug bounce. "If you think I'll agree to a divorce, you're nuts!"*

*It took a second for me to understand: he'd interpreted my statement to mean that because he'd been unfaithful, I no longer considered myself to be his wife. I was dumbfounded as he glowered, warning me, "Just because you have a trust fund doesn't mean you'll be able to make ends meet. I've seen the figures and that money won't last very long. And then how do you suppose a secretarial school dropout like you is going to be able to support a child?"*

*"Oh, she'd find a way," I muttered to myself, thinking about Rose. She wouldn't have let anything or anyone interfere with her raising her son to the best of her ability.*

*When Robert's face blanched, I realized I'd said, "she," instead of "I." But all he seemed to hear was my defiance. "Is that a threat?*

*Because if it is, I have one for you, too." As he straightened his posture, his mouth twisted into a ruthless sneer. "If you so much as utter the word 'divorce,' I'll tell my attorney you're unfit to care for a child. That you're a danger to yourself and should be put in an asylum. Considering your recent behavior, half of the people on this island would back me up."*

"He was *evil*," Brooke declared. "That man was just plain evil."

"*That's* an understatement!" Jill exclaimed.

*I was mortified, my mind reeling. If Robert could blackmail his grieving wife with a claim of emotional instability, I could only imagine how he might intimidate me. I'd been posing as a deceased person for several days! I wasn't sure if he could have me institutionalized, but I was 100 per cent positive at the very least he'd prevent me from ever seeing my nephew again. The possibility of Robert and Daisy getting married and subsequently neglecting my sister's child was more than I could stomach. I ran into the bathroom and retched.*

*When I was done, I rinsed out my mouth, blotted my lips and looked into the mirror. My sister's pale, tear-streaked face stared back at me. That was the moment I made the conscious decision to take her place. To become Jimmy's mother…*

*I realize I still have much more to explain, but for now I hope you won't begrudge me the privilege of signing this,*

*as always,*

*Your loving Nana*

Rachel's arm dropped to the side of her chair, as if the emotional gravitas of the letter had made it physically heavy, too.

"I knew it. I knew Nana was of sound mind when she decided to impersonate her twin." Jill wasn't gloating; she was relieved.

"She didn't do it because she was unbalanced—she did it out of love for Dad."

"And out of fear. Robert was a total brute." Brooke spat out the words. "*He's* the one who should have been locked up for threatening Nana like that."

"Yes, I can see why she pretended to be her sister," Rachel allowed. "I probably would have done the same thing."

"I hope Nana didn't put up with him for very long before they got divorced," Brooke replied. "For Dad's sake, as well as for her own."

"When I was younger, I always felt sorry for Dad because he never knew Robert. But that was because I naively assumed he'd missed out on having the kind of wonderful father that *we'd* had. Now I'm relieved he didn't have to grow up with an apathetic, merciless, money-grubbing man like Robert," Rachel said. "Although I'm still not sure Nana should have kept her own identity a secret from Dad for his entire life."

"But we haven't heard her whole story yet. She wrote that she has a lot more to explain, so I'm sure she had good reasons for never telling him," Jill insisted. "We just have to trust her about this, too. We'll find out what it was eventually."

For over an hour, the three sisters continued discussing their nana's plight. They reread passages of her letters aloud or to themselves and commented about how lonely and frightened she must have felt. Yet they all admired her courage and her commitment to protecting their father, too.

"If it hadn't been for Nana, who knows what might have happened to Dad," Brooke remarked. "We probably never would have even been born."

Jill dared to hope her sister's gratitude might cause her to change her stance on selling Nana's estate. There was still the question of whether the twins would receive scholarships, and Jill would have to pull off some impressive financial maneuvers, but she felt so much more optimistic now than yesterday.

So after a while, when Brooke asked if anyone wanted to go to the boardwalk with her, Jill said, "I do—it sounds like fun. We can take our minds off everything poor Nana had to go through, at least until we get another letter." Going into town with her sisters would also be a fun distraction from thinking about her job situation. Maybe not quite as enjoyable as going out with Alex would have been, but Jill only had herself to blame for turning him down.

"The boardwalk on a rainy afternoon sounds like torture," Rachel objected. "Every tourist on the island will be there."

"No they won't. It's Saturday, remember? There's always a quiet window of time between when last week's vacationers leave and this week's arrive."

"Besides, we haven't taken our annual trip to Lucy's Tees," Brooke reminded Rachel. "I told the girls I'd bring them both a couple of shirts."

Every year, the sisters and their daughters went to the island's best known T-shirt shop and bought three to five shirts apiece in various designs and colors. The soft, cool cotton tops were a staple of their summer wardrobes; they wore them to run, beachcomb, sleep and even over their suits when they went swimming. But because of the weather, this year the women hadn't gone to town for the purpose of making their traditional clothing purchases.

"As long as we're going to the boardwalk, let's stop at the souvenir shop and get saltwater taffy," Jill suggested. "We can do all of the touristy things."

"Not *all* of them. We can't play mini-golf. It's pouring."

"Well, we could but we'd have to wear garbage bags." Jill laughed as she reminded her sisters of the summer when she was nine, Brooke was eleven and Rachel had just turned thirteen. They'd all wanted to go mini-golfing but it was raining even harder than it was today. Their umbrella was broken and they hadn't brought any rain gear. So Nana had outfitted them in clean plastic garbage bags by simply cutting a hole in the bottom and an arm hole on each side. Then the girls had turned them upside down and pulled them over their heads, just as they would have done with any shirt.

Brooke was too self-conscious or vain to wear hers and she took it off as soon as they were out of Nana's sight. By the time they got down to the boardwalk, her clothes were soaked and her bright pink butterfly underwear showed through her white shorts. As it turned out, nearly half the other kids at the mini-golf course were wearing garbage bags, too. It was probably the only time in her young life that Jill had felt "cooler" than her older sister.

After reminiscing about their childhood expedition, Rachel decided she wanted to accompany her sisters to the boardwalk after all. "We can stop and redeem our bottles on the way and then use the change we get back as spending money."

"Okay." Jill chuckled because she thought Rachel was joking, since that's what they used to do when they were kids. But after Rachel left the room, she asked Brooke, "You don't think she was serious, do you?"

Brooke shrugged. "Maybe. You know how conscientious she is about the environment."

"It's not the environment I think she's concerned about. It's the money. She's obsessed about every cent she spends—I mean, more than usual. She's supposed to be on vacation but she's fixated on those financial spreadsheets that she has laid out all over the dining table. I don't get it. If anyone needs to worry about money, you'd think it would be *me.* Especially now that I—" Jill stopped herself just in time from letting it slip that she'd lost her job, but Brooke picked up her flub anyway.

"Now that you *what*?"

"Now that I might be contributing to Nana's estate." Jill hastily insisted, "Not that I couldn't afford to, because I'd make it happen, no matter what. I'm just saying that compared to Rachel, you'd think *I'd* be the one pinching every penny."

Brooke shrugged. "Rachel has always been frugal—it comes with the territory of being the firstborn. She thinks she needs to do everything perfectly, including staying within a budget."

"Hmm. Maybe." Jill hadn't really thought of it that way. She'd just felt that Rachel had gotten really cheap. Or really greedy. "But just so you know, I do *not* want to stop so she can gather bottles from the side of the road to add to her collection."

"In that case, we'd better take your car instead of hers," Brooke joked, laughing.

The sisters made an entire day of their trip. Since they were already out, after they'd finished shopping on the boardwalk they figured they might as well browse the shops in the other three town centers, as well. By then, it was four o'clock and they felt famished, so Brooke and Jill convinced Rachel they should treat themselves to the early bird special at Captain Clark's in Port Newcomb. On the way home, they circled past the ferry dock. Traffic flowed freely in their lane, but the vehicles heading in the other direction were at a standstill.

"Look at all those people trying to catch a ferry home. They didn't have a single day of sunshine this week," Rachel sympathized. "I feel so sorry for them."

"I do, too. But I'm always kind of happy when it rains on my final day of vacation," Brooke said. "It makes it easier to leave when the sun isn't shining."

*There aren't enough clouds in the sky to make me feel that way about leaving Dune Island*, Jill thought. *Especially not if it's our final summer here.*

"The only thing that has ever made it easier for me to leave Nana's place has been knowing I'd be coming back the following summer," she asserted. She expected her sisters to tell her not to pressure them about the estate, but instead, they both nodded, as if deep down they felt the same way she did.

# CHAPTER ELEVEN

## *Sunday – June 26*

*Dear Rachel, Brooke and Jill. I wish I could be there at the summer place to make supper for you. I was never as good of a cook as Rose was. But you and the kids always felt starving after frolicking on the beach so you appreciated whatever I set in front of you.*

Jill had barely finished reading the first paragraph when Brooke interrupted her to say, “Hold on. This letter is making me hungry. I need to get something to eat.”

Jill waited impatiently for her to get up and serve herself another slice of apple walnut bread that Rachel had baked after they’d returned home the previous evening. Meanwhile, Brooke had chatted on the phone with her daughters. And the Wi-Fi signal was strong enough that Jill had been able to spend several hours researching tech writing positions, with little success. Thinking about it made her testy and she grouched, “Can’t you wait until we’re done reading to eat again?”

“I’m *starving*. I could devour the rest of this loaf by myself and I’d be hungry again in two minutes.”

"I wonder if it's possible you picked up some kind of parasite when you were camping," Rachel suggested, a frown etched across her forehead.

"Thanks for that. You just ruined my breakfast." Brooke scowled but then she took another bite of bread. "My second breakfast, that is," she admitted, with crumbs bouncing from her lips.

"May I continue now?"

"Please do."

*If you can believe Robert's nerve, after warning me what would happen if I ever tried to divorce him, he waited for me to come out of the bathroom and then suggested I make him supper. (That was the first of many times I panicked, fearful he'd discover I wasn't Rose.) Fortunately, the fridge was nearly empty. Robert acted disgruntled and said he'd get a burger and milkshake at a diner on the boardwalk, instead.*

*In retrospect, I think he knew we were low on food; he was just contriving an excuse to get away from the cottage. Maybe he was rendezvousing with Daisy one last time since we were supposed to leave the island in the morning; who knows? In any case, I was just relieved he was gone. That night I slept in Jimmy's bed. That is, I lay there very still—I didn't sleep a wink all night—agonizing over what to do next, now that I'd assumed my sister's life.*

*By daybreak, I decided I was going to cancel the funeral service my friends and theater colleagues had planned and arrange for a private burial instead. I recognized this would seem ungrateful, but how could I bear to hear anyone offer their condolences or worse, eulogize me? I didn't deserve praise; Rose did. It would have been unthinkable to allow my friends to pay me homage when I was robbing hers of the chance to acknowledge her passing.*

*Robert was surprisingly tolerant when I told him, although perhaps "indifferent" is more accurate. He didn't even seem ruffled when I said I wasn't ready to return to Connecticut. I told him I needed another week before I could face our friends or receive well-wishers into our home. (Which was true, but even more than that, for some irrational reason I felt like I'd be abandoning Rose if I left our summer estate.)*

That didn't sound so irrational to Jill—she felt like if they sold Nana's estate, they'd be deserting her memory. But she knew if she expressed that to her sisters now, they get off-track and she wanted to hear the rest of the letter before they started discussing it.

*Also, I wanted to put as much distance between him and me as possible, as quickly as I could. I figured he'd need to get back to work or at least he'd want to get back to his mistress. Unfortunately, Daisy must have been vacationing longer on the island, because Robert stayed until the following Saturday, too.*

*Most days, he'd go golfing, or so he said. At night-time, I was the one who lied, claiming Jimmy wouldn't go to sleep unless I was in bed with him. Then I'd pretend to doze off, remaining at the baby's side until morning.*

*There were a couple of close calls when I thought Robert could see right through me. The first was when I made him eggs and toast for breakfast, at his request. "Did you do this on purpose?" he asked after I set the meal in front of him.*

*"What's wrong?"*

*He pushed the plate away and stood up. "How many times have I told you I like them hard boiled, not soft?"*

*Can you imagine? My sister had recently died on the same day I caught him kissing another woman, yet he had the nerve to complain I'd made his eggs too runny! When I ran into the bedroom and fell face first onto the bed, he probably thought I was crying because he'd criticized me or that I felt sad I'd displeased him. But I was crying for my sister. "If only I had tried harder to convince Rose not to marry him," I lamented silently. "Or if only I hadn't left so soon after Mother and Father died, she wouldn't have been so lonely. She wouldn't have fallen for a lout like him."*

Jill's breath caught. *Did* I *fall for a lout like* Brandon *because I missed reconnecting with my sisters every summer at Nana's place?* The issue wasn't that simple, but there was definitely something about her situation that was similar to Rose's.

Jill wasn't blaming Brooke and Rachel for her decision to get involved with Brandon, nor did she think Nana should have felt guilty that Rose chose to marry Robert. But once again, Jill recognized that her perspective had definitely suffered during the three years she and her sisters hadn't been able to spend time on Dune Island together.

"Sorry, I got distracted," she said because Brooke and Rachel were looking at her oddly. They must have wondered why she'd stopped reading.

*I nearly slipped up again a couple of days after that. The weather was so unbearably muggy that I decided to put on the pair of shorts and blouse still hanging on the line from the morning Jimmy cut his toe on a razor clam. Since everything I'd brought to the island had been destroyed in the fire, I'd been wearing Rose's clothes, which tended to be warmer than mine. So I was relieved to discover I still had one outfit of my own left over, despite its negative associations with the day I last wore it.*

*The garments were wrinkled, but since Jimmy and I were just going down to the beach, I figured no one would see us and truthfully, I wouldn't have cared if they did. This had become part of our daily routine, our mourning process. At low tide, he'd run along the rivulets or splash in the tidal pools, hollering with glee, while I trailed behind him, usually weeping.*

*That particular day, we walked farther than we normally did, so we were both very hungry by the time we climbed the stairs to the cottage again. When we reached the upper landing, I'd always drop my head and watch my feet as I walked because I didn't want to catch a glimpse of the wreckage from the fire. So I didn't notice Robert had returned from the club and was lounging in a chair on the patio until I was standing right in front of him.*

*Looking me up and down, he asked, "What do you think you're doing? Why are you pretending to be your sister?"*

"Oh, no. He figured it out?" Rachel wondered aloud. She had a habit of talking to the screen in the theater, too, right during the most nail-biting moments. The other moviegoers would shush her, but Jill and Brooke were used to it.

*If I could have moved, I literally would have thrown myself at his feet and begged for mercy, but I froze, aghast. In the nick of time, it struck me: because of my clothes, he'd thought I was Rose pretending to be Hattie, not vice versa. My secret was still safe.*

"Phew." Rachel audibly exhaled.

*"I-I'm not pretending anything. I needed something cooler to wear and I found these hanging on the line." I was about to add, "I should*

*have packed more pairs of shorts," when I remembered why Rose rarely wore them: she didn't like people seeing her scar. And there I was, standing bare-legged in broad daylight, my thighs almost even with Robert's eye level. I would have dashed into the house, but I was afraid I'd draw even more attention to myself.*

*"Your own clothes are nicer." He reached out and touched the faded stain on the hem of my shorts, his hand inches away from where Rose's scar would have been. "What's this? Dirt?"*

*(I trust you'll understand how imperative it was for me to distract him.)*

*"Probably," I said, putting a finger beneath his chin to tilt his head upward. "You're home early—how was your round of golf?" I hoped to catch him off guard by feigning interest, but my plan backfired in the worst way.*

*"It was okay," he said. "But I missed you." He grabbed my other hand and pulled me down onto his lap. At first, I was too surprised to resist.*

Brooke commented, "I feel so bad for Nana. It must have made her sick to her stomach to have him pawing her."

*Then I tried to stand, telling him, "I need to go start supper." But he wrapped his arms tighter around my waist. I couldn't wrest them away because I had to keep one hand covering the spot on my bare thigh where Rose had burned herself as a child.*

*"No. You need to sit here with your husband," he half-whispered, half-growled into my ear. "You're the one who's always complaining I don't show enough affection."*

*I felt as sickened by his nearness as I did by the sense I was eavesdropping on an intimate conversation between him and my sister. "Don't forget about Jimmy," I suggested brightly. "He likes to cuddle, too."*

*I was sure Robert would object and allow me to get up, but instead he beckoned the baby, who was drizzling handfuls of sand in small piles on the patio a couple feet away. "Come sit on your mama's lap," Robert instructed him. "C'mon, son. Here you go."*

*He helped Jimmy climb up and I positioned him so he was covering my left thigh. "Want a horsey ride?" I asked and bounced my leg up and down, desperate to annoy Robert into letting me go. Now that I had Jimmy in my arms, I figured I could carry him into the cottage in a way that shielded my leg from Robert's view.*

*Again, my plan was thwarted. Robert pressed his palm against my knee to hold it still. "Rose, stop it. I need to talk to you about something." My flesh crawling, I focused on inhaling the scent of Jimmy's hair, still the sweetest smell in the world. Robert continued, "Your birthday is coming up in October and I've been giving a lot of thought about what to do. I think I've made up my mind."*

*I'm embarrassed to say that for a moment, I actually thought he was talking about making plans to celebrate the occasion. Admittedly, it would have been terrible timing for him to bring up the subject of a party so close to the time his wife's twin supposedly had died, but at least it would mean he'd been trying to make amends to Rose. I was so desperate to believe he had a modicum of remorse about his behavior toward my sister—especially about the affair—that I asked, "Really? What are you planning?"*

*"Since you'll be inheriting Hattie's half of the trust, as well as your own, I want to purchase a new car, for starters. And I've been talking to a realtor from Connecticut who goes to the club. He suggested buying a home over in the Sycamore Street neighborhood. It's a nicer area and we shouldn't continue renting when we can own."*

*How could I have been so stupid? Robert hadn't been planning to celebrate Rose's birthday; he'd been planning to spend her trust fund—and mine, too! That was the reason behind his sudden display of affection toward his wife and son. Talk about a facade—Robert was a better actor than half the male leads I'd seen perform on Broadway.*

Jill chuckled; she loved Nana's sense of humor, particularly in the face of situations like the one she was describing.

*"What do you think, baby? Wouldn't you like to move into a bigger house?" he asked, caressing my knee in a slow circle with his thumb.*

*Heaven help me, girls, but I did the only thing I could think of in that moment to get away from him: I tweaked the underside of the baby's leg. Not hard, mind you—just enough to startle him. I knew if Jimmy began to fuss, even a little, Robert would let us go. But my darling boy was hungry and overly tired, so he screamed something fierce, flailing his arms and kicking his father right where it hurt. Robert yowled and pushed us both from his lap.*

*"I'll go start supper," I offered over my shoulder as I carried my little hero into the cottage.*

"Way to go, Dad!" Rachel hurrahed.

"Nana was right, he *was* a little hero," Brooke declared before Jill continued reading.

*"Don't bother on my account," Robert said with a groan. "I'm going out with some people from the club tonight."*

*I'd lost my appetite, but I made Jimmy's favorite meal; noodles and spaghetti sauce, with lots of parmesan cheese on top. Before I sat down with him at the table, I changed out of my clothes and threw them in the garbage bin. And I decided I'd never wear shorts again.*

*Love, Nana.*

"Ohhh," Brooke said as if something had just dawned on her. "Nana never wore shorts because she *didn't* have a scar on her leg, not because she did."

"Yeah, that must have been the reason," Rachel acknowledged. "And now we know why she always told us that noodles and spaghetti sauce with lots of parm on top were Dad's favorite meal when he was young. She made the same remark every time she served it to the kids, too. I remember one time Noah whined at her, 'We know that, Nana. You already told us a hundred times.' She got this really hurt expression on her face and I was mortified. She just said, 'Did I? I must have forgotten I mentioned it.' But she'd probably been repeating the same comment all those years because it brought back the memory of how Dad saved the day by kicking Robert. After Noah complained, I never heard her say how much Dad liked the dish again."

Noticing how forlorn Rachel looked, Jill tried to console her. "Noah was only a little boy. Nana understood that most children don't have a lot of tact."

"Yes, but what makes me sad is that this letter emphasizes that Nana was carrying this enormous burden that she felt like she couldn't share," Rachel explained.

"She didn't have a choice—she *had* to keep it a secret. Who knows what Robert would have done if he'd found out about her charade, even years and years later? Besides, Nana didn't have anyone to turn to when she was young because her entire family was gone," Brooke pointed out. "Think about it, Rachel. You can hardly even stand to *listen* to Nana's story because the suspense stresses you out. But she had to *live* with that kind of anxiety every day. On top of that, it must have been agonizing for her to discover she'd been right about Robert—he'd only married Rose for her money. I don't know how Nana managed to keep it together. I would have cracked under that kind of pressure."

All of a sudden, Jill felt as if *she* couldn't take the pressure of keeping *her* secret to herself any longer. "I lost my job," she blurted out. Rachel and Brooke stared at her as if she were talking gibberish. "Our entire department was terminated because the company was acquired by a large corporation. They already have a big tech writing team, so there's too much duplication between our roles and theirs."

"That's awful, Jill," Brooke exclaimed.

"I'm so sorry to hear that," Rachel empathized. "Did they at least give you a good severance package?"

"I-I don't know all the details. I only spoke to my coworker, not to human resources. But I'm not all that worried about being unemployed. It might take a while, but eventually I always find another job."

"How long have you been searching?" Brooke asked.

"Not very long at all. I just found out I'd lost my job on Friday evening." Jill admitted, "I would have told you both sooner, but I was afraid if you knew, it would tip the scales in favor of selling Nana's estate and I really don't want that to happen."

"But the last thing you need right now is another financial obligation," Rachel said. "Not only are you unemployed, but now you might have to relocate to a new city. Moving can be expensive."

"You don't have to tell *me* that," Jill barked. "I've been through it a lot more times than you ever have."

"Jill! I'm only considering what's best for you."

But Jill didn't want to listen to Rachel's unsolicited advice again. "What's best for me is if you let *me* decide what's best for me and *you* can decide what's best for you. I only told you about losing my job because I know it bothers you that Nana never told anyone her secret. So I hope you'll honor your agreement to wait until you've been notified about the outcome of the scholarships and make your final decision based on that, not on my situation," Jill said. "And Brooke, you said you'd give it a few more days to hear what else Nana has to say in her letters before you make up your mind."

Rachel released a big breath and made a spluttering sound before conceding, "All right, fine."

Just then, Brooke's phone vibrated on the breakfast bar. Jumping up to answer it, she promised that Jill's unemployment situation wouldn't figure into her own decision about Nana's place. Then she dashed from the room.

"I'm going to drive to the fish market to buy fresh scrod for lunch—unless you want to talk about this more?" asked Rachel.

"No, thanks. There's nothing else to really talk about." In fact, Jill regretted telling her sisters her secret in the first place.

# CHAPTER TWELVE

*Monday – June 27*

Brooke served herself fruit salad and scrambled eggs. It must have been her third breakfast so far today and it was only nine-thirty.

"Maybe you're always so hungry because you're pregnant," Rachel suggested, still obviously concerned about her sister's health.

"Not a chance."

"You never know. Sometimes women can seem to get their periods even when they're pregnant," her older sister reminded her. "Didn't you lose a lot of weight the first few months when you were pregnant with Kaylee?"

"That's because I had severe morning sickness. This is different. I'm definitely not pregnant." Brooke giggled saucily. "But who knows, maybe after Todd and I take our second honeymoon…"

"Hold on," Jill said. "You're actually taking a second honeymoon? Where are you going?"

"To Banff, in Canada. Todd loves it there—I told you that."

"You told me Todd loves to go fishing there, but you never mentioned a honeymoon." *I would have remembered because it would have annoyed me that you're calling it a honeymoon since you claim the vow renewal isn't a second wedding.*

"It's gorgeous. After we're done reading Nana's letter, I can show you photos of the resort where we're staying."

"Hopefully you'll get better weather in Canada than we've gotten on this vacation." Rachel complained as the rain drummed against the deck and windows. "Tonight will be the tenth evening in a row that we didn't get to see a sunset. We haven't had this many consecutive days of rain since that year Mom took us to see *Fiddler on the Roof.* I'm afraid we might even break that record. There's a slim chance the sun will peek through the clouds at suppertime tomorrow, but otherwise it's not supposed come out until Friday. I hope it really does, because we've never left the island without watching at least one sunset together."

Jill refrained from suggesting that if the weather didn't cooperate during this vacation, they could all return later in the season and watch a sunset together then.

"Yeah, that would be a first." Brooke carried her plate into the great room and sat beside Jill. "Do either of you remember the only time we ever watched the sunset from *inside* the house? It was when we were kids and Mom and Dad had a huge argument right after supper."

"I remember, because they hardly ever fought," Rachel quietly answered. "Jill, you were only seven or eight and you got really upset and started crying, so Nana rather emphatically suggested they should take their argument outside. While she read you a story, Mom and Dad went for a walk down the beach. I could still hear them—not their words, but their voices—shouting at each other. It was awful."

"Yes, it was. But then they came back right before sunset and they were holding each other's hands, standing near the dune. We wanted to run out and watch the sunset with them, but Nana said they needed their privacy and she made us stay inside. We watched the sun go down from her bedroom." Brooke had a faraway look in her eyes as she gestured toward the back yard. "Now when I picture them standing there, I think it's so romantic… not just because of the setting or because they were holding hands, but because they'd made up after such a bitter argument."

*That's why she regretted not being married on the dunes at sunset,* Jill realized. Taking advantage of the quiet pause while Brooke lifted a spoonful of eggs to her mouth, she suggested that Rachel should start reading. "You said you were expecting a few important calls this morning, so maybe we should keep our comments to a minimum until we've read the entire letter. Otherwise, we might get sidetracked. Then if you have to leave to answer the phone, we'll feel frustrated that you're leaving us with a cliffhanger about what else Nana wrote."

"Good idea," Rachel agreed. "Let's read as much of the letter as we can before I'm interrupted."

She began:

*Dear Rachel, Brooke and Jill,*

*Your vacation is more than halfway over now. I remember when you'd come to visit me for two weeks as children and each morning at breakfast you'd announce something to the effect of, "We still have eight more days here." But once you passed the halfway mark, your phrasing would change and you'd whine, "We only have six days left at Nana's house." Your parents would tell you to stop complaining, but I understood. I relished your time on Sea Breeze Lane as much as you did.*

*When I last wrote, I described a couple of times when I feared Robert would discover I wasn't Rose. Even though he was probably too focused on covering up his own tracks to notice mine, I couldn't take any chances. The stakes were too high.*

*If you've ever done something—even as a child—you shouldn't have done and worried that someone would find out about it, you'll understand a fraction of the anxiety I experienced that week at the cottage. The guilt and fear consumed me to such a degree I hardly had any emotion left over to grieve Rose. My low-tide walks with Jimmy were the only opportunity to let my guard down and weep. The rest of the time, I kept my feelings bottled up the best I could, terrified of what I might inadvertently admit if I started crying.*

*The day before we were supposed to leave, it rained cats and dogs, and Robert didn't take off for the club or for Daisy's place, the way he usually did. Jimmy was irritable from being cooped up inside and I was having a terrific struggle trying to keep myself from going to pieces emotionally. I still couldn't fathom the thought of leaving Dune Island, but it was time to pack and in those days, women took care of such things.*

*So I was retrieving Robert's clothes from the dresser drawer to put them into the suitcase when Jimmy got underfoot. I tripped over him and yelped and the clothes went flying. Jimmy immediately began to cry, so I sat on the bed and picked him up. "Mama's sorry I frightened you," I cooed.*

*He pushed my face away with his chubby little hand, wailing, "No, Mama. No."*

*From the next room, Robert barked, "Even the kid thinks you coddle him too much. Back off already."*

*But that's not what Jimmy had meant; he was trying to say that I wasn't his mama. I was his aunt. He wasn't quite two years old, but he recognized who Rose had been better than her husband did. I knew right then I couldn't bring that child back to his home and sadden him all over again when he realized his mother wasn't there, either.*

*After the rain lifted, I walked with Jimmy down the beach to the pier and bought lobster and scallops, Robert's favorite seafood. Then I went to the liquor store and purchased a bottle of the expensive chardonnay Rose once mentioned he preferred. That evening, I fed the baby and put him down for the night before serving Jimmy and me our supper.*

*Once his meal was gone and Robert had nearly emptied the bottle, I told him I liked his idea about buying a new car and moving to a more upscale neighborhood. "The only problem is, I don't trust myself to make sound decisions yet. Or to attend to any of the details involved in moving. Maybe if I stay here on Dune Island with Jimmy for the summer, I'll be able to able to get my head on straight. At the very least, I won't get in your way and you won't have to worry about me."*

*Robert's eyebrows shot up. It was as if he'd won the lottery and the prize was two trust funds and an unlimited amount of time with his mistress, no questions asked. Of course, he immediately agreed that my proposed arrangement would be best for all of us. He even volunteered to look at a few houses in Connecticut. "Who knows? Maybe if I see something I like, I can make an offer. The trust won't be available until October, but it's as good as gold."*

*He was so ecstatic he'd gotten his way with virtually no hassle that he came around to my side of the table and cupped my face in his hands. As with so many other insufferable experiences in my life, I've shut the kiss that followed out of my memory...*

*However deplorable it was, it was a small price to pay to remain on Dune Island for the next two months without him. What I'd do after that, I had no idea; I was making up my plan as I went along. But once Robert was gone, I felt as if I could release my breath again. I could stop looking over my shoulder—at least when Jimmy and I were alone.*

*In public, I became an object of scrutiny: I imagine that people wanted a glimpse of the woman who was so emotionally distraught she canceled her twin sister's funeral. Maybe they were expecting me to dissolve into tears in the market or to run crying from the bank. Or perhaps they simply felt sorry for me. But the more they stared, the more self-conscious I became. I was sure that sooner or later, someone would recognize I wasn't my sister.*

*So, I limited our trips into town as much as possible. When we did go buy groceries or run an errand, I'd wear a hat or scarf and sunglasses, regardless of the weather, as a way of preventing anyone from examining me too closely. Fortunately, our section of Lucinda's Hamlet wasn't residentially developed and few people ever walked from the public beach all the way down to the cottage. Jimmy and I could go for days without seeing anyone except each other.*

*However, one afternoon Lawrence Rutherford called on me, much to my surprise.*

"Hold on," said Brooke. Her sisters looked at her impatiently. "I know you two said no interruptions, but who on earth is Lawrence Rutherford?"

"How could you forget him?!" Rachel asked. "He was the man who hosted Nana, Dad and Robert after the fire."

"Mr. Rutherford was also the uncle of the boy from the theater who had a crush on Nana," Jill added.

"Oh, that's right. I'd just forgotten that his first name was Lawrence, that's all. Don't look at me like that! Go on, Rachel."

*I was sitting on the patio with my back turned, as always, to the debris from the fire. So I didn't know he was making his way along the sandy path, which couldn't have been easy, since he had to use a cane. Jimmy had a slight fever—he was teething, if I recall—and he was miserable, so I was trying to rock him to sleep while singing, "Oh, What a Beautiful Mornin'", just like I'd been doing since he was a newborn. But he kept whining and wailing, and I was so tired and distressed that I was on the verge of tears, too.*

*When Mr. Rutherford hobbled around in front of us, he smiled and greeted me in a hushed voice. "Don't get up," he said. "It looks like you're winning the battle."*

*He was right; Jimmy's lids were getting heavier by the second. I continued rocking back and forth. "I have lemonade in the fridge if you'd like it," I whispered.*

*Mr. Rutherford poured us each a glass and brought it out. You have to understand; men usually didn't do that kind of thing back then—it was considered women's work. That one little gesture was so kind and unexpected that I started to cry.*

*"There, there," he said and patted my arm a few times. But other than that, he just let me weep.*

*When I finally stopped, Mr. Rutherford asked if there was anything he could do to help me. I thanked him and said he'd already done so much by allowing us to stay in his home immediately after the fire.*

*"Do you know why I moved to Dune Island year-round?" he asked.*

*I had no idea; he was just an acquaintance. Prior to staying in his home after the fire, I'd only met him twice. Once at a reception after a performance, and the other time was at the beach party on his waterfront. I shook my head.*

*"I couldn't abide living in the same house where my wife died of carbon monoxide poisoning," he said. I gasped to learn about his sad history, but he continued talking, gesturing toward the remains of the other cottage. "I can arrange to have that cleared away, if you'd like."*

*"Thank you. That's very generous, but it isn't necessary." I added wryly, "I've learned to keep my head down when I pass by it."*

*"The fire wasn't your fault," Lawrence murmured. "Your sister wouldn't want you to torment yourself. She'd want you to remember how she lived, not how she died. She'd want you to look up. To appreciate the beauty that's all around you still."*

*Only someone who'd been through an experience similar to mine could have said something so insightful. Could have understood what an odious smudge the fire had left on my conscience. For as much as I couldn't bear to look at the sooty detritus on the dunes, having it there served as a kind of penance. It was a way to "torment myself," as Mr. Rutherford put it.*

*But he was right: the fire wasn't my fault. I had plenty of things to feel guilty about, but the fire wasn't one of them. So I accepted his gift and two days later, when the excavator arrived, I took Jimmy down to the beach. By the time we returned, the spot where the cottage once stood was a flat, smooth patch of soil. Its color didn't match the blondness of the surrounding sand, but it was several shades closer to blending in with it.*

*My grief, too, faded a little bit that day. Later, Jimmy and I relocated* Rosa rugosa *shrubs to that corner of the yard in honor of Rose. There have been some growing there ever since.*

*Please go clip a few sprigs and set them in bud vases in every room. And when you do, think of your loving Nana and her sister, both. XO*

"Ohhh," Brooke cooed. "I'm going to do that as soon as the rain lets up."

"I wouldn't hold my breath waiting for that to happen," Rachel pessimistically remarked about the weather, just as Jill's phone vibrated on the coffee table. She glanced at the number.

"I don't believe it. Someone's calling me from work. Are they actually going to fire me over the phone—while I'm on *vacation*?!"

"You should answer it," Rachel urged. "Find out what kind of severance package you're getting."

"Oh, okay." Jill groaned as she stood up. "But don't discuss Nana's letter until I get back. I want to be part of this conversation."

She picked up the phone and said hello. The HR specialist introduced himself as Douglas Slater. Surprisingly, the connection was crystal clear, so instead of running outside to talk in the car, Jill headed upstairs to her room.

"I understand you're out of town on vacation," Douglas said. "Are you staying somewhere special?"

Jill didn't have any inclination to engage in chitchat about Nana's place with the man who was about to fire her. But she knew how vital it was to obtain a good reference from her employer, so she said cordially, "Yes, very special—I'm in Lucinda's Hamlet, on Dune Island."

"Aha. I spent three days in Hope Haven last week. The island was beautiful but the weather was awful. I hope it has stopped raining by now?"

*Now he's driveling about the weather? How obtuse can he be?* She answered, "Not yet, but I've heard the sun's supposed to come out on Tuesday afternoon."

"That's great. Really terrific," Douglas replied with forced gusto. Jill wished he'd cut to the chase and tell her what her severance package included. With any luck, it would be substantial enough to ease whatever concerns Rachel still had about Jill paying her share of the estate expenses.

Finally, he got down to business and told her about the layoffs in her department. "As you know, your colleagues are a talented and dedicated group of individuals. However, business needs drive all our decisions, which is why I'm calling you now… Although your position as a technical writer has also been eliminated, we'd like to offer you a promotion to a management role."

Completely taken aback, Jill stared out the window with her mouth hanging open as Douglas described the responsibilities of the position, which included overseeing a team of tech writers from the acquiring corporation, who weren't as familiar with her company's products as she was.

"It will mean a lot more responsibility, but there will also be a significant increase in your salary—somewhere in the range of twenty-five per cent," he said. "I'll email all the details to you, so you can think it over and inform us of your decision when you return. We would have waited until your vacation was over to make the offer, but we were concerned that one of your coworkers might tell you about the changes in the department before we had a chance to speak with you."

Pinching her thigh so she wouldn't sound as euphoric as she felt, Jill thanked him for the offer and indicated she'd be pleased to consider it. Not that there was much to consider: a 25 per cent increase in salary far outweighed any qualms she had about working in management. Now she wouldn't have to worry about being able to cover both hers and Rachel's estate expenses. Jill chatted a few more minutes with Douglas and as soon as she disconnected she flew down the stairs, whooping and hollering along the way.

"Brooke! Rachel!" she shouted, interrupting their conversation. "Guess what?! I didn't get fired. I got *promoted*! I won't have any problem covering my share—and yours, Rach—of the estate expenses!"

Because the lighting was dreary and she'd barged into the room so abruptly, Jill hadn't noticed her sisters' expressions until her announcement was met with silence. Only then did she see that Brooke was crying and Rachel's mouth was a taut, thin line.

"What's wrong?" Jill asked, her stomach clenching. "Are the kids okay? Are Todd and Derek?"

"Yes. They're all fine. Congratulations on your promotion," Rachel said, but her sentiment sounded perfunctory.

"Yes, that's terrific, Jill," Brooke wept the words into a tissue.

"Thank you. But what's wrong?" she repeated. "Why are you crying?"

"I just found out..."

When Brooke didn't finish her sentence, Rachel explained, "Todd missed the deadline for putting down the deposit for the rooms at the resort. Now their guests can't stay there before the vow renewal ceremony and everything else in the area is booked."

"That's really lousy," Jill said. She understood why Brooke was disappointed, but it puzzled her that Rachel appeared so upset about it, too. "Can you move it to another date? Like a week earlier? Or later?"

"No. It's booked the weekend after Labor Day. And if we hold the ceremony the weekend earlier, Rachel's family won't be able to come because that's when Densmore has orientation for new students."

Densmore. As soon as Brooke mentioned the prep school, Rachel averted her eyes toward the sliding doors. That little flicker of movement was all Jill needed to see to figure out why her eldest sister looked so somber: someone from Densmore must have called while Jill was upstairs. "Noah and Grace didn't get scholarships, did they?" she asked.

Rachel shook her head. "No."

The cruel irony of the situation made Jill feel as if someone had doused her head—had doused her *dreams*—with a bucket of ice water. She stood frozen and blinking, her mouth agape.

Brooke must have thought Jill was staring at Rachel because she was angry, and she tried to make peace by saying. "It's not Rachel's fault, Jill. I've done my best to keep an open mind, but to be honest, I still would have voted to sell the house, whether or not the twins got scholarships."

*Is hearing that it was inevitable somehow supposed to make me feel better*? Jill wondered. Clutching at straws, she argued, "But we haven't finished reading Nana's letters yet. Maybe there's something in one of them—"

"No, Jill," Rachel interrupted, putting an end to her last hope. "We've both given your perspective a lot of consideration, but we have to put our families' needs first. It isn't practical to keep the estate just because it had sentimental value to Nana and us or because we enjoy vacationing here." She waited and when Jill didn't respond, she prompted, "Can you please say something? Tell us what you're thinking?"

"I think... I think I need to go for a drive. Alone." She started to leave the room, but Brooke stood up and touched her shoulder.

"Don't go, Jill. Sit back down and talk to us."

"What's there to talk about? How disappointed I am? That will only make you two feel guilty and me feel sadder," she said quietly. "I really do understand why you have to put your families' needs first. And I've had fair warning that selling the estate was a strong possibility. But now that it's a reality, I need some time and space alone so I can come to terms with it." *Like a death*, she thought, as she hurried from the house.

Because of the deluge and tourist traffic, it took Jill twice as long as usual to drive entirely around the island. She didn't have a destination; she followed the flow of traffic in a stupor, almost as if she were driving on autopilot. As she neared the turnoff for Sea Breeze Lane, she still felt numb, so she circled the island again, but in the reverse direction.

By the time she'd made it back to Lucy's Ham a second time, she was getting hungry for lunch, but the eateries were packed. She still wasn't ready to return home to her sisters and it was raining too hard to take a walk on the beach or to do anything else outdoors.

As she approached The Clam Shack, she thought of Alex. *I bet he isn't working in this weather.* It wasn't the first time he'd popped into her mind since she'd turned him down on Friday. Maybe he'd want to go out for lunch with her once the crowds were gone? This could be kind of like a second chance at a second chance to get together. Even if they just hung out as friends for the afternoon, being with him was fun and it always made her feel better. She impulsively turned off Main Street and headed toward his house on Driftwood Avenue.

"Hey, Jill," he exclaimed, obviously surprised when he opened the door and let her in. "It's great to see you. But I hope this doesn't mean you lost your power again?"

"No. Just my job as a tech writer." She hadn't meant to blurt that out or even mention it at all; she'd been trying to forget about it.

"You lost your *job*?" he echoed. "That's awful."

He looked so distraught that she quickly consoled him, "It's okay. I got a promotion."

"Wow. Congratulations." Alex tilted his head to the side, eyeing her. "You don't seem very happy about it."

"That's because I also lost my Nana's house." Without warning, Jill burst into tears, which made her feel foolish. Maybe coming here wasn't such a bright idea after all, but she'd feel even more foolish if she left all of a sudden. She had to get a grip on her emotions. "May I use your bathroom?" she asked.

Alex directed her down the hall. By the time she'd regained her composure and returned to the kitchen, he was serving them each a bowl of tomato soup and a grilled cheese sandwich. "Rainy day comfort food," he explained. "Seems like you could use it."

His thoughtfulness reminded her of what Nana had written about Mr. Rutherford bringing her a glass of lemonade. And thinking about Nana nearly triggered another spate of tears, but the soup smelled good and Jill didn't want to let it get cold while she was weeping, so she held them back.

After they taken their seats, Alex asked, "You want to talk about what's been going on?"

So as they ate she told him about her job situation, as well as about how much she'd wanted to keep Nana's house, but that her sisters had decided to sell it. When she'd finished speaking, he let out a low whistle. "You've really been on a rollercoaster ride, haven't you?"

"Yes, but thanks for listening. Usually, I can talk to Brooke and Rachel about these kinds of things, but this is one of those rare instances when we're on opposite sides of the fence."

"You should have heard the disagreements Sydney and I had about our parents' place—and there were only two of us. It must be even more challenging with three people sharing one inheritance." They had both finished eating and in his usual easygoing manner, Alex leaned back in his chair and asked, "So, do you know what you're going to do now?"

"There isn't much I *can* do. Even if I refuse to give up the house, my sisters could force the sale legally. Besides, my nana trusted us to come to a unanimous decision. I could never do anything that would dishonor her memory or create that kind of division between my sisters and me. And ultimately, I understand why they have to do what's best for their families." Jill felt so comfortable being open with Alex that she barely paused before admitting, "But I have to say, it's going to take me a long, long time to work through my disappointment. And right now, I'm just plain steamed."

"No one could blame you for that," he replied with an empathetic smile. "But what I meant was what are you going to do about your job situation? The other day you told me how glad you were that you didn't work in management. So, now that you don't need a bigger salary to cover the costs of keeping your nana's estate, does that mean you're not going to accept the promotion?"

Jill shrugged. "If I don't, I'll have to scramble to find another job. From what I can see from my research, there aren't a lot of opportunities out there right now. Not only that, but turning down the promotion would make me ineligible to receive unemployment benefits. So I wouldn't have any income at all until I found another position."

"Yeah, I can see how that could create a hardship." Alex jiggled his leg beneath the table, giving Jill the feeling there was something else he wanted to say. She kept pressing him to tell her what it was until he finally gave in. "Listen, I don't have any idea what your financial obligations are, and they're none of my business. It's just that after the way I heard you talk about working in management, I wish there were a way for you to hold out a little while until you found another tech writing position. It seems that would be better in the long run than committing to a position you know you definitely won't like."

Once again, he looked so concerned on Jill's behalf that she found herself trying to ease his mind. "To be honest, I'm not crazy about tech writing, either. So it's six of one, half dozen of the other—except the management position comes with a better salary."

"In other words, at least you'll be well-compensated for being unhappy?"

Jill laughed. "Something like that." She started to stand so she could bring the dishes to the sink, but Alex clasped her forearm, giving it a gentle tug.

"Hold on. Just play along with me for a second," he said and she promptly sat back down. Not so much because she wanted to continue talking about her employment situation, but because the weight and warmth of his touch was making her weak-kneed. "If you could have any job in the world, what would it be?" After he'd asked the question he withdrew his hand from her arm, his fingers trailing across her skin and momentarily causing her to lose her focus.

"Oh, I don't know… professional beachcomber?" she proposed, thinking of the moments when she was most content, looking out over the bay with the sand between her toes. "Do you know anyone who's hiring for that?"

"Noo… But how about lifeguarding?"

"Water, water everywhere, nor any drop to drink," she replied, quoting Samuel Taylor Coleridge's poem, "The Rime of the Ancient Mariner."

Alex seemed to understand the reference immediately. "Yeah, when I was a lifeguard, I resented sitting in a chair while everyone else got to go swimming, too. And I definitely wouldn't recommend becoming a deckhand, either. Let's see, what other kind of beachy jobs are there…"

She smiled at his optimism. "It's okay, Alex. I appreciate that you're trying to be helpful, but the embarrassing truth is, I don't know what I'd want to do if I could have any job in the world."

"Why is that embarrassing?"

The sincere puzzlement in his eyes was disarming and Jill stopped kidding around. Even though she knew he wouldn't judge her, she felt vulnerable and her voice dropped to a whisper as she admitted, "Because I'm too old to be trying to find myself and too young for a mid-life crisis. I should know what my calling is by now, but I don't think I have one."

"Or maybe you just haven't found it yet. Like I told you the other day, I had to eliminate a lot of potential occupations—and by that I mean over twenty—before I found my niche," he reminded her. "Sometimes figuring out what you *don't* want to do takes you one step closer to discovering what it is you *want* to do."

Jill nodded pensively. She gazed toward the slightly ajar slider to the deck as she considered his remarks. For a while, she was so lost in thought, she didn't register that the torrential downpour had diminished to a light sprinkle, until she heard a bird singing.

"Hey, sweetie," she mumbled.

Alex sat straight up. Clearly he thought she'd been addressing him—and he actually looked rather hopeful. "What did you say?"

Jill suppressed a giggle as she explained, "The bird that's singing is a black-capped chickadee, calling to its mate. It sounds as if it's saying, 'Hey, sweetie. Hey, sweetie.' Doesn't it?"

Alex listened and when the bird repeated the notes, he said, "Yeah, it does. That's really cool. I've heard that song a thousand times but I never knew what kind of bird was singing it."

"The chickadee was one of the first birds my nana taught me to identify by sound. I was about six years old. She and my dad were avid birders and they used to let me go birding on the beach with them in the morning. Or sometimes we'd hike at the sanctuary."

"Aha, so that's why you knew so much about piping plovers by the time you were a teenager," he said. "Do you still go birdwatching?"

"Not as often as when my nana was alive. Right up until the summer before she fell and broke her hip—she was in her late eighties then—we'd go almost every day whenever I visited her here on Dune Island." Thinking about those walks, Jill was overcome with nostalgia and her teary eyes smarted. But all at once, the room seemed brighter. Was that…?—it *was!*

"Look," she cried. "A sun shower."

They both darted to the sliding glass door. They stood so close together that Jill could feel the little hairs on Alex's arm brushing against her skin as they admired the slanted, watery beams of light emanating from a break in the clouds. In that moment, it seemed as if there was a clearing in Jill's mind, too.

Turning to Alex, she announced, "I've just decided there are two things I'm absolutely positive I don't want to do."

He grinned. "What are they?"

"I don't want to leave Dune Island until the end of the summer… And I don't want to leave here today without kissing you."

It was nearly ten-thirty in the evening when Jill tiptoed up the deck stairs and into the dark house, nearly dizzy with giddiness.

As she was slipping off her wet sandals, Brooke startled her by asking, "Where have you been all this time?"

"Oh, hi, Brooke. I was at Alex's." Jill squinted toward the sofa in the great room. She didn't want to elaborate any further on Alex. "Is Rachel there, too?"

"Yes, I am. That wasn't very considerate of you not to call and at least let us know you were hanging out with your boyfriend."

Resisting the impulse to remind Rachel that she wasn't her child, and ignoring the 'boyfriend' jibe, Jill said, "I forgot my phone in my room. But—"

"You could have used Alex's."

"I tried. His connection is even worse than ours. But I sent a text. I guess it didn't come through?"

"No, it didn't." Rachel's tone softened. "I'm sorry. It's just that we knew how upset you were when you left this morning and we've been worried about you."

"There's no cause for concern. I'm fine. But I do need to talk to you about something." Jill felt her way toward a lamp and clicked it on, causing her sisters to shield their eyes. She didn't know why they'd been sitting in the dark, but she didn't want to take the time to ask them. "As I told you this morning, I respect your decision to do what's best for your families. Since you believe that includes selling Nana's estate, I'll support you in that. However, I also need to do what's best for *my* family—even if I'm only a family of one."

"You're not a family of one. You have us," Brooke said.

"I know—and I'm very grateful for that. What I mean is that I don't think it's fair that just because I'm outnumbered, we should do *every*thing the way you two want to do it. I'll agree to sell the house, but not until September. I want to spend the summer here."

Rachel immediately objected. "You can't do that. What about your promotion?"

"I'm not going to accept it."

Rachel looked at her incredulously. "Why not? It would be such a great career move."

"If you want it, then *you* should apply for it. But it's not what *I* want to do. I've always hated the idea of working in management and bossing other people around," Jill said pointedly.

"But if your company extends an offer and you don't take it, you'll also forfeit your unemployment benefits."

"So what? I'll take a part-time job here if I have to. Besides, as you've said, once the estate sells, I'll make a small fortune and I'll receive it in one lump sum," Jill reminded her sister.

"You're going to throw away a career advancement opportunity and then dip into your inheritance instead of investing it, just so you can stay on Dune Island for two more months?" Rachel asked, her tone growing more and more disbelieving.

"Yes—although I wouldn't put it that way. And frankly, Rachel, I don't see how it's any of your business what I do with my career or my money," Jill replied, nettled but resolute about her plan.

"It's my business, first and foremost, because I care about what happens to you." Red-faced, Rachel set her glasses atop of her head. "Secondly, if we postpone selling the house until the fall, I won't be able to get a discount for paying the twins' tuition in full at the beginning of the school year."

"There's no guarantee the house is going to sell that quickly anyway," Jill argued. "Besides, I'm agreeing to give up the estate even though I really, really want to keep it. All I expect as a compromise is for you and Brooke to postpone putting it on the market for two months. Losing out on a measly, five or ten per cent discount is nothing compared to—"

Rachel butted in to clarify, "It's a *twelve* per cent discount."

"You just want to stay here because of Alex, don't you?" Brooke asked out of the blue before Jill could respond to her eldest sister. "I thought you said you weren't interested in casual dating any longer."

"I thought *you* said I should go out with him because I never know where or when I might meet The One."

"Go out with him, yes. But I didn't mean you should rearrange your whole life just to have a summer fling with someone you've said is definitely never going to relocate off-island. As you've put it, your heart is going to get involved and then you'll be miserable when you inevitably break up at the end of the season."

Jill resented it that Brooke was using her own words against her, even if there was a chance she might be right. "It's not *inevitable* that we'll break up. We might decide to have a long-distance relationship. I could come here on the weekends. I only live in Boston."

"How convenient—for him. But why should you be the one who's going to make all the concessions? Trust me, you don't want that kind of disparity in a relationship."

*Funny you should say that, because that's exactly how I feel about you, Rachel and me in regard to our inheritance*, Jill thought. But she replied as calmly as she could, "For the record, I'd want to stay here for the rest of the summer whether or not I see Alex again. And I'd want to stay here even if I have to deplete my entire retirement account or go into debt for the next ten years. Regardless, I'm not asking for your opinions or approval about that. I'm proposing a fair compromise about the house."

Technically, it would have been futile to refuse her proposal, since it would require legal action to force Jill to give up the house before September. By the time all of those procedures had been followed, summer would be over anyway. But Jill wanted to give both her sisters the opportunity to willingly agree with her plan.

"Okay, if that's what you want to do, go ahead," Brooke muttered. "But don't say I didn't warn you."

Jill waited for Rachel to agree, too.

She huffed in exasperation before finally capitulating. "Fine," she said.

It wasn't until she was stretched out in bed fifteen minutes later that Jill allowed herself to revel in the chain of events that had transpired since this morning. It was still crushing that she couldn't keep Nana's estate permanently, but at least she didn't have to give it up for two more sumptuous months.

She owed a world of gratitude to Alex for that, because his questions had helped her see she was at a crossroads, professionally. *I might not know where I'm headed next, but turning down the management position is a step in the right direction,* she thought.

Jill had meant what she'd said when she told her sisters she'd want to stay on the island even if she never saw Alex again. But as her mind wandered back to that first tender kiss she'd shared with him—and all the luscious, longer kisses that followed—she could hardly wait to get together with him tomorrow.

# CHAPTER THIRTEEN

## *Tuesday – June 28*

*Polite, but strained.* That's how Nana had described her interaction with Rose after they'd had an argument about Robert. And that's how Jill would have described her sisters' attitudes toward her on Tuesday morning, too. They made obligatory small talk as they fixed their coffee and breakfasts, but there was none of their easy, good-natured bantering.

So, in an effort to smooth things out between them, Jill asked Brooke if she needed help brainstorming a backup plan for the vow renewal ceremony. But her sister immediately shut the conversation down, snapping that she didn't want to talk about it.

Then, still trying to be helpful, Jill offered to call the attorney to let him know what they'd decided about the estate. But Rachel told her there was no hurry. "Let's sleep on it for a few more days, so we're absolutely sure of our plans before we call him."

Jill's heart ballooned with hope. "You're having second thoughts about selling?"

"No, none at all." Rachel answered. "I'm one hundred per cent certain we should sell the estate."

Brooke was every bit as conclusive. "So am I."

That's when Jill caught on: they thought *she* might change *her* mind about staying there through the summer. As maddening as that was, she didn't want to create any more friction between her and her sisters by telling them off. "And I'm a hundred per cent certain I'm staying here for the summer," she said evenly. Then she quickly changed the subject by volunteering to read Nana's most recent letter.

Her sisters silently settled into their places in the great room and Jill began:

*My dears,*

*Time is running out, but I'm determined to finish my story.*

*The summer of the fire, I only left the island twice, once in July and once in August, to take Jimmy to visit my grandfather in the nursing home. Since I was familiar with most of the staff, I felt confident posing as my sister in front of them. And because they lived in East Hartford instead of West, I knew there was virtually no chance any of the nurses or aides would cross paths with Robert and mention that they'd seen me.*

*Getting to Connecticut and back without a car was all-day endeavor. We had to take a bus to the ferry and then I'd rent a car in Hyannis, which was expensive. I didn't want Robert to know I'd rented it, so I had to pay for it with cash, which was allowed back then. It had broken my heart to do it, but I'd pawned Rose's gold class ring to get the money.*

*My plan was to drive with Jimmy for almost three hours to the nursing home, stay an hour or two and then drive back to Hyannis. We had to hurry in order to catch the last bus from Port Newcomb to Lucinda's Hamlet, otherwise I would have had to walk from the ferry dock to the cottage in the dark. (I wasn't afraid of anyone bothering me; I was afraid I might disturb a skunk!)*

*I rather doubt my grandfather was even aware of our presence. As usual, he showed no sign of recognition; he didn't even open his eyes. But Rose had faithfully visited him twice a week and so had I, whenever I came home from New York. If he had any comprehension about what was going on, I didn't want him to think we'd both forgotten all about him.*

*I didn't tell him about the fire or about Rose's death. For one thing, I didn't want him to have to grieve alone, the way I had. Also, I couldn't lie to him about something like that. So I didn't say, "Hi, Grandpa. It's me, Rose," when I hugged him hello, the way my sister always did. All I could utter was, "Jimmy and I are happy to see you, Grandpa."*

*After visiting him a second time, in August, Jimmy and I were headed toward the car when a thin, brunette woman with a poodle-cut hairstyle stopped me in the parking lot. "Rose? Rose Sampson? What are you doing here? Robert said you were summering on Dune Island. You poor thing, how are you?"*

Jill paused in anticipation of Rachel uttering some sort of apprehensive sound, but her sister remained quiet. So she read on:

*"I-I'm getting by," I answered carefully. I had no idea who the woman was. "It-it's been too long since I've seen my grandfather, so I returned for a quick visit. How have you been lately?"*

*I hoped she'd offer information that would give me a clue about how she knew Rose and Robert, but she just said, "I'm fine. It's my turn to visit my mother—her hip is getting better. She'll be coming home a week from Thursday." She bit the corner of her lip before adding, "You don't have to put on a brave face, Rose. Everyone thinks the whole situation is just terrible. All the girls in the neighborhood will support you, however we can, you know that, don't you? If you want to talk about it or need a shoulder to cry on..."*

*Realizing she must have been one of Rose's neighbors, I said, "Thank you for your concern—it's really kind. But talking about it seems to make it worse. It's better for me if I put it out of my mind and carry as normally as I can. It was nice seeing you again, but if you'll excuse me, Jimmy's getting antsy."*

*She gave me a peculiar look before saying goodbye. As I drove away, I realized there was a good chance Rose's neighbor would tell Robert she'd bumped into me at the nursing home. Then how would I explain why I'd returned to Connecticut without telling him? There was no way around it: I was going to have to have to spend the night at Rose's house, and explain to Robert myself.*

*Reversing my direction, I concocted a story about how I'd called the nursing home and discovered my grandfather had taken a turn, so I rushed home to see him. I planned to claim I was so upset I didn't take the time to call Robert and let him know I was coming. For effect, I'd even admit, "But Grandpa was fine, so I guess you're right—sometimes I overreact." (It would be stretching my acting skills to the limit.)*

*But since Robert was still at work at that time in the afternoon, I decided to take Jimmy to the cemetery where all of my family members, except for Grandpa, were buried. It was a park-like setting and I thought we'd take a stroll to stretch our legs, since we'd been in the car for so long that morning. Also, although I know it seems a peculiar thing to say, I missed my family so much that I felt desperate to be around them.*

*The bright grass had overgrown my parents' plots long ago, but there was a fresh mound of dirt above where Rose rested. As expected, her headstone was carved with my own name: Hattie Jean Coleman. October 7, 1930 – June 24, 1955.*

*Never in our entire lives had my sister and I tried to switch places, the way twins are apt to do—yet in death, she had permanently taken on my identity. The irony struck me as funny and I started to giggle.*

*When a person is grieving, there's a fine line between hilarity and hysteria. I sank to my knees and laughed until I was sobbing. "I'm sorry, Rose. I'm sorry," I wailed. I would have done anything to change places with her again…*

*I cried out to my mother and father, too. "I'm sorry for all the ugly things I said before I ran off to New York. I'm so sorry. Please forgive me."*

*Jimmy, meanwhile, was strolling along the row of headstones nearby, patting the top of each one, as if he was playing the child's game, "Duck, Duck, Goose!" Maybe it was disrespectful of me to allow him to do that, but his touch was gentle and his footfall light and I was too depleted to chase after him.*

*As I was weeping, my head bowed, I sensed him standing beside me. "Pity. Pity," he said and at first I thought he'd meant me; that I was pitiful. But when I glanced up, I saw him sniffing a lily he must have plucked from a graveside vase. Just as Mr. Rutherford had done, my little boy reminded me to look up. To appreciate what was still beautiful around me. Not least of all, him.*

Touched by this description of her father comforting Nana, Jill said, "Dad was such a sweet, sensitive little soul, wasn't he?"

"Mm-hm." Brooke's lukewarm reply was barely audible and Rachel didn't respond at all.

Jill supposed her sisters might have just been tired or preoccupied, but she suspected it was more likely that Brooke was irked at Todd for messing up their reservations. And Rachel was probably peeved because Jill wouldn't back down about staying on Dune Island for the summer.

She knew they'd both work through their emotions in time, but meanwhile, she didn't want reading their grandmother's letter to be an unpleasant occasion for any of them. So she said, "You guys seem kind of preoccupied. Do you want to stop here and read this later?"

"No. Keep going," Rachel curtly instructed her.

*Yes, ma'am*, Jill thought, resisting the urge to salute. She read on:

*I sniffed the lily. "Yes, Jimmy. It's very pretty. Let's put it back and then we'll go to the pond and feed the ducks."*

*We stayed at the pond until almost five o'clock and then we headed to Rose's house. As irrational as it was, I didn't want to pull into the driveway because then Robert would pull in behind me and I'd feel trapped. So I parallel-parked beside the front curb. I was so worried about how Jimmy would react to being back at his home that I didn't notice there was already a car in the driveway.*

*Since I was using Rose's purse, I had a key and we entered through the front door. Jimmy didn't seem to search for his mother—maybe he'd already forgotten her. Or maybe, like me, he was utterly befuddled to find Daisy cooking supper in the kitchen and her son making a tower with the blocks I had bought for Jimmy the previous spring.*

*"I-I just came over to make a meal for Robert," she stammered. "I thought he'd appreciate something homemade. He's-he's had to eat out a lot while you've been away."*

*I couldn't believe her gall! Here she was, practically accusing Rose of neglecting her husband, when Daisy was the one who was brazenly carrying on an affair with Robert in broad daylight. I felt enraged on*

*Rose's behalf. It was disgraceful enough that her husband was unfaithful, but to do it in such a public manner was particularly humiliating.*

Jill stopped and raised an eyebrow at Brooke, who asked, "What's that look supposed to mean?"

"Nothing. It's just that usually when Robert acts like a jerk, you let loose a stream of invective. So I was waiting for you to say something."

She shrugged. "You're the one who's always telling me I interrupt too much."

*Wow,* Jill thought. *And you have the nerve to complain about your children sulking!* Fed up, she decided she'd read the rest of the letter without trying to engage her sisters in any remarks about it.

*Then the light dawned. This was what the neighbor at the nursing home had meant when she'd said, "Everyone thinks the whole thing is just terrible." She'd been referring to Daisy showing up at my sister's house while Rose was supposedly out of town, grieving.*

*I couldn't have asked for a better solution to my problem! Don't you see? Robert might have known a few islanders who'd claim I'd been acting erratically, but I had an entire neighborhood who'd witnessed his flagrant affair with Rose. Now that I had something to hold over his head, divorce was suddenly an option.*

*Calm as a clam, I replied, "Oh, don't mind me. Keep doing what you're doing. I'm just here to get a few things."*

*I went into the bedroom, took a suitcase from the closet and methodically began packing. There wasn't much I wanted; mostly books and clothes for Jimmy, along with his birth certificate and baby photo album which I found in a drawer. I also took a couple of pairs of shoes for me, a winter coat, the jewelry my parents had given to my sister and the photo of Rose and me the year we graduated high school: we were in our bathing suits on the beach in front of the cottages, throwing our mortarboards into the air.*

*When I returned to the kitchen, Daisy was talking on the phone to Robert, apparently tattling on me. I moved past her and began taking the china my grandmother had left to Rose from the china cabinet, which I wrapped in dish towels and arranged in a laundry basket.*

*I set the luggage and china on the front step so I wouldn't have to come back inside the house once I'd left. All this time, Jimmy had been standing beside Rose's son, watching him. He held a red block in his hand and when I told him it was time to leave, he reached up to place it on top of the tower. But he set it down too hard and the entire column toppled and skittered across the floor.*

*"Uh-oh," Jimmy said, tipping his hands upward innocently.*

*"Look what you did," the other boy whined. "It took me a long time to build that. You wrecked everything!"*

*"I know how you feel," I said, directing my remark more to his mother than to him. "But those weren't really yours to play with in the first place, were they?"*

"You tell 'em, Nana!" Jill exclaimed, refusing to allow her sisters' sour moods to temper her own delight in Nana's story.

*As I collected the blocks and deposited them into their plastic bucket, the boy ran to his mother and buried his face in her skirt, sniveling.*

*Daisy reached over him to extend the phone to me. "Your husband wants to talk to you."*

*"I don't have a husband," I replied. I picked up the bucket, took Jimmy's hand and exited that house forever.*

*Do you girls know, those are the same blocks you and your kids played with? It used to drive your parents to distraction when you'd build something and it would come crashing down on the hardwood floor. But the clatter always gave me a little thrill.*

*"I guess that block was the last straw," I'd say, a private joke with myself about the day I decided Rose and Robert were getting divorced.*

*Just remember, girls; you have to laugh a little at life in order to survive it. Love, Nana*

Considering how much tension there was between the sisters, the last line of their grandmother's letter was a timely reminder. It reminded Jill of the not-so-subtle advice Nana used to slip into conversation when they were growing up. She was right: laughter had helped them through countless difficult circumstances. On more than one occasion, it had also bridged the distance between them after they'd bickered with each other.

But instead of sharing a chuckle today, as soon as Jill finished reading, the three women drifted from the room and further apart from each other than they had already grown.

# CHAPTER FOURTEEN

*Wednesday – June 29*

Jill patted her open mouth, yawning as she waited for Rachel and Brooke to fix their coffee and join her in the great room on Wednesday morning. Alex had taken her to Captain Clark's restaurant the previous evening, followed by a jazz performance at Encore, a bar in Rockfield. She hadn't gotten home until half-past midnight.

Their date had been a welcome diversion from the tense atmosphere at Nana's house on Tuesday. Not that Jill had seen her sisters much during the day—they'd all stayed in their rooms and gone on separate jaunts into town. Or, in Jill's case, for a solitary stroll down the beach in the rain. But the very fact that they'd isolated themselves had been a kind of stressor, especially considering that they only had a few days left to be together on the island.

But her time with Alex had been lovely. Jill smiled to herself, thinking about how he'd requested a table on the restaurant's canopied balcony because the sun was forecasted to make an appearance at the end of the day. He'd hoped they could watch it set over the bay in Port Newcomb and was deeply disappointed that the thick cloud cover never lifted.

However—although she'd never admit it to him—Jill had been secretly pleased. Because in spite of her sisters' crabby moods, she still wanted the first sunset she watched on Dune Island to be with them, because that was their tradition.

And now, as Brooke and Rachel came over and perched on the sofa and armchair respectively, their small smiles indicated their frosty attitudes were melting, just a little. Relieved, Jill relaxed against the sofa cushion and closed her eyes as Rachel began reading Nana's letter.

*Dear Rachel, Brooke and Jill,*

*As I write this, my penultimate letter to you girls, I'm tethered to an oxygen tank. I'm not telling you this to make you sad—I'm telling you so that right now, you'll pause to inhale the scent of the salt spray roses, the honeysuckle and the ocean, as deeply as you can.*

*Marvelous, isn't it?!*

*Okay, back to my story…*

*I don't think any bride was ever as eager to get married as I was to get divorced. But I knew I was in for a fight. Since I didn't have a phone at the cottage, the Saturday after I visited my grandfather, Robert arrived on Dune Island in person to threaten me. Not physically—he wasn't that kind of man. He was the kind who'd hurt a woman by taking away her child.*

*But I was prepared and I beat him to the punch, so to speak. I proposed that if he agreed to an amicable divorce, I'd sign over my trust fund over to him, as well as my sister's, on my birthday. He could keep all of our material possessions: the car, the furniture, the major appliances, everything.*

*What I wanted was the cottage on Sea Breeze Lane. I knew he'd relinquish it easily because after the fire, the insurance company told him that filing a claim for the little structure wouldn't be worth the cost of the paper it was printed on.*

*I also said that for the duration of the winter, I needed to receive the same weekly grocery allowance I'd been spending during the summer and I wanted to have a propane heater installed. Incredibly enough, Robert balked at that! He stood to gain over 300 times that amount from my inheritance, yet he was nickel-and-diming me about a measly expenditure to pay for food and a source of heat for his son.*

*I'm pleased to say, I met his bluff with a bluff of my own. "If you think that's unfair, I know an attorney on the island who offered to help us draft a different agreement. He's a friend of Lawrence Rutherford's and he goes to the club. You may know him, his name is Gordon Nelson?"*

*There was no Gordon Nelson; I made him up so Robert would believe that I'd been rubbing elbows with wealthy summer residents. It was important to insinuate that I knew people in high places who didn't believe I was an unfit mother and who would support me in getting a divorce. Predictably, Robert granted my requests.*

*I'm aware that most people would think I was incredibly foolish to give my inheritance away the way I did, essentially serving it up to Robert on a silver platter. They'd say that I should have fought tooth and nail to hold on to what was rightfully mine. But the way I saw it, Jimmy was rightfully his son. We both had something the other person desperately wanted and my offer made it easy for both of us to have it. To those who'd argue it wasn't a fair exchange, I'd agree: I stole something far more precious from Robert than what he received from me.*

At this point, there was such a long pause that Jill opened her eyes to see why Rachel had stopped reading. Apparently, the passage she'd just read had struck a chord with her, because she was blotting her cheeks with a tissue. Jill and Brooke both waited in patient silence until she continued:

*Although I choked on the words, before he left, I promised I'd never stop him from seeing Jimmy. "Once he's a little older, he can visit you overnight, if you want him to," I suggested.*

*"Right." Robert picked his child up and tousled his hair, then set him down again.*

*He opened the door and stepped out onto the patio, furrowing his brow and looking off into the distance as if he had something important to say. I held my breath, terrified he might change his mind about the conditions of the divorce. Worse, that he might apologize and plead for forgiveness, asking me to take him back. "Where did you get the money to raze what was left of the other cottage?" he asked.*

*I was so relieved, I grinned, in spite of my disgust. "Mr. Rutherford cleared the dune as a gift to me." I took the opportunity to issue one final veiled threat, which also happened to be the truth. "He knew how much I was suffering and he wanted to do something helpful on my behalf."*

*Having the debris removed wasn't the only thing Mr. Rutherford did that was helpful; he'd hobble up to the cottage every week or so to say hello and ask if I needed a ride to the market or laundromat. Usually, I'd just pour us cool drinks and we'd sit in the lounge chairs on the patio and look out over the water. Jimmy would play nearby or else I'd hum a tune, lulling him into an afternoon nap as I rocked him in my arms.*

*With the exception of the day Lawrence told me about how his wife had died, we rarely discussed anything of consequence (although I did confide that Robert and I were divorcing). Mostly, we'd chat about the weather or comment on Jimmy's antics or other trivialities, but it wasn't what we talked about that mattered. You see, that summer I felt as if I'd been shipwrecked and washed ashore on Grief Island. But Lawrence's presence gave me hope that I'd survive, regardless of whether I was ever rescued.*

*Little by little, I began to feel stronger emotionally, especially once I no longer had to dread returning to Connecticut to live with Robert. I'd never stayed on Dune Island during September, but it turned out to be my favorite time of the year there. The vacationers left for the season but the weather was still warm enough for long morning walks and afternoon swimming. (How often have you heard me boast that your father learned to swim before his second birthday? In that regard, he was just like his mother! That's why it so delights me that you and your children also love being in the water.)*

*During my first year in Lucinda's Hamlet, the longest time I spent off-island was nine days spanning the week of my birthday in October. That's when I returned to Connecticut to attend to the paperwork regarding my trust funds and the divorce. Also, we visited my grandfather and went shopping for warmer clothes for both Jimmy and me.*

*I knew we'd be in for a cold winter in our little cottage on the dunes, but I didn't care: it was worth it to be free of Robert. Right up until the very last time I saw him at the attorney's office, I was afraid I'd do something to blow my cover and he'd be able to prove I was emotionally unstable after all. (I may well have been, but not in the way he'd accuse me of being.) I must have practiced Rose's signature a thousand times, but my hand still shook as I signed the necessary documents. The attorney noticed and asked if everything was okay. "I'm just very emotional," I answered truthfully.*

*I figured once we finalized the transaction and I put as much distance as I could between us, I'd breathe a lot easier. After all, people on the island didn't know Rose nearly as well as those in Connecticut did. So if I inadvertently snubbed one of her acquaintances in town, they chalked it up to the trauma of losing my sister.*

*"With all you've had on your mind, it's no wonder you've forgotten my name," they'd say and then they'd re-introduce themselves, as if I had amnesia. In that way, the island was the perfect place for me to hide while I tried to determine where to go from there.*

Jill couldn't help but compare her situation to her grandmother's. Although the particulars were different, they'd both bought themselves more time in Hope Haven until they could decide what to do next. *Nana figured out a plan, so I'm sure I can, too*, she thought, drawing courage from her grandmother's example.

*However, two days after Jimmy and I returned after our nine-day absence, Lawrence's housekeeper, Christina, paid a visit to share terrible news with me. Mr. Rutherford had suffered a minor heart attack and he'd had to be transported to a hospital in Boston. While he was there waiting for surgery, he experienced a second, more severe heart attack, which killed him.*

"Oh, that's terrible," Brooke moaned and her sisters echoed her lament.

*His funeral had already been held and he'd been buried in Longmeadow, his hometown. Christina had come to deliver a sealed note that was among those he'd written while in the hospital.*

*I was severely saddened that someone I'd cared about had died and dismayed that I didn't get the chance to say goodbye to him. (That is why, even though I know it's been painful and you'd rather deny what's going to happen, I've been so upfront about my prognosis. I haven't wanted anything important to go unsaid between us—this belated confession notwithstanding.)*

*It took two weeks before I could bring myself to open Lawrence's letter. I read it so many times I can repeat it here in its entirety, almost sixty-five years later. The salutation said, "Dearest Lori." Since the letter wasn't addressed to me, I shouldn't have read on, but my eyes scanned the page. He'd written:*

*Your talent is a rare gift in someone so young; it's inimitable. You were undoubtedly on your way to fame and fulfillment as an actress. While I'm surprised by this new path you've taken, I can guess some of your reasons for pursuing it. I wholeheartedly believe it will be worth the sacrifice and I have nothing but good wishes for your happiness.*

*For that reason, I feel compelled to warn you that others might not look at your decision the same way I do. They might think it's a shame—some might even call it criminal—for you to do what you're doing instead of what they'd expect from you. In time, they'll lose interest, but meanwhile, such attitudes are destructive and I urge you to keep your guard up.*

*Keep your head up, too—remember; there's still beauty all around. I very much enjoyed sharing glimpses of it with you.*

*Sincerely,*
*Your friend,*
*Lawrence J. Rutherford*

*On first reading, I figured he had put the wrong note in my envelope. I admit I felt envious of this actress whose talent my elderly companion admired so greatly and I was curious about why she'd given up acting.*

*But when I read the lines about keeping my head up, I knew the letter really was intended for me.*

*I knew he knew. It was a terrifying feeling.*

Rachel gasped at what she'd just read, as if she was equally terrified. She turned to the next page and kept reading.

*I realized why he'd referred to me as Lori—Laurey was my character's name in* Oklahoma!, *the play I'd been in on the island. He'd written to me in a kind of code so that if anyone else read the note, they wouldn't understand its meaning. They'd simply think he was writing to a talented young woman who'd given up acting. But in reality, he was warning me. He was telling me to be careful, lest someone else find out my secret, the way he had.*

*But how? How had he known? The question tormented me. Was it something I'd said while I was medicated and staying in his home? That seemed most likely. But it could have happened afterward, during one of his visits. As I obsessively ruminated over our every encounter, I recalled the first time he dropped by, I'd been singing, "Oh, What a Beautiful Mornin'" to Jimmy. Had my voice given me away? If not, then what had? I was plagued by the possibility I might repeat my mistake in front of somebody who wasn't as sympathetic as Mr. Rutherford was.*

*A chill ran through me as I re-read his line, "Some might call it criminal." There was no question about it: he was referring to my impersonation of Rose. As naive as it seems, up until then, I'd been so concerned about Robert claiming I was an unfit mother, that it hadn't actually occurred to me that what I was doing was illegal. Even as I was practicing Rose's signature, I didn't really consider it forgery and punishable by law.*

*All of my new-found peace—my relief at knowing I was free of Robert for good—dissipated immediately. I couldn't shake the fear that I'd be found out and put in jail. Then what would happen to Jimmy? It was a fear that beset me throughout your father's youth, beginning immediately after I received the note from Mr. Rutherford.*

*Girls, mark my words: the more a person has to lose, the more extreme her behavior will become to keep it. That evening after Jimmy was asleep, I carried a kettle of boiling water with me outside to the staircase by the dunes so he wouldn't hear me when I cried. Then I sat down in the dark and splashed the water across my left thigh. I knew my scar wouldn't match Rose's, but I figured I could explain that away by saying I burned the same leg a second time as an adult. Only a doctor would be able to tell the difference.*

"I think I'm going to be sick," Brooke mumbled. At first Jill thought she was speaking figuratively, meaning it turned her stomach to imagine Nana burning herself like that. But when Jill noticed how peaked and clammy her sister appeared, she got up and brought her a glass of ice water.

"I can stop reading if you want me to," Rachel offered.

"No, you can't leave us with a cliffhanger," Brooke insisted, so Rachel continued.

*That evening, I also made up a plan to become even more of a hermit than I already was. Fortunately, the island was practically deserted during the off-season so I didn't come into contact with many people anyway. But whenever I had to interact with others, I'd wonder, "Is that who Lawrence was warning me to avoid? Did that person say something to him about my behavior?"*

*I especially suspected Christina, since she took care of me when I was loopy from medication immediately following the fire. It was a shame I wasn't sure I could trust her, because she was the closest person I might have had to a female friend on the island. She stopped by a couple of times after delivering the note from Lawrence, but because I didn't want to encourage her to visit, I wasn't very welcoming. It was a huge weight off my shoulders when she told me she'd finally closed up Mr. Rutherford's house for the off-season and she'd taken a job as a live-in maid in Newport, RI. Lawrence's relatives sold his estate the following spring, so Christina never did come back to Lucinda's Hamlet again.*

*Even in private, I was careful to imitate Rose's behaviors and tone of voice. I'd pinch the bridge of my nose when I was trying to make a decision; take my coffee with milk, instead of cream; or brush the ends of my hair before brushing the roots—those kinds of things. In a way, imitating my sister made me feel as if I had her back with me again. I practiced everything I could remember her doing until her habits became second nature and my own felt foreign to me. Yet that first year, I still worried constantly that someone would find me out.*

*Twice a month when the weather allowed, Jimmy and I visited my grandfather in the nursing home. During the winter, the ferry only ran on Saturdays and Wednesdays. We usually went on Wednesday so we could stock up on picture books from the public library to take back to the cottage. It's no wonder Jimmy learned to read by the time he was four—whenever we weren't hiking on the beach or playing in the snow, I was reading to him.*

*It was a quiet life and we were shielded from the public eye. Yet I knew we couldn't live there indefinitely. What would I do for work? Most of the jobs were seasonal. Besides, Jimmy seemed to be growing up so quickly. Even though I needed to be reclusive, I wanted him to have lots of little friends and eventually to attend a bigger school than the tiny one in Lucinda's Hamlet.*

*Also, that first year we wintered on Dune Island, I was consumed with the fear of being discovered. To be honest, I was literally worried sick, as well as being lonely. Those feelings were so negative that they poisoned me against ever wintering in Hope Haven again.*

"Oh, so that explains why Nana always left Sea Breeze Lane by late September," Jill said softly. On occasion, she had asked her grandmother why she hadn't moved to Hope Haven year-round, especially after she'd retired. Nana had usually made a vague reference to the harsh island winters and the high cost of heating a house with so many windows in it. Or else she'd claim the island was too deserted for her comfort in the off-season.

It saddened Jill to learn the real reason was that her grandmother had developed such negative associations with wintering on the island her first full year there, she never got over them.

*The next April, my dear grandfather passed away and as his sole beneficiary, I inherited a small fortune. It was so surprising to me. For one thing, my grandparents' house had already been sold to cover Grandpa's nursing home expenses so I thought his savings had been depleted. For another, Nana and Grandpa lived so frugally that I hadn't realized they'd amassed quite a bit of wealth.*

*Jimmy and I stayed in Lucinda's Hamlet until October of that year and then we moved into a small apartment in Worcester, Massachusetts. The reason I chose that city was because it was far enough away from West Hartford that I wouldn't cross paths with people who'd known Rose. Yet it was close enough to Dune Island that we could travel there easily. And although I could have afforded to buy a home instead of renting an apartment, I was afraid if I did, Robert would come sniffing around and accuse me of holding out money on him.*

*Since I wanted to stay home with Jimmy until he was old enough to go to kindergarten, I kept our expenses low. I only used the inheritance to pay the rent; I took in sewing and earned enough money for groceries and utilities. Once Jimmy was enrolled at school—my smart boy skipped ahead to first grade—I found a job as a receptionist for the insurance company. (Later, as you know, I became a secretary and then a claims adjuster, working there for a total of thirty-eight years before I retired.) When Jimmy was seven, we moved into the duplex on Greendale Street.*

*Every summer, we'd go to the cottage for at least two weeks. The winter your father turned twelve, the cottage was lost to the bay in a nor'easter. At first it was devastating to lose it – like losing a piece of my sister, and my family memories all over again. So I decided to use my inheritance to have a house built on Sea Breeze Lane, figuring I'd been working long enough by then that Robert wouldn't wonder how I financed it. The summer after the new house was completed, Jimmy and I spent as many weekends on Dune Island as we could, in addition to our two-week vacation there in July.*

*I always allowed him to bring a friend along with us. The boys were crazy about the beach and about hanging out on the boardwalk as teenagers. I guess I was trying to make up for the fact that Jimmy didn't have a father or brother. But for a year after we moved into the duplex, he did have an important male influence in his life; Edward Brooks—the man he named you after, Brooke.*

*Your father undoubtedly told you how fond he was of Ed, the furnace repairman whose parents lived next door to us in the duplex.*

*Ed was about eight years older than I was and his wife had tragically died after just three years of marriage. He lived in Millbury, south of the city. We met when his parents, our neighbors—their names were Ralph and Marjorie—invited Jimmy and me to supper the same evening Ed was there. After we ate, Edward went out into the small back yard and helped your father refine his pitching technique until it got dark. He wasn't a man of many words, but he was very patient and encouraging. And when he showed up to watch Jimmy's game that Saturday, your father was so pleased he didn't even mind that his team lost.*

*After that, Ed would frequently stop by whenever he was visiting his parents. Sometimes we'd all have cookouts together and other times, he, Jimmy and I would walk to the park. He'd play catcher so Jimmy could practice pitching, or the two of them would join the other young men playing basketball.*

*Do you know how when you love something or someone—say, the ocean or your children—and someone else treasures it, too, it endears that person to you? I think that's what happened with Ed and me. Because of the interest he took in Jimmy, I became especially fond of Edward. So when Marjorie and Ralph announced they were retiring to Florida a year after Jimmy and I moved into the duplex, I was disappointed. Not only because it meant Edward wouldn't have a reason to come around any longer, but because Marjorie and Ralph were such a warm, pleasant couple that I had come to think of them more as in-laws than as neighbors.*

*I didn't think I'd see Edward after that, but he stopped by one late afternoon in the fall. I had just gotten home from work and was about to begin preparing supper. "Jimmy should be home from soccer practice in another hour," I told him. "If you can wait that long, you're welcome to join us for supper. He'll be thrilled to see you."*

*"Actually, I've come to talk to you." Edward looked so serious that I was concerned something had happened to his parents. But instead, he told me that he'd enjoyed getting to know me that year and he wondered if I'd ever consider going out with him.*

*As much as I liked him and would have loved for your father to have a consistent male influence like Ed in his life, I had to turn him down. I knew our relationship wouldn't ever go anywhere. We couldn't get married—what if I got pregnant? A doctor would have been able to tell I'd never had a child. I couldn't risk anyone finding out I wasn't Jimmy's mother.*

*Nor could I deceive a man into believing he was falling in love with me when I wasn't me: for all intents and purposes, I was Rose. (In my mind, pretending to be Jimmy's mother was different—it was necessary in order to protect him. But tricking someone as kind and sensitive as Edward into thinking he loved me would have been so inauthentic it seemed cruel.) Ed took it well and he even came to Jimmy's soccer championship game that season, but I could see the disappointment in his big brown eyes when I told him I had decided to remain single for the rest of my life.*

"I remember Dad telling me he named me after a friend," Brooke said. She still appeared very wan and sweaty. "When we were growing up, I always felt envious because Rachel was named after mom's mother but I was named after a man. But now that I know a little more about Edward Brooks, I'm glad I was named after him."

*Robert, on the other hand, married Daisy a couple of months after the divorce was finalized. They never had any children and sixteen years after their wedding, she suffered a seizure and died. I never would have known but her son—whose name was Brian—had requested his attorney contact me. By that time, Brian was twenty-one and apparently, Robert had been unfaithful to Daisy, too. They'd started divorce proceedings before she died. So the two men were embroiled in a bitter dispute over property Daisy had inherited from an uncle. The attorney thought I'd serve as some sort of character witness, but I declined to have anything to do with the situation.*

*As your dad undoubtedly told you, he had absolutely no recollection of his father. The entire time Jimmy was growing up, Robert never once came to see him. He never wrote. Never called. I wouldn't have discouraged Jimmy if he had been the one who wanted to get in touch with his dad. I never spoke against him. I didn't tell Jimmy about the fire or about the trust fund. I only said that Robert had left me for another woman, whom he eventually married.*

*There were even times when your father was an adult that I encouraged him to seek Robert out, but he had no interest in getting to know him. "Why bother? I've managed this long without him," he'd say with a shrug. He wasn't bitter; he was indifferent. Which wasn't surprising, considering how indifferent his father had been toward him.*

*While your dad was alive, I'd often wondered whether I'd cheated him—and you girls—of having a relationship with Robert. "After all, he may have changed," I thought. And, "No matter how I feel about him, he's still Jimmy's father." But when your Dad died six years ago, I felt it only right to contact Robert to let him know.*

*I'm sorry to tell you girls that he didn't express sadness or ask me when the funeral was or how your dad had died. He didn't even inquire whether Jimmy was married or had children. His only question was, "I don't suppose he left me anything in his will, did he?"*

"Ug!" Brooke clutched her chest. "He makes me so angry I feel like I'm having a heart attack," she said.

Usually, Jill took her sister's theatrical complaints with a grain of salt, but she could see that Brooke was absolutely beside herself and her shirt was drenched with sweat.

"I'll get you more water," she offered. "Rachel, I think we should stop here. This is making Brooke too upset."

"No it's not," Brooke argued. "Just keep reading."

"Okay. It'll be quick—there's just one more paragraph," Rachel told them. But what a paragraph their grandmother had written:

*In that instant, every concern, every doubt and every misgiving I'd ever had about posing as my sister was put to rest… and soon, my darling girls, I'll be put to rest, as well. Although I'm sad because I know you'll mourn my absence, I can't tell you how much I'm looking forward to seeing Jimmy in his mama's arms again!*

"She signs it, *Love, Nana,*" Rachel said, her voice so garbled that her words were barely discernible. Jill was moved to tears, too. She stole a look at Brooke, who was bent at the waist, hugging herself and rocking up and down.

"Not right," she whimpered. At first, Jill thought she meant she was referring to Robert's behavior but then she repeated more distinctly, "Something's not right."

"Brooke!" she placed a hand on her sister's bony shoulder. Her skin was slick with sweat. "What's wrong? Are you in pain?"

"My heart. It's racing."

Rachel checked her pulse."183." She looked at Jill. "We need to call 9-1-1."

# CHAPTER FIFTEEN

## *Wednesday – June 29, continued*

The call wouldn't go through from the great room, so Jill raced out into the hall with her phone. As it was ringing on the other end, she could hear Rachel telling Brooke she was probably anxious and overheated. "Let's do some deep breathing."

"I am." Panic was rising in Brooke's voice. "But my heart won't slow down."

The operator came on the line and asked, "What's your emergency?"

"My sister—" The phone dropped the call. *No, no, no, no, no*, Jill thought. She tried again. Nothing.

Returning to the living room, Jill started to panic. "Rachel, the phone, I can't—"

"We're going to have to go to the ER in the car," Rachel decided. "I'll drive. Brooke, you're going to need to lie down in the back seat."

"I'm too hot," she gasped. "I want to be in the front by the air conditioner."

So they reclined the front passenger seat as far as it would go and blasted the cold air. Rachel sped so fast down the dirt road that when she hit a pothole, Jill bounced up and smacked her head against the ceiling. A minute down the road, the phone rang.

"This is emergency services. Did you call 9-1-1?" the woman asked. Jill gave her all of the necessary information about what had happened. Then she reported to Rachel, "They want us to stop here and wait for an ambulance. What's the name of the closest cross street?"

"I don't know but I'm not stopping anyway." Rachel, the ultimate rule-follower, stepped on the gas. "Ask her to call the hospital for us and let them know we're coming."

When Jill repeated Rachel's instructions, the woman argued, "Ma'am, it's better if—"

Rachel hung a right so sharply that Jill dropped the phone and it slid beneath the reclined passenger seat, beyond her reach. She could hear the dispatcher's voice for another mile, before she either hung up or they lost their connection again.

Meanwhile, Brooke had begun tossing her head from side to side, so Jill leaned forward and said, "We're almost there. You're going to be okay."

"No, I'm not. I'm having a heart attack, just like Dad did," Brooke cried. "It's genetic and I've always looked like his side of the family."

"No, you haven't. You have Mom's crooked toes." Jill tried to make her sister lighten up even though she herself felt as if she was going to collapse under the gravity of the situation.

Brooke persisted. "If I die, will you both care for my children like Nana did for Dad?"

"You're not going to die."

"But if I do, will you?"

"You're not going to die," she repeated. "But yes, I promise I'll help Todd raise your children and so will Rachel. Won't you, Rach?"

"Of course." Rachel pressed on her horn and held it down until the three cyclists in front of them shifted into a single file and she sped past them.

"Todd doesn't want to raise the kids. He's checked out on our family. He doesn't care about us. He's totally apathetic," Brooke said.

Or maybe it was *pathetic*, Jill wasn't sure. But she was alarmed by Brooke's sudden confusion, because she knew it could signify a critical condition. So, she prompted, "You mean Robert, don't you? He didn't care about Rose and Jimmy. But Todd loves you and your children very much. You're having a vow renewal ceremony, don't you remember?"

"Of course, I remember—I'm not *delusional*!" She was so indignant that Jill would have laughed if she weren't so concerned about her sister's health. "The only reason we're having a vow renewal ceremony is because I'm trying to recreate the romance we used to have. Things have been… really bad between us."

Brooke began to convulse with sobs. Jill unbuckled her seatbelt and slid closer so she could hold her shoulders from behind. "It's okay, Brooke," she whispered into her ear. "Everything's going to be okay. Take it from me. I know a lot more about breaking up than… Brooke? Brooke! Rachel—she passed out. What are you doing? Don't stop driving!"

"Calm down, Jill." Rachel pointed to the window. "Look. See? We're here."

All at once someone pulled Brooke's door open and two men lifted her onto a stretcher. Jill raced inside with them, reporting everything she knew about her sister's current symptoms and health history. A nurse stopped her from following the men through a wide set of double doors, so she waited in the lobby until Rachel came in after parking the car.

"The nurse said she'd give me an update as soon as they can," Jill told her. "She told me that Brooke is in really good hands. The cardiology department here is excellent."

"I hope so." Then Rachel said her legs felt weak and she dropped into a chair.

"I'll go get you some water." When Jill returned, Rachel was staring at her blank phone screen.

"I tried calling Todd, but I couldn't reach him, so I left a message."

"Oh. Good idea. I didn't even think of doing that." Jill said. "You handled this entire situation expertly, Rachel. I don't know what Brooke and I would have done without you."

"That's how I feel about both of you—all the time, not just in emergencies," she replied, with tears beading on her lashes. She gave Jill's hand a squeeze and Jill leaned her head against her sister's shoulder, closing the distance between them.

It must have been over an hour later when Dr. Laurent came out to tell them that Brooke was doing well. He said that her heart itself was very healthy; the problem had originated with her overactive thyroid gland.

"Brooke experienced something we call thyroid storm, which caused her heart to go into atrial fibrillation, so we had to cardiovert her. By that I mean we used an electrical current to restore a normal sinus rhythm. Now that her heart is beating exactly as it should, we'll monitor her for a few hours and if everything checks out okay, she can go home this evening. She'll have to follow up with an endocrinologist so this doesn't happen again. We cardioverted her under anesthesia, so she's still groggy, but a nurse will take you back to see her soon."

After the doctor answered all their questions, Jill and Rachel chorused, "Thank you. Thank you!"

His handsome, tired face crinkled with a smile, "You're welcome."

After he left, the women spontaneously embraced each other and then Rachel suggested they call Todd to give him an update. "But I really need to use the restroom, first."

"If you give me your phone, I'll call him."

As she handed it to her, Rachel asked, "Do you think Brooke really meant what she said about him?"

"It would explain why she's been so weepy and so obsessed about the vow renewal ceremony. That's not like Brooke at all. She usually wouldn't spend half a second online here. Plus, she becomes really angry whenever Robert is mentioned in Nana's letters. I don't like our grandfather, either, but she seems to take his behavior personally."

"Unfortunately, I think you may be right."

While Rachel was in the restroom, Jill found Todd's name in her contacts list and tapped his number but he didn't pick up. She left him a cheerful, reassuring message. She was just about to hang up, when she thought of how upset Brooke had been at him and she added, "The cardiologist said thyroid storm has a fifty per cent mortality rate in the US. So we feel very blessed we didn't lose her."

*Sometimes, a little well-placed guilt is as effective as a kick where it hurts,* she thought, remembering what Nana had written about Jill's dad Robert.

After the stream of physicians, fellows and nurses had flowed in and out of the room and the three women were finally alone, Brooke told her sisters she actually felt better than she had in two months. She looked better, too. "It sounds funny, but I finally feel relaxed enough to sleep. I can't wait to get back to Nana's place so I can go to bed."

"Do you want to use my phone to call Todd?" Rachel extended it to her, but Brooke shook her head.

"I'm fine, now. There's no reason he even has to know this happened."

"Uh-oh. We already called him to let him know you were in the ER."

"That's all right. What did he say?" There was a hopeful note in Brooke's voice.

"He didn't pick up—but we left messages."

Brooke smoothed the sheet over her legs with swift motions, indicating her annoyance. "He's probably playing some stupid video game again. You know, when we were reading Nana's letters, I was so angry about how dismissive Robert was of Rose. But in a weird way, I was actually *envious* of her that her husband was having an affair with another woman. At least that explained his indifferent behavior. But there is no 'other woman' for Todd. He has just totally checked out of our family. If he's not working, he's gaming or shooting pool with his pals. He hardly spends any time with the kids and me, no matter how hard I've tried to entice him to get involved with us. Why do you think I planned a so-called second honeymoon in Banff? It's so he can go fishing."

Jill suddenly understood why her sister had suggested that she'd be sorry if she made too many concessions in order to be in a relationship with Alex. *It's because Brooke feels like* she's *been deferring to Todd's preferences too often and she resents it*, she realized.

Brooke continued ranting. "I *hate* fishing. To be perfectly honest, I didn't want to go to the mountains for our entire family vacation this summer, either. I mean, I enjoy camping but I wanted to spend at least half of our vacation here, on Dune Island. But do you think Todd cares about what *I* want?" She shook her head in disgust, as if answering her own question. "I really don't get it. I have so many happy memories of us being here together. I even remember bringing him here to meet Nana for the first time. He always used to love it here…"

Once again, Jill was struck with an epiphany. She recalled Brooke saying that now their parents and Nana weren't alive, it felt almost unbearable to remember their joyful times together on Dune Island. But it just occurred to Jill that it was probably unbearable for Brooke to remember happier times on Sea Breeze Lane with her husband, too. *Is that part of the reason she wants to sell Nana's place?* she wondered. *Does it upset her too much to remember what her relationship with Todd used to be like?*

The machine Brooke was hooked up to started to go *ding, ding, ding*, indicating her heart rate had shot up. So Jill swiftly suggested, "Maybe we should talk about something else. I don't want them to have to defibrillate you again. Dr. Laurent said you were sedated, but do you remember feeling it at all?"

"Not consciously, but I must have felt it on some level because I had a dream I was with both of you in the car and we came to a sudden stop and I hit my chest against the dashboard. That was probably when they jolted me."

"I wouldn't be so sure that was a dream, considering how Rachel was driving on the way here. You were lying down, so you couldn't see what was going on." Jill laughed. "Our rules-are-meant-to-be-followed sister broke at least half a dozen laws driving here. If there were traffic cams along the way, she's going to be in a ton of debt from fines."

"Perfect Rachel might get fined?" Brooke taunted, "Sounds like you're going to have to redeem a lot more bottles this summer."

Noticing the look on Rachel's face, Jill thought they were teasing her too hard, so she tried to turn the humor on herself. "Don't worry, Rachel, if you have to pay off tickets, I'll help. Oh, wait, I can't—I'm unemployed!"

Rachel took her remark the wrong way. "I know you two think I'm cheap and overly concerned with money," she began, her eyes welling with tears for the second time that evening.

"I was only kidding, Rach—"

"No, it's true. I *am* obsessed with money. But it's because Derek and I are in debt up to our eyeballs. I think we might have to declare bankruptcy. That's why I wanted to sell Nana's estate. It isn't just so the kids can go to Densmore. It's also because I'm trying to get us out of the hole."

Jill was momentarily stunned. "You're serious?"

"Yes," she mumbled, bobbing her head as she lifted a small box of tissues from the tray beside Brooke's bed.

"Oh, Rachel. You must be so stressed out. Why didn't you tell us?"

"Because I've felt so ashamed. If only we hadn't opened a second shop, we wouldn't be in this mess. My intention was to bring in more money so the twins could go to prep school." Rachel blew her nose. "At the time, business was great and the risk of opening another store seemed very mild. But my assessment must have been inaccurate. I should have been more careful. I've always tried to be a good example to you two."

"Uh, Rach? We're in our forties now," Brooke pointed out. "The days when you had to be a good example because you're the oldest and you should know better are long over."

"*I'm* not in my forties yet," Jill jokingly reminded her. Then she turned to her eldest sister. "But even if I were, those days will never be over, will they Rachel? You'll always feel responsible for guiding Brooke and me. Just like we'll always look up to you and admire your success."

"Success? I've totally made a mess of things."

"You think your life is a mess? At least once the estate is sold, you'll be out of debt. But there's no repairing my marriage," Brooke said woefully.

"There might be, Brooke," Rachel reassured her. "Have you tried couples' counseling?"

"Of course we have. We've tried everything. At least, *I've* tried everything. Todd doesn't even seem to want to work on our marriage. And I can't *make* him care about it. Renewing our vows was sort of my last attempt to revive our relationship. But now that we've lost our rooms at the resort, I've decided to cancel the ceremony. Todd would just be saying empty words anyway." Brooke started to cry and Rachel grabbed several more tissues before handing her the box. "I think… I think it's time for a separation. The kids are going to be devastated."

"Oh, Brooke." Jill got up and patted her shoulder, at a loss for what to say that might comfort her.

"Maybe we should keep Nana's estate after all, so the children and I can live there," Brooke suggested through her tissues. She gave a wry little laugh that turned into a cough and then more tears.

Rachel approved of Brooke's idea, drolly remarking, "That's fine, as long as you don't mind sharing the house with me and my family once we go into foreclosure on ours."

Even though Jill knew her sisters weren't being serious about moving to Dune Island, she could hear their genuine despair about their situations. Her eyes stung as it occurred to her that Nana wasn't the only one who'd been bearing a secret burden. Jill and her sisters had been hiding their troubles from each other, too. She chimed in, "If you're all going to live at Nana's house permanently, so am I. Then I won't be a family of one and I won't feel so lonely any more." Grabbing the last tissue from the box Brooke was holding, she added, "And all of our problems will be solved."

Just then, Dr. Laurent returned. "Excuse me?" he said tentatively, standing at the door. "Is everything okay, Brooke? Are you in any discomfort?"

"No, I'm fine," She wiped her eyes and Jill and Rachel averted theirs, embarrassed. "I feel a lot better, in fact."

"Yes, my wife and sister always say the same thing after they've finished crying together, too," he said with an understanding smile. "But how about your physical health? Is that better now, as well?"

Brooke chuckled. "Definitely. My heart isn't racing at all any more."

"Can I take a listen?" He asked and Brooke nodded, so he did. "Yes, it sounds good. And your EKG looks great. I wish all of my patients' hearts were as strong as yours."

"Strong hearts run in my family," Brooke said, winking at her sisters.

"Is anyone hungry?" Rachel asked when they returned home shortly before eight o'clock that evening. "I could make something for supper."

"For once, I'm more tired than hungry," Brooke answered. "I just want to go to bed."

"Okay. But promise you'll wake us up if you feel even a little bit like you did earlier today?"

Brooke promised she would and then both her sisters went to their rooms, too. Jill wasn't exactly tired, but she needed to think.

As the light faded from the sky, she lay in bed, contemplating everything that had happened since she'd first gotten up that morning. The day may have begun with petty, lingering grievances, but it had ended with profound gratitude. Jill could hardly resist the urge to go wake her sisters and tell them for a second time this evening how much she loved them and how glad she was that Brooke was okay now.

Yet her relief was also tinged with regret. The more she thought about Brooke's marital strife and Rachel's financial hardship, the sorrier she was that she'd been adding to their distress. First, by pushing them to keep Nana's place. And then, when that didn't turn out, by insisting she was going to stay there for the rest of the summer, no matter how her sisters felt about it.

Granted, she hadn't known about Brooke and Rachel's troublesome circumstances. Not in detail, anyway, although she'd had an inkling something had been seriously bothering both of them. But that wasn't the point. The point was, now that Jill was aware of the challenges her sisters were facing—about Rachel's debt, in particular—she wanted to be more supportive.

*Nana sacrificed almost everything for her sister and her sister's child*, she realized. By comparison, Jill felt very stingy. *I've had almost forty summers on Dune Island. My spending two more months here isn't worth my sisters' health or happiness.*

Nothing else was worth that, either. Not even the opportunity to have a brief relationship with someone Jill liked as much as she liked Alex. *It isn't going to be easy to say goodbye to him sooner than I planned to*, she acknowledged to herself. In fact, it was going to be downright painful.

Regardless, the issue was settled. Jill still wasn't going to accept the promotion. But she decided to tell her sisters in the morning that she'd changed her mind; they could call a realtor and put the house on the market right away.

# CHAPTER SIXTEEN

*Thursday – June 30*

Rachel and Jill had taken turns quietly peeking into Brooke's room every hour throughout the night to be sure she was okay. She never woke and they hadn't wanted to disturb her rest, so it was a relief when she finally shuffled into the kitchen at half-past ten on Thursday morning. "How are you feeling today?" Jill anxiously asked.

"Fantastic. That was the best sleep I've had in ages."

"It's no wonder you've had insomnia," Rachel said. "Hyperthyroidism can cause weight loss and heat intolerance, too. It also might be why your hair's been falling out and you've been weepier than usual."

"Me? Weepy?" Brooke was kidding, but the next instant, her eyes abruptly filled with tears. "I feel so dense for not recognizing the signs that my thyroid function was off. I'd received a clean bill of health in January, so I attributed my symptoms to… to being upset about other things."

"That's understandable. You've had a lot on your mind." Jill reached out and gave her sister's hand a sympathetic squeeze. Brooke's comment was the perfect introduction to Jill's announcement that she wanted to sell the house right away instead of waiting until the end of summer. But before she could bring it up, Brooke asked what smelled so delicious.

"Baked oatmeal with cranberries and almonds. I was actually kind of chilly this morning so I wanted to eat something warm," Rachel replied. It was drizzling out but the humidity was lower and the temperature was fifteen degrees cooler than it had been on previous mornings. "Do you want a bowl?"

"Yes, please, and fill it to the brim. My heart rhythm may be back to normal, but my appetite is still twice as big as usual."

After eating breakfast, the sisters moved into the great room with their coffee. Brooke took one sip and wrinkled her nose. "What's in this?"

"Nothing. And by that I mean no caffeine—or very little." Since the doctor had advised Brooke to avoid caffeine or strictly limit her intake for now, Jill had dashed out and bought decaf as soon as the store opened. "Drink up. It's good for you."

"You obviously haven't tasted it."

"See?" Rachel pointed a finger at Jill. "I suggested we should drink decaf as a supportive gesture, but you refused."

"I'm all for solidarity, to a point. Caffeine is where I draw the line," Jill retorted. "But there's nothing stopping *you* from drinking decaf, Rachel. Is that what's in your mug?"

"No. It's regular." She sheepishly justified herself by joking, "Since you and Brooke both needed different things, I could only show solidarity with one of you."

Brooke laughed, but Jill seized the opportunity to transition to the subject that was pressing on her mind. "Speaking of solidarity, I have something important I'd like to discuss with both of you," she announced.

"I have something I need to say, too."

"That makes three of us," Brooke said. "Who wants to go first?"

Rachel set down her mug. "I will. I'm the oldest."

"No, *I* should, since I was the first one to say I had something important to discuss," Jill argued.

"*I* should start. The middle sister never gets to be first," Brooke griped.

Jill chuckled at this obvious parodying of their younger selves. "I think we should hear what *Nana* has to say before any of us takes a turn talking." She indicated the envelope lying on the coffee table.

"Good idea." Brooke plucked up the letter. "I'll read today. I'm going to prove that I'm as emotionally resilient as both of you are."

"You don't have to prove anything, Brooke," Jill said.

"I still want to read it." So she began:

*My dearest Rachel, Brooke and Jill,*

*This will be my last letter to you. Thank you for indulging my rather tortuous trip down memory lane during your vacation. I can imagine how upsetting it's been for you to read this, but I wanted you to know the history of this place and your family's background, for better and for worse.*

*Even more importantly, I needed you to know what I'd done and who I really I am. You girls have always been so open with me about who* <u>you</u> *are; about your faults and strengths, your failures and triumphs, and your struggles and hopes. Thank you for trusting me enough to share your authentic selves. It was an honor to be your confidante, just as it has been a privilege to confide in you through these letters.*

*My secret, like the estate, is yours now to do with as you wish. You don't have to worry about Robert finding out; I was notified that he died the week before I began writing these letters. It seems like one of life's cruelties that he outlived Rose and Jimmy by so many years—he was over 100 when he died. I suppose his death was what finally gave me the courage to tell you about my past; I knew he couldn't somehow claim your inheritance for himself.*

*In my last letter, I wrote that when Robert asked what Jimmy had left him in his will, it confirmed for me that I'd made the right decision to pose as my sister all these years. But that wasn't entirely true.*

*Deep down, I knew I'd made the right decision even before I made it. I knew it the moment Jimmy ran into the back bedroom in Rose's cottage, calling for his mother, who wasn't there.*

*At least, it was settled in my mind. You girls might not agree with what I did. But I hope—as mothers and aunts and especially as sisters—that you can understand it.*

*All my love,*

*Nana*

There were tears dribbling off of Brooke's chin. "So much for proving I'm as strong as you two are—I'm bawling like a baby again."

"Rachel and I are both babies, too," Jill said, sniffling.

Her oldest sister passed the tissue box around. "Nana's right—as a sister, a mother and an aunt, I understand why she pretended to be Dad's mother. I've even come to appreciate why she kept it a secret from him all of his life… but I still wish she had told him, at least after he became an adult. Not for just Dad's sake, but for her own."

"Because then she wouldn't have had to bear so much fear and guilt?" Brooke questioned.

"Yes," Rachel confirmed. "And because she was so worried that if Dad found out she'd kept it a secret from him for so long, he'd doubt her love for him. But knowing what kind of man Dad was, I think he would have understood all she'd sacrificed for him. And he would have appreciated the depth of her love even more than if he'd never known that she was his aunt and not his mother."

Jill admitted that she'd been contemplating the sacrifices Nana had made for their father, too. She counted on her fingers as she listed them, saying, "She gave up her inheritance from her parents. Her dream of acting. The opportunity to have close relationships, including marriage. And, not least of all, she gave up her *identity*." She took a deep breath and continued, "I understand that her secrecy was partly driven by fear and guilt. But her *actions* were inspired by the love she had for Dad and Rose. She would have done anything for them and for us, too."

"That's why—" Rachel started but Jill cut her off, insisting she needed to finish what she was saying first.

"Yesterday when we were in the ER waiting to find out…" She swallowed, unable to complete her thought aloud. She started again from a different angle, saying, "You know how Nana wrote that her sister was the other half of her heart? Well, the three of us really are like a braid and if anything ever happened to either of you, I'd come completely unraveled. I don't want you to be unhappy or stressed out. I don't want our inheritance to come between us, either. I'm sorry that I was so self-centered about it. Since we haven't told the attorney what we decided yet, I think we should inform him we want to sell the estate as soon as possible. That way, you won't be so pressured financially, Rachel. And you can get the discount for paying Noah and Grace's tuition in full at the beginning of the year."

Having said her piece, she sat back in her chair. Just as her nana had written in this morning's letter, Jill knew deep down that she'd made the right decision.

But Rachel frantically waved her hands. "No, no, no. This is exactly what *I* wanted to talk to *you* about." She blew air out through her lips. "I've decided Grace and Noah don't need to go to Densmore. It's ridiculous to send them to private school when we're in so much trouble financially. I've also figured out a way for Derek and me to meet our business and family's expenses until we recover our losses—we a can take out a second mortgage on the house. Then we'll have enough cash to help you out, too, Jill, so you won't have to find some dreadful seasonal job. You should take the entire summer off and thoroughly enjoy your last summer at Nana's place."

Jill was floored. "You're not serious."

"I am, too. I've been thinking a lot about Nana writing that she didn't mind if Robert got her inheritance because she received something in exchange that was even more precious—she was able to raise Dad as her son. Her attitude made me realize how tight-fisted I've become. I don't think it's because I'm greedy—at least I hope it's not, because I don't want to be anything like Dad's father. I think I… I felt so awful about failing financially that I was terrified of it happening again, so I started watching every penny. I even tried to impose my perspective on both of you—especially on you, Jill. But when you said you were willing to withdraw from your retirement account or go into debt just so you could stay here for a couple months, I finally understood how much Nana's place means to you. And when Brooke got so sick yesterday—well, let's just say I realized I'd lost sight of what is truly precious in my life. I'm really sorry and I hope you'll accept my apology—and my financial help this summer."

"I appreciate the offer, Rach, I really do. But I can't—"

"There aren't any *buts* about it," she scolded, just like their mother used to say when they were children. "Refinancing the house won't be a problem. In fact, I was going to suggest we could even take out a big enough loan to cover your share of the estate expenses until you could get on your feet. But I know how upsetting it is for Brooke to be here, so I'm torn between—"

"Wait a second, who said it's upsetting for me to be here?" Brooke's question caused her sisters to look wide-eyed at each other.

"*You* did," Rachel reminded her.

"About a million times," Jill added. "Because the memories make you too sad."

"Well, that was before my near-death experience." Brooke's melodramatic response made Rachel and Jill chuckle, but she insisted she was serious. "Stop laughing, you two, and just listen… When I was lying on that hospital gurney yesterday, my mind was racing as fast as my heart, but there were two things that brought me comfort. The first was that you'd both promised to help take care of Kaylee, Ella and Zach if I died and I knew you'd love them as much as Nana loved Dad. The other thing that calmed me down was imagining myself floating in the bay with both of you when we were girls. That was literally the last image that flashed through my mind before the sedation kicked in."

Jill blinked and reached for another tissue. She set the box on the coffee table, but Rachel picked it up and pulled out two tissues for herself.

Brooke continued, "You've both mentioned the sacrifices Nana made, and I'm grateful for those things, too. But what strikes me is that there's one thing she absolutely refused to give up. This place. She loved summers on Dune Island so much that even though this was where her sister died—maybe even *because* it was—Nana was still strong enough to return here every year. The three of us love summers on Sea Breeze Lane, too. And even though I've been wallowing in my sorrows lately, I found out yesterday that I was a lot stronger than I thought I was. So I vote that we should keep the estate."

Jill's elation was tentative. After all, didn't hospitals advise patients not to make any legal decisions within twenty-four hours after being sedated? "You may feel that way now, Brooke, but will you still feel that way—"

"If Todd and I end up getting divorced?" Brooke completed her sister's sentence for her, but that wasn't what Jill was going to say. "Yes, I'll still feel that way. It might not be easy, because being here does remind me of when… well, when things were different. But not all of those memories make me sad—like the one I remembered of the three of us while I was in the hospital. And I'm looking forward to creating new memories here with our family, just like Nana did with us every summer."

Astounded, Jill looked at Rachel and then at Brooke, who were both grinning. That her sisters had had such huge changes of heart was almost more than she could take in. As much as she wanted to keep Nana's estate, she couldn't open herself to the possibility again unless her sisters were completely certain it was what they wanted to do. She heard herself saying, "Maybe you should both mull it over another day or two. We still have time before we need to tell the attorney what we decided."

"Are you kidding me?" Rachel was obviously nonplused. "All this time you've been trying to persuade us not to sell the house and now that we've agreed, you're *arguing* with us?"

"I'm not arguing. It's just that… it feels almost too good to be true. And I don't know if I could bear it if something happened to make you change your minds again."

"Like what could possibly happen?" Rachel asked.

"I don't know. Maybe you'd talk to your husbands about it and they'd convince you that keeping the estate is a bad idea."

"Pbft." Rachel made a dismissive noise. "Derek will be thrilled we're keeping it."

Simultaneously, Brooke said, "Believe me, Todd doesn't get any say in this matter."

As if she'd summoned him, all of a sudden Brooke's husband appeared on the deck stairs. "Are you kidding me?" she uttered, standing up as he came through the slider and crossed the room.

"Brooke." As he embraced his wife, Jill noticed that Todd's face wet with tears. His voice cracking, he said, "I'm so sorry I wasn't here for you—and I haven't been. I'm so sorry. I couldn't bear to lose you."

Jill tried to leave the room to give them privacy but they were blocking her way. Brooke shook herself free of Todd's arms and although Jill couldn't see her face, she recognized the guardedness in her sister's voice when she asked, "Where are the children?"

"My parents are picking them up from camp and then they're putting them on the next red-eye flight to Boston."

"Why did you have them do that? The kids are going to be upset. You should have texted or called me if you were worried and I would have told you I was fine."

"I did. I called and texted you and Jill and Rachel. I even called Derek, but he didn't answer. No one did." Until Todd mentioned it, Jill hadn't realized her phone was still under the car seat where it had fallen yesterday.

"My battery must have died," Brooke said at the same time Rachel mumbled something about the connection being especially bad this year.

"I made sure the kids knew you were all right, but they wanted to come anyway. We should have been together here in the first place—I know how much our Dune Island vacations mean to you. I'm so sorry, Brooke," Todd repeated.

She made a scoffing sound, before beckoning him toward the door. "C'mon. It's only sprinkling and the tide is out. Let's go for a walk."

"Did the doctor say it was okay for you to exercise?"

"It's fine. We're only going for a stroll." Brooke addressed her sisters. "I'll see you in a while. I hope you'll call the attorney while I'm gone and tell him what we've decided, because I'm not going to change my mind and that's final."

Watching them leave, Jill chewed on her thumbnail. "Do you think their marriage is going to make it?" she asked once they were out of earshot.

"I think it has a chance now that Todd showed up. Otherwise, it wasn't looking good." Rachel said, rising from the sofa. "If I can get a connection, should I call the attorney or do you want to do it?"

Jill hesitated. "Are you absolutely sure you want to keep Nana's place? I thought the kids had their hearts set on Densmore?"

"Derek and I had our hearts set on it for them. They were never crazy about the idea." She gave Jill a crooked smile. "As you've said, they're brilliant. So they'll do fine in public school. But I am still concerned about *you.* Please tell me you'll accept some… financial aid?

"Thank you, Brooke. It means a lot to me that you'd offer. But as I've said, I've got enough in savings to keep me afloat through the summer and I can always take a part-time job on the island. Oh! That reminds me. I need to get my phone out of the car and call the human resources department at work to tell them I'm not accepting the promotion." But first, she intended to call Alex—she couldn't wait to tell him her great news, which was the exact opposite of the conversation she'd been dreading ever since she'd gotten out of bed this morning.

She went outside and retrieved the phone from beneath the seat of the car. As she was shutting the door, she noticed Alex's truck pulling to a stop at the end of the driveway. *Could this morning get any better?* she thought as he strode toward her. Even though it was misting out, the bleached sky must have bothered his eyes because he was wearing sunglasses. But she could tell what kind of mood he was in by the width of his grin.

"Good morning, Jill."

"It sure is," she purred. *For so many reasons.* "What a wonderful surprise to see you."

"I wouldn't have shown up unannounced, but I've been texting and calling since last night and I couldn't get through. I've been dying to tell you what happened when we were taking down a diseased oak over at the bird sanctuary yesterday," he breathlessly explained. "The director came out to make sure we didn't disturb an eagle's nest in a nearby conifer."

Jill thought she could anticipate what he was about to say. "Did you get to see a hatchling? They're quite rare on Dune Island."

"I know—the director gave me a long, impassioned lecture about it, which reminded me of a certain teenage girl I used to know." Alex nudged her arm affectionately. "Anyway, we got to talking and he told me the sanctuary is urgently looking to hire shorebird technicians to help with things like monitoring, tracking, research and a bunch of other responsibilities I can't remember now. The positions are supposed to be year-round, but the sanctuary is so desperate he said they might be able to hire you on a temporary basis until they find a permanent replacement. There is one caveat though… The shift starts at four o'clock, so you'd literally be waking up with the birds."

Jill was so ecstatic she could hardly get any words out. "You have *got* to be kidding me!" She threw back her head and laughed.

Alex must have misinterpreted her reaction, because his face fell. "Yeah, I suppose four o'clock in the morning is awfully early. But other than that, I really thought this job sounded like a good fit for you."

Jill quickly explained that she was laughing because she was deliriously happy. "This job doesn't just sound like it might be a good fit—it sounds as if it might be my *calling*." Then she told him about what had happened to Brooke and how her sisters had decided they wanted to keep their nana's estate after all. "So this means I potentially could accept a permanent position and live on Dune Island year-round."

"That's fantastic!" Beaming, he gave her a congratulatory hug. Then he slid his hands to her waist and she rested hers flat against his chest.

"Thank you again for listening to me the other day. And for telling me about this opportunity now."

"You're welcome."

The drizzle had turned to a light shower and Jill knew Alex probably needed to leave for work. But she wanted to prolong the comfortable closeness of this moment and as usual, he seemed in no hurry. "It's my turn to make a confession about when we were kids," she told him.

He cocked his head quizzically. "What is it?"

"I might not have recognized you when we met again as adults, but I've never forgotten your eyes. I just couldn't figure out where I'd first seen them. I actually thought they were familiar because the color reminded me of a shark's eyes."

"A shark?"

"Yes. When I was a girl, I saw a dogfish shark washed up on shore. It had the most beautiful eyes I've ever seen."

"That's nice, I guess… although I'm not sure how I feel about being associated with a predatory animal," he joked. "Especially considering our unfortunate miscommunication about the shower situation."

Jill laughed. "If it helps to know it, the blueness of your eyes also reminds me of the horizon between the sea and sky on a sunny day."

She had made him blush. "Thank you," Alex said. Then he leaned down and by the time he'd stopped kissing her, she was blushing, too.

# CHAPTER SEVENTEEN

## *Friday – July 1*

"The guys will be back with the takeout soon." Rachel dunked herself in the tepid water and came up again, slicking her hair back as she suggested, "We should go up to the house and get the table ready for supper."

"Yeah, we should," Brooke agreed, floating on her back. She was wearing a T-shirt over her new bikini so her stomach wouldn't burn. "But I can't stop staring at the sky. I don't think I've ever seen such a glorious shade of blue. And the beach grass is so chartreuse it's almost blinding."

"Oh, the difference sunshine makes." Jill languidly bobbed in the water beside her sisters, paddling her hands and cycling her feet just enough to keep her chin above the surface. "I feel as if I've lived an entire lifetime in just one day."

And what a perfect day it had been. Temperatures were in the mid-eighties with low humidity and a mild breeze dimpled the bay. Todd had picked Kaylee, Ella and Zach up from the airport in Boston that morning, and Derek and the twins arrived three or four hours ago. Everyone was finally together again. Or almost everyone.

As she peered toward shore, Jill's gaze traced a path up the dunes to the landing at the top of the stairs. She could imagine Nana standing there and looking down at them, smiling as she watched their antics in the water. Jill smiled back.

"The best part is, we get to repeat it all again tomorrow," Rachel said. She and Derek had decided their family would stay on the island for two more weeks. They'd take a second vacation at Sea Breeze Lane in August. Brooke and her children were remaining at Nana's place almost until Labor Day. Todd was returning to Oregon after the July Fourth holiday to take care of a few things, since he'd left the house in such a rush, but then he'd come back to Hope Haven for the duration of the summer. Jill only intended to leave once—for a day—to move her belongings out of her Boston apartment.

"Mm. Repeating all of *this* is the one kind of starting over I never mind doing." Jill stretched her arms out to indicate she was referring to everything she did at Nana's place, surrounded by her family.

"You might not be saying that by the end of the summer," Brooke cautioned. "I've told you how chaotic our household is at home."

"I remember what it's like to share a living space with your family—it's only been three years since the last time we all vacationed here."

"But this is for a lot longer than two weeks. My kids can only sustain their good behavior for so long."

Jill laughed. "It'll be good training for me before I get roommates."

She and her sisters had agreed that Jill would rent out a couple of rooms at Nana's place to someone who needed affordable housing on the island, until the following June. She'd give their rent money to her sisters, which would help Rachel out financially until she and Derek got on their feet again. And in lieu of paying rent herself, Jill would cover both her and Rachel's full share of expenses for the estate.

"We really should let the kids know it's almost time to eat," Rachel urged. "Otherwise, the food will get cold while we're waiting for them to come off the beach."

Brooke cupped her hands around her mouth. "Kaylee, Ella, Grace! Time to go upstairs!"

Rachel beckoned to the boys, "You, too, Noah and Zach!"

One by one the children popped their heads up out of the water, like cormorants. They bypassed the three women, who were wading slowly out of the water, and dashed up the stairs.

"Is Alex going to join us?" Brooke asked Jill as they reached the spot on the beach where they'd left their clothes and towels.

"He might. But usually on Friday nights he brings his sister and her friends to the concert at the pavilion."

"You should have invited him to bring them here, too. They could have eaten supper with us, first."

"I did, but Sydney is shy about meeting new people—I haven't met her yet. Also, Alex said she has a difficult time adjusting to changes in her routines."

Jill wished Alex could have made it there, but she understood why he couldn't, especially with such short notice. Yesterday evening she'd called to tell him she'd been hired on the spot at the bird sanctuary, so she was definitely moving to the island long-term. That's when she'd also shared that Brooke had decided rather than having a vow renewal ceremony in Oregon, she wanted to hold a "celebration of life" in Nana's memory on Sea Breeze Lane.

"I'm honored you'd invite Sydney and me, but that's your family's special time," Alex had replied.

"Trust me, this is very casual. We're literally going to come up from the beach and eat takeout from The Clam Shack and ice cream from Bleecker's. We might play a game of volleyball or go swimming after that and then we'll watch the sunset. That's it. We don't even plan to say anything formal about Nana—enjoying ourselves together here *is* our celebration of her life. It's the only tribute she would have wanted."

Alex had nodded and said, "I'll see what I can do."

But it was already past six, which was when Jill had told him they'd eat, so he probably wasn't coming. She pulled her T-shirt from Lucy's Tees on over her swimsuit, and then slipped into her shorts and followed her sisters up to the house.

They were scrambling to gather glasses, plates and utensils to bring outside when Jill heard a knock on the front door. "I'll get it," she said excitedly, assuming it was Alex.

But when she rounded the corner to the entry way, she saw the courier standing on the other side of the screen door. Bewildered to receive another delivery, especially on a Friday evening, Jill assumed the cardboard envelope the courier handed her contained business documents that Rachel and Derek must have needed for work next week.

However, as she carried it into the kitchen, she noticed it was addressed to her, Brooke and Rachel. Nana's attorney's return address was printed on the label, just like it was on all the other letters they'd received. *It might be an official reminder that we still need to inform him of our decision about the estate*, she thought.

"We got another letter," she announced to her sisters. "It's from Nana's lawyer. Should we read it or do you want to wait until later?"

"The guys still aren't back, so we might as well open it now. It might be urgent."

Jill pulled the tab on the outer pouch and removed a smaller white paper envelope from inside it. *To be delivered Between 6 and 7 p.m. on the last evening of Rachel, Brooke and Jill's vacation*, it read in familiar handwriting.

"Oh!" Jill immediately became choked up. "Look. It must be another letter from Nana."

Brooke and Rachel squeezed in close on both sides so they could see it. "What in the world…?" Rachel marveled after reading the note on the outside.

"Hurry up and open it," Brooke urged Jill.

Her hands were shaking and she felt as if she was unsealing the envelope in slow motion. She carefully removed its contents and all three of the sisters gasped at once. Instead of a letter, inside were two photographs. The first was a black and white graduation snapshot of Nana and her sister on the beach, throwing their mortarboards into the air. Printed beneath them in faded ink was the phrase, *Sweet Summer of '48*.

"Look at how young and beautiful they were," Brooke murmured.

Rachel added, "And how joyful."

"Which one is Nana?"

"It's hard to tell. It's too faded to see a scar," Jill answered, squinting at the twins' long, bare legs. "But Rose must have been so exuberant she didn't even bother trying to cover it with her hand."

The trio studied the photo with a kind of respectful, fond regard for several more moments before Jill flipped to the second picture. It was of Nana, their parents, the three sisters, and Brooke and Rachel's husbands and children, all standing together on the cusp of the dune at sunset.

"I remember when this was taken." Brooke sighed. "Kaylee wasn't even a year old yet."

Jill automatically turned the photo over to check the date. Instead, she found an inscription. *No regrets—it was the role of a lifetime*, Nana had written.

Jill immediately pressed her fingers hard against her lips, but a sob escaped them anyway. Brooke and Rachel's eyes welled up, too, and the three sisters' faces were so close together it was difficult to tell whose tears were whose.

"Uh-oh," Kaylee commented to Grace and Ella a few minutes later when the girls entered the kitchen and found the women dewy-cheeked and sniffling, with their arms wrapped around each other. "This always happens when the three of them get together."

"Shush, you," Brooke scolded but her daughter's remark made the sisters chuckle and release each other. Brooke handed them each a napkin from the stack she'd been holding, so they could dry their eyes.

"Aunt Jill, there's a guy here to see you," Noah announced indiscreetly from the deck. "And Dad and Uncle Todd are back with the food."

Within a few minutes, Jill had introduced Alex to everyone he hadn't already met, and they'd all taken their seats. After serving the drinks, Rachel proposed a simple toast, saying, "To Nana, who isn't with us at this table but who will always be with us in our hearts."

"Cheers," and "To Nana," everyone chorused. The meal that followed was boisterous but warmhearted, and afterward, the kids challenged the adults to a game of volleyball on the beach.

"My stomach's too full for that level of activity. I'll stay up here and clear the table," Rachel volunteered and her sisters stayed behind to help her.

As they were finishing loading the dishwasher, Brooke remarked, "I have a feeling Alex might be The One, Jill."

*I hope you're right, but time will tell.* "What makes you say that?"

"He likes trees and you like birds," Brooke said, as if the perfectly logical conclusion was that they therefore must be meant for each other.

"Some birds nest on the ground."

Her sister rolled her eyes. "Yeah, I know—like piping plovers. I still remember your diatribe word for word."

"I'm glad Shane wasn't the only one who made an impression on you that day." Jill mockingly batted her lashes in an impersonation of her sister as a teenager.

As usual, pensive Rachel ignored their silliness and redirected the conversation. "I think I understand why Nana instructed her attorney to arrange for those photos to be delivered to us between six and seven o'clock this evening. I think the timing was her subtle way of urging us to carry on the family's sunset tradition. Not just for tonight, either. I think Jill was right from the beginning—Nana wanted us to keep the house. But she didn't want to pressure us into it."

Brooke nodded thoughtfully and Jill pointed to the bay, where the sun appeared to hang a foot or two above the horizon. "We'd better call everyone up to the deck."

But the gang was already clambering up the stairs and bounding across the yard. The kids perched on the deck railing, and Rachel and Derek dropped into the wicker chairs, deliberately leaving the love seat for either Brooke and Todd or Jill and Alex.

"Go ahead, you two can sit there," Todd offered. "I'm going to dance with my bride, if she'll accept me."

He extended his hand to Brooke and she took it, allowing him to usher her across the yard to the edge of the dune. Embracing, they swayed to the music that trickled down the beach from the pavilion. Their children acted embarrassed, but Jill suspected they were secretly pleased. One day, like their mother, they might even confess that they found it romantic to watch their parents dance against the backdrop of the setting sun.

After settling into the love seat beside Alex, she whispered, "I'm so glad you came, but I'm kind of surprised that Sydney was okay with it. Who drove her and her friends to the concert?"

"Actually, I did. I have to pick them up, too."

"They're at the concert alone?"

"No, their home manager agreed to go in my place. Since I never sit with her anyway, Syd didn't mind too much if I wasn't there during the concert. But she insisted I take her and her housemates there and bring them back home, just like always. So unfortunately, I'm not going to be able to stay here very long after the sun sets."

"That's okay. I'm impressed Sydney was willing to change even one part of her familiar routine. I hope it doesn't make her feel too anxious."

"She was a little nervous this time, but in a few weeks, she'll be completely adjusted. That's assuming you'll want to keep going out with me on Friday nights?"

"Absolutely," she answered, smiling. And when he wrapped his brawny arm around her shoulder, all she could think was that Brooke was right: Jill felt like a bird nestled within the crook of a branch, the perfect pairing.

*Whoever said clouds are necessary for a dramatic sunset has never been to Dune Island*, Jill thought as she gazed toward the water. The sun had ignited the cloudless sky with color—it burned a bright, unadulterated orange—and silhouetted Brooke and Todd's forms in the foreground. Now the golden disc was multiplying itself in the mirror of the bay, illuminating a yellow path across the dark water.

*This is our first sunset on Sea Breeze Lane without Nana*, Jill realized. Staggered by unexpected loneliness, she dipped her chin to her chest so Alex wouldn't notice her expression. Yet before any tears could fall, she remembered what Mr. Rutherford had said to Nana after her twin had died. So as the glowing sphere began to slip behind the horizon, Jill looked up to appreciate the beauty that was all around her still.

# A Letter from Kristin

I want to say a huge thank-you for choosing to read *A Letter from Nana Rose*. If you enjoyed it and want to keep up to date with all my latest releases, just sign up at the following link. Your email address will never be shared and you can unsubscribe at any time.

*www.bookouture.com/kristin-harper*

I began writing this book during the early months of the pandemic, when travel restrictions prevented one of my sisters from joining our extended family on Cape Cod, Massachusetts, for our annual summer vacation. I finished writing it shortly after the restrictions lifted (yes, it took me that long). We were all a little worse for the wear, but we considered ourselves very blessed when we were finally able to get together again. Like Rachel, Brooke and Jill, my sisters and I floated in the bay, bought T-shirts and ice cream cones, and laughed and cried together. (Fortunately, our weather was better than theirs.) I hope you and yours have been enjoying your favorite simple pleasures again, too.

If reading *A Letter from Nana Rose* was a fantastic experience for you, I'd really appreciate it if you'd share what you loved about it in a review. Your perspective means a lot to me and your enthusiasm makes a big difference in helping new readers discover one of my books for the first time.

Keeping in touch means a lot to me, too, so please don't hesitate to reach out through Twitter, Goodreads or my website.

Thanks,
Kristin

# ACKNOWLEDGMENTS

I'm delightedly indebted to:

Ellen Gleeson, editor extraordinaire, for her perseverance, brilliance and enthusiasm.

Bookouture for being such a creative, innovative and ambitious publisher.

Alex Holmes, Peta Nightingale, Natalie Edwards, Sally Partington, Loma Halden and Sarah Hardy, as well as each and every member of the Bookouture team for doing what you do so expertly.

The friends who listened to me complain and yet remained. (I'm sorry.)

J. & D., who cooked so I could write.

S., for floating and for keeping me afloat.

D., for plodding and plotting with me – through so many stages.

My genius father, who restored my laptop twice.

My mother, for everything and for always. Happy Birthday!